A

Little

Something

Richard Haddaway

New York

Harvard Square Editions

2014

Published in the United States by Harvard Square Editions

ISBN: 978-0-9895960-6-0

Cover photo: © Zurijeta,
'Happy kid enjoying in nature at sunset'

Harvard Square Editions web address:
www.harvardsquareeditions.org

We shall not cease from exploration
And the end of all our exploring
Will be to arrive where we started
And know the place for the first time.
Through the unknown, unremembered gate
When the last of earth left to discover
Is that which was the beginning;
At the source of the longest river
The voice of the hidden waterfall
And the children in the apple-tree
Not known, because not looked for
But heard, half-heard, in the stillness
Between two waves of the sea.
Quick now, here, now, always —
A condition of complete simplicity
(Costing not less than everything)
And all shall be well and
All manner of thing shall be well
When the tongues of flame are in-folded
Into the crowned knot of fire
And the fire and the rose are one.

— 'Little Gidding', T.S. Eliot

In the beginning was a little something,
A mustard seed of atomic fire,
The boiled down essence of everything.
From it sprang an abundance of light and emptiness,
The glory and the distance,
The Earth and the spotted sky of night.
Into it, eventually,
All things, and time,
Return.

— Richard Haddaway

For Kay,
Always

ONE

The baseball might as well have been a fist. In less than a blink it hammered the boy's face, bursting his vision into slivers of light. It knocked him back, his helmet tumbled away and his bare head slammed into the ground. The dark came down.

"Shit!" With the shout, Brian Singleton jumped to his feet, and Sam Moore, who sat next to him in the bleachers, rose too, not yet sure why. His attention was ripped loose from the messages in his BlackBerry.

"Justin," Brian said to Sam, moving with quickening sideways steps toward the concrete stairs between the rows. "It's Justin."

"He's not moving, Brian. Shit." Sam could see the crumpled boy off to the side of home plate. It was his son. Taking the stairs two and three at a time in his giant stride, Sam passed Brian before they reached the bottom.

By the time the two men threaded their way through the gap in the fence and onto the field, the umpire had called time and was helping the ten-year-old to his feet. Sam took the other side, bending his huge frame, and together they led the dazed boy to the dugout bench.

"Jus, you all right?"

"Dad?" He looked up uncertainly. His voice was weak and small. Sam and the ump eased the boy to a sitting position.

"It looked like you were knocked out for a little bit," Brian said, squatting in front of the boy and assuming his role as the physician he was.

"Really?"

"Todd was up — remember? — and you were on deck. He hit a foul off the side of his bat." Todd was Brian's son. They shared the same blond coloring and slender body type.

"And it hit me smack in the face."

"Right here," Brian said, gently touching a point next to Justin's nose. "Big red mark. And it cut your lip. Knocked your helmet off, too."

Justin was a good-looking kid. With his olive skin and dark, curly hair, he was mostly Sam. He got his mother's walnut-burled eyes and both their height — Sam was six-four, Justin's mother was a solid six feet, and Justin was the tallest kid in his class. His perfectly ordered, milk-bright teeth set off a wrap-around smile.

Todd — aka Toady, Justin's neighbor, fellow fifth-grader at St. Alban's Episcopal Day School, and best bud — rushed up with a towel wrapped around a handful of crushed ice. "Here, Dad."

"Thanks, guy," Brian said.

A trickle of blood was running from the corner of Justin's mouth. "You look like a vampire," Toady said.

A crowd of teammates had gathered. "Yeah, cool," somebody added.

Justin smiled enough to give Brian an opening to carefully move his index finger inside the boy's upper and lower lip. He ran his finger over the teeth. As he helped Justin guide the towel of ice to the side of his mouth, Brian gently ran his hand through the jumble of dusty black hair at the back of the boy's head, checking for swelling. "Open your eyes wide," he said, looking from different angles into Justin's eyes, checking pupil dilation.

It was a sun-strong, late spring day in Texas, and Sam and Brian wore the weekend uniform of suburban fathers — Polo shirt, khaki shorts, tennis shoes, Polaroid sunglasses, brimmed cap. A middle-age thickening showed around Sam's waist. His jaw line wasn't a line anymore. The bags under his eyes and the lines tracing his face added a couple of years to his actual forty-two.

Sam phoned his wife at the pediatrics clinic. After a friendly moment with Jonesie, the nurse/receptionist, Sam was greeted with a chorus of wails in the background as Katherine answered, "This is Doctor Warren."

"Kath, it's me. We've had a little problem with Justin at the ball field."

"Yeah?" Katherine was as steady as always, even as a particularly urgent shriek pushed through the receiver. She pulled the stethoscope from her ears, and with one large and authoritative sweep of her arm she handed the diapered baby back to its mother. Dr. Warren turned away from the noise and pushed a finger into her free ear. "So what happened?"

Sam went through the story. As she listened, she leaned against the wall. When Sam had finished she asked to talk to Brian, one doc to another.

"I'd say he was unconscious thirty seconds max, Kath," Brian said. "No disorientation. Pupils equal, reactive. I'm no neuro guy, but I'm not seeing any harm here. A little swelling in the back of his head, some tenderness, I'm guessing a hematoma. Suppose it wouldn't hurt for a once-over from a specialist."

"Bleeding?" she asked.

"Minor," Brian said. "Small cut, lip versus teeth, typical sort of thing. I don't see a need for stitches. Just an icepack. I expect he'll have a spectacular black eye."

She smiled through the phone. "Justin'll love that. The black badge of courage."

Brian smiled back, continued. "What I'm worried about is his teeth, Katherine. One of his main front teeth feels a little loose. I can see a little blood around the roots. Who knows how many other teeth need attention, too."

"Damn it." Katherine decided the tooth needed to be stabilized, and everything needed to be checked out. They couldn't afford to wait around, either.

Sam took back the phone, and Katherine brought him up to speed. "You think we should go to the dentist now?" he asked.

"Yeah, Sam, I do. That new guy, I can't remember his name. I'll get Jonesie to call ahead for you, then call you with the particulars. After that, bring Justin over here to the clinic. I want to check him out myself, and if I see anything amiss I can get him in for a neuro workup with Goldstein at Children's."

Justin heard enough of the one-sided conversation to know that an adult intervention was a probability. He asked his dad for the phone.

"Can I go back in the game, Mom?" His words were muffled from the icepack. "I'm fine, Mom. Really."

"Honey, I think we need to get you to the dentist right away," she said.

Katherine could hear him curling his tongue up to the loose spot. "It doesn't feel like it's that bad, Mom."

"Maybe. But I think . . ."

"Mom, it's no big deal. Really. Just a stupid tooth. Can I go back in the game? Please? I promise I . . ."

"No, Justin."

"But Mom, really, I gotta get out there, it's eleven to zip, we can't...all the Twins need is three grand slams and we can beat 'em! Please, Mom? Please?"

"No whining, Justin. It's unbecoming."

"I'm not whining, Mom. That's not my *whining* voice, that's my *begging* voice. Please? Please? Really, it's just a little loose, a tiny, tiny bit. Besides, if it fell out, I could spit a lot better. Please? Just an hour . . . ?"

"No deal. Let me talk to your dad again."

"God, Mom. *God!*" He handed the phone back to his father.

The man who'd been Katherine's dentist since childhood, and had been treating Justin and Sam, too, had recently retired and handed all his patients to a new guy. They hadn't used him yet. It was about time for an exam anyway, and she'd asked Sam to get something scheduled for the three of them, but he had not gotten around to it.

"And by the way," she said to Sam, "if Justin gets listless or seems disoriented, call me right away. Even if it seems like just a little something, I want to know about it. If he suffered more than a mild concussion, I don't want to take any chances."

"I understand, Kath. I'll keep a close eye on him."

"Please, Sam. I'm deadly serious."

He hesitated, swallowed, pushing down on his resentment at what felt like a questioning of his judgment. He was never good enough. "I hear you, Katherine."

TWO

Katherine wasn't deeply worried about Justin. Another day, another scrape. That was her boy, like most boys. Besides, she trusted Brian and his judgment. Yes, the concussion could be a problem, but Justin sounded perfectly normal over the phone and she was sure Sam would call her if he noticed anything out of the ordinary. Well, pretty sure. He could get preoccupied.

She was in the middle of a typical Saturday morning at the North Side Fort Worth/Tarrant County Pediatrics Clinic: Every day began with the same crying swirl of misery when she opened the back door to the clinic. Bleary-eyed parents would be waiting with their distressed kids in the three exam rooms when she arrived at nine. Mothers — almost always mothers — would have been up all night with kids in pain from earaches, stomach distress, asthma. Some days the misery index doubled and tripled, as when a stomach virus marched through the neighborhood. For those time Katherine and her nurse/receptionist Kirby Jones had a saying: "Shit happens. Bring a shovel." That fortified them. They could handle anything.

Saturdays were usually a bit less busy than other days because, without school to dodge, the kids' health seemed to take an upswing. But Saturdays were also a day for immunizations and general checkups.

This morning, like all the others, began with the screamers. Katherine would set down her purse on the desk in her office, ignore the phone messages, wash her hands and get going. It usually took an hour to get the decibels down to an acceptable range. Then she could answer her phone messages and maybe squeeze in half a cup of coffee. After that, she could start working on the not-so-distressed patients.

Katherine Warren, M.D., was one big slump of a woman, intense, warm, lumpy, huggable. She started and ended each patient visit with a hug or a touch. In between, each kid got the benefit of a keen and deep diagnostic onceover.

Well-rounded, she liked to call herself — wide bottom, heavy bosoms, pudgy face and eyes so tired they rested on their own little dark pillows. A disgrace to physicianhood, she called herself in her worst moments. Her Body Mass Index was in the unacceptable range, no doubt, and what kind of message was that sending to her patients? She was thirty pounds overweight, at least. Thirty-five, max. Well, except for holidays. Forty, then. She'd starve off five, ten pounds, and then a grateful mother would bring her a lemon pound cake with a beckoning, sugary glaze, or one of the guys from the firehouse next door to the clinic would drop off a box of warm doughnuts. Bushwhacked! When the stress was high, her resistance was low. Before Katherine knew what hit her, she'd be brushing crumbs off her lab coat.

It wasn't all bad. The pounds made her approachable, unlike her angular, severe-looking, "healthy" colleagues. The children seemed to trust Katherine, to open up to her, and to easily respond to her big fat mom smile. She had arms worth falling into, a soothing voice in a lower range, a brown mop of random, neglected hair. "Show me where it hurts, honey," and they did, again and again.

She could also be a mother bear, and neglectful parents or unprepared hospital residents had the bite marks to prove it. Sam had been chewed on plenty of times, too.

By the time Katherine prepared to see the last of the major noisemakers, it was approaching ten-thirty. She folded her stethoscope into the side pocket of her white doctor's coat and walked toward Exam Three. The boy's torrential screams were down to hiccups.

Three-year-old Jackson McDermott sat on the edge of the exam table, swinging his legs and working on the sugarless sucker that Jonesie had given him. Except for some redness around one nostril and a few last sniffles, the ordeal was over. His mother Linda had wiped the Vaseline from his nose and the extracted dried bean had been tossed in the trash.

Bean In Nose. BIN. It happened often enough that Jonesie had given it an abbreviation for the clinic records.

The nurse stepped back as Katherine came in with her otoscope to take a look. "This won't hurt, honey," she said, partially squatting to get even with the boy's face. She gently held his curly head and slid the pointed plastic end of the instrument into his nose. The light showed no damage. "All clear, Jack," she said. "Mr. Jonesie has gotten you all fixed up."

"He doesn't look like a nurse," said seven-year-old Randy, Jackson's brother. His hair was burred; a tough guy in the making.

Kirby Jones, R.N., in neat green scrubs, was two inches taller than Katherine and fifty pounds lighter. He put his hand up to his coiffed blond head and said, "Oh, dear! I forgot my nurse's cap again!"

Both boys laughed. Jackson's tears were long gone.

Their father was Lt. Chris McDermott, in charge of the firehouse next door to the clinic. "I'm surprised Chris didn't hear Jackson yelling and come on over," Katherine said.

"They're out on a call," Linda said with a smile. "Otherwise he probably would have."

Katherine leaned back against the stainless steel countertop on the other side of the exam room. The boys were regulars. She'd known Jack since infancy. "So what made you decide to put a bean in your nose, Jack?" she asked.

"Wandy," the boy explained. "He said he bet I could get at least ten in each hole. I got in three and then I sneezed and two came flyin' out. The other one got stuck."

"Randy?" his mother began. "How many times…"

"Wandy said I was gettin' a bud in my butt."

"A *what?*" Katherine asked.

"I was just teasin'," Randy said.

"He made me pull my pants down," Jackson said. "He said sure enough he could already see a leaf growin' out of my butt. From the bean."

"I told him not to worry about it," Randy said. "I said it was just a bud. Didn't amount to a hill of beans. That's when he really started screamin'."

"You were torturing your brother," Linda said. "We've talked about this, Randy. You're going to be grounded."

Katherine raised an index finger, gesturing for a reconsideration. "Jonesie, bring me Randall McDermott's file, would ya?"

"Sure thing." He left the room.

Katherine looked at the older boy, then at his mother. "I thought this might be a good time to check Randy's records. Make sure his immunizations are up to date."

"You mean a *shot?*" Randy's face suddenly scowled in fear.

Jackson broke out into a grin of triumph and pumped his little fist. "Yessss!"

At last Katherine arrived at her midmorning break. Behind the closed door of her little office at the end of the hall, with a cup of coffee in her hand and a sigh on her lips, she leaned back in her government-issued, faux-everything, semi-executive chair. She thought back to the beginning of her morning, before her workday began . . . .

The Great Awakening, DEFCON Five. "Justin? Time to get up, honey!"

Katherine paused at the open door of his bedroom. No response, either from the boy or the Labrador. Gracie was curled in her spot at the end of his bed, where she'd been all night.

It was six-thirty. Because it was Saturday, Katherine could afford to give Justin another half hour of sleep. His game wasn't until nine, but he had to have breakfast and a shower, and she already knew his objections, which they'd have to negotiate through: "Before a game, Mom? Are you crazy? It's a waste of water when I'm gonna get dirty in another hour anyway." And she'd say something like, "Not to worry, my friend, we can afford the water." Katherine needed to leave by seven-thirty to take in rounds at the hospital and get to the clinic by nine.

That meant Justin needed to get up by seven, which would give her and Sam time for a second — and very necessary — quiet cup of coffee. No response to her first wakeup call? No problem. She'd be back. Consider this a shot over the bow.

Katherine went into the living room, where she slumped onto her designated end of the couch. Sam, in his leather recliner next to her, was looking through the business section of the *Fort Worth Star-Telegram*. She reached for the local section. This was their usual division of the world — the couch, the chair, the paper, the chores. Today began as typically as any Saturday.

Sam liked to check for news of his Fort Worth clients' businesses. Katherine needed to know what the local politicos were up to, since they shaped the county budget that kept her clinic going and had such an impact on what she considered her second child, Fort Worth Children's Medical Center. Her most recent project was kick-starting a separate emergency room there. If she detected a fiscal threat, she'd have to make some calls. She knew where the power was.

She breezed through the section. No red flags. She also panned across the obituaries, looking for familiar names. She tried to keep abreast of what was going on with her patients' parents and grandparents. Grief invariably opened the door to ailments in the small bodies she treated. Besides, it was a connection. The more connections with her kids, the better.

Her kids, her families, her old, familiar neighborhood. She wanted to do her part to make a community out of the crumbling, weedy side of town that had been her first home, a shelter in her ragged growing up, and she was not going to abandon it. The north side of Fort Worth was home to most of the city's substantial Hispanic population, with a few Anglo stragglers like her grandmother and the McDermotts.

Sam looked over at her from his outfolded paper. "I was thinking of spending a few hours at the office this afternoon after the game, since Justin's going to spend the rest of the day at Toady's. That's still the plan, right?"

She folded down her paper into her lap. "Right. I talked to Marcie last night, remember? The pool opens at the club today. They want to take Justin."

"What's wrong with our pool, by the way?"

"Justin says it's too cold."

"For God's sake."

"I know."

"Anyway, what about your schedule, Kath?"

"The usual — clinic till three, rounds at the hospital till four, maybe five. If all goes smoothly."

"It never goes smoothly."

"It might. Sometimes it does, Sam. Then I was thinking about us all getting a pizza."

"Sure, if it's not too late. Call me if you're gonna be late. Justin and I'll go on and go, and we can bring you a doggie bag."

"Sure, Sam. Whatever. Me and Gracie. *Woof.*"

It wasn't supposed to be this complicated. The clinic was supposed to be something Katherine could leave at the end of the day, the way Sam could leave his accounting firm (except during the springtime tax crunch). But it hadn't worked out that way.

At the clinic, the last person to leave punched in the burglar alarm code and locked the deadbolt, and that was usually Katherine. Closing time was supposed to be at five, but often it was six, sometimes seven, paperwork, phone calls, late arrivals at the clinic. Then rounds at the hospital, which could keep her busy until eight or nine or ten at night, or committee meetings, so many meetings. And the two a.m. emergency calls to her cell or her pager beside her bed. The dreams, the figuring out of a patient's hidden malady, the fears of figuring it out wrongly. Her heart never closed, her days never ended. She couldn't blame Sam and Justin for resenting the leftovers of herself they so often got. Warmed-over, bone-tired, doggie-bag leftovers.

DEFCON Three. "Justin, time to get up!"

She stood at the bedroom doorway again, flinging double the decibels at him this time. He didn't wiggle, and neither did Gracie — hardly even a snort in their sleep. Six forty-five. She was running low on time and was going to have to escalate her tactics in a hurry. She turned on the stereo and directed the CD player to a certain aria. She reached just inside his bedroom door and turned up the volume to the speakers in the ceiling above his bed. They released a piercing soprano with a jackhammer vibrato.

"Mom! Please! It's Saturday!"

Justin pulled the pillow over his head, smothering his ears and groaning. Gracie was unmoved.

"What about your game, Jus? It's a biggie." She was almost yelling.

"Please shut off that noise, Mom. Please? I promise I'll get up if you turn it off."

"Promise?"

"Cross my heart."

She didn't believe him, of course, but she went back into the den and pushed the button that brought Verdi to a mid-note stop. Katherine loved opera, but this little ditty — she wasn't sure what work the aria was from — was enough to loosen the plaster, and Katherine wasn't upset when the silence resumed.

She returned, leaned back on the doorjamb of his bedroom and took in the scene. A gorgeous day poured in from the skylight and between the slats of the high windows' shutters. Layers of beaming morning covered the bed, brightening the dog's black fur and Justin's pajamaed chest. The light blanketed her child, cherishing him, as it had every day for all of his almost-eleven years.

The vision reminded her of why she had pushed Sam to buy this old mansion and give it a new life. The first time she saw it, it spoke to her. She spoke back. "Welcome, home, Sam," she told him as they walked through it for the first time and before they had even made an offer. "Get out your checkbook."

In 1910, a Texas oilman built the residence as a gift to his mistress, an amateur opera singer. It was a prairie-style house with grand Art Nouveau touches and an angular, Frank Lloyd Wright feel.

The great room, where Katherine and Sam drank their coffee each morning, had been the mistress's performance space. It was massive. The ceiling was seventeen feet tall and the room forty feet long. There was room for two sitting areas. Katherine filled the room with her opera recordings through giant stereo speakers, and the music seemed at home.

Katherine called it the God Room. When newcomers walked in through the front door, turning the corner from the sunroom, "Oh my God!" was the typical awed response. It was a thrill to see so much unexpected space, cheery in the daylight with its pale lemon walls and stained glass in the wall-high bank of windows. Katherine compared the ten-foot-tall marble fireplace mantel to an altar. With the room's cathedral breadth and auditorium acoustics, her metaphor was complete.

Sam got swept up in her vision. The house itself wasn't too expensive, but what she wanted to do to it was going to cost more than the original mortgage.

He wanted to make her happy. She had worked so hard, come so far, starting in that little house on the North Side, orphaned, taken in, then working her way to the top of her class at the Johns Hopkins University School of Medicine. She deserved a castle, Sam believed, and this house, by the time they finished, came close. His father backed the note and they borrowed their way to beauty.

Wiring was replaced, hardwood floors reworked, kitchen remodeled, grounds landscaped. The house had a separate two-story servants' quarters. They connected it to the main house with a tiled utility area and a second porch. They turned the bottom floor of the servants' quarters into a garage and made a large office for Sam above. It was far from the center of things, quiet, isolated. He spent hours there when he wasn't at Moore & Assoc., Accounting and Investments, downtown.

The house became Katherine's refuge, just as she imagined it would. Every high-windowed room was a shelter of light. Every morning was a grand opening, every evening a quiet closing, every night a safe dark. As hard as she worked and as much as she loved her job, she always couldn't wait to get home.

As a final touch she had hired decorators — friends of Jonesie's — to give the newly remodeled house a sophisticated polish.

Justin let Kenneth and Franklin arrange the furniture in his room, but he took over the walls. He hammered into place his Texas Rangers pennants, the Billy Bass musical fish and the bug collection. Kenneth, in the spirit of compromise, kept his mouth shut, except for one gasp.

Katherine overheard this conversation one morning between Justin and his father:

"Dad, Franklin says I'm going to have pillow shams to match the walls. What's a pillow sham?"

"Hell if I know."

"Do I have to have 'em?"

"Yeah, Justin."

"What would happen if Gracie accidentally ate 'em?"

"Your mother would throw a walleyed fit, that's what. Don't encourage Gracie, or at least not for a while."

Standing at the door now, Katherine could see those frilly, mauve-toned pillows piled into a corner of the all-boy room. Some had teeth marks. Canines.

For the second time she retreated. Fifteen more minutes of probation for Justin and that was it. She went back to the master bath and took her shower. Sam was in his office upstairs, buried in stock reports.

She returned to just what she expected. Neither boy nor dog had moved.

That was it. DEFCON One. She went to the pantry and came back with two dog snacks in the shape of bacon. When she went into Justin's room, he was sleeping on his back with the covers at his knees. She slipped one strip under each buttock, with just the tips showing. The aroma would be enough to wake Gracie, and she'd do the rest.

Katherine quietly closed the bedroom door and went to the kitchen to set out breakfast. She heard the first giggly scream before she got to the refrigerator.

Within minutes he came into the kitchen. The dog ambled in behind him.

"Gracie bit me, Mom. I hope you're happy."

"On your lazy butt?"

"Yeah."

"I gave you fair warning."

Justin and his mother moved to the dining room. She was suited up in her uniform of the day, blue scrubs, lab coat and running shoes. He was still in his pajamas. Soon they were smacking down their bowls of Cheerios, and Gracie was standing by, at the ready for spillage.

"Any blood loss?" she asked.

Justin pulled back on the elastic waistband, looked back and down, kept chewing.

"Nope."

"Do you need a Band-Aid?"

"I don't think so."

"I guess you're gonna pull through then, huh?"

He let the waistband snap back. "I guess."

Both mother and son ate desperately fast. He, because that's how boys ate; she, because she was running late.

The dining room was on the east side of the house. Because the shutters were closed, the blast of light from the new morning couldn't score a direct hit on them, but plenty got in anyway, more than enough to brighten Justin to a rich glow. They crunched and breathed and slurped. Gracie whined a little, her snout propped across Justin's thigh, her caramel eyes expectant. Justin passed a tiny portion of cereal to her, and the dog inhaled it.

"You haven't seen a single one of my games this year," Justin said.

Katherine was standing at the table next to him. She'd finished her cereal, and he was tilting his bowl to his lips for a final gulp.

"I know, honey, I know. And I'm sorry. But I've told you, Dr. Lydia is on maternity leave." Lydia Rojas was her partner at the clinic.

Katherine had filled her go-cup with coffee and was pushing the rubber lid on. She had her purse hanging from one arm, her car keys in her hand. All aboard the guilt train.

"You can't get somebody else to take your place, Mom? Just one Saturday?"

"Maybe, honey. Maybe. But not today. Probably just one more month and Lydia will be back."

"No more Little League games by then. Are you gonna miss *all* my games?"

"But summer vacation, honey. We'll go somewhere neat. Promise. In July. I'll get some time off then."

"OK."

"Be thinking about where you want to go. We'll go for sure."

She grabbed a drive-by kiss from him, a smear of a smooch, as she walked toward the door. "I'll hear about the game this evening, honey. OK? Over a pizza?"

"OK, Mom."

She was halfway out the front door but still leaning back to get in her last words.

"Hit one out of the park for me, Justie!"

"You got it, Mom!"

That sunrise smile of his fanned out to her, and then she was gone.

THREE

Something's wrong. Sam looked up from his magazine. Had he said anything aloud, or was it just a very loud thought that had interrupted his reading?

He looked around the dentist's nondescript waiting room. Nobody seemed to have noticed. A woman with a child in her lap was pointing at the pictures in a cardboard book. An old man sat in a chair across the low table from him, staring down. Other people, no reaction. Sam looked back down to the Nasdaq chart he had been studying, a breakout of the top-tier Internet stocks, their year-earlier lofty P/E's and their downward, jagged plunge. The headline asked, "Have the Dot-Com Darlings Lost Their Appeal for Good?"

The closed door of the treatment area was across the room. Nothing seemed amiss. He looked at the dentist's receptionist behind the counter. Her dark bubble of hair was immobile, her attention captured by her computer screen. If there were anything wrong she'd be looking away, into the hall behind her. Wouldn't she?

Weird what comes into your mind, Sam thought. *So much bouncing around. Random crap.*

Justin had been adamant that he didn't need his father to accompany him back to the big chair where the dentist worked. "Really, Dad, I'm eleven years old."

"Ten, Justin."

"OK, almost eleven. I can handle this."

Sam smiled at the recollection. Justin was his mother's kid; his independent streak was a mile wide. His father reluctantly let the boy follow the receptionist by himself when his name was called. Justin's eye was darkening and he walked with a bit of a swagger. The wounded warrior. Sam smiled again.

Sam had been so unlike Justin in his own growing up. Sam's father had been a lot different, too.

It was hard to get much more formidable than U.S. District Judge Leonard Samuel "Leo" Moore. Or more formal, or traditional, or powerful. And no matter how much taller than his dad Sam eventually got, he could never seem to outgrow his father's shadow.

Sam was the only child, born late in his parents' lives after their stately ways had been established. Sam's natural reserve helped him fit in; he was balancing a teacup on his knee by the time he was twelve. His timid and sheltered mother taught him that.

From the beginning Sam's shyness and shame had a chokehold on him. He bumbled his way through adolescence in an obvious way. It wasn't easy to hide six feet four inches of awkwardness. It didn't go unnoticed when he tripped on his laces going after a grounder, or when he let a basketball whack him on the head as he jumped to block an opponent's shot. His mistakes were monumental.

Prep school helped some with the shyness. Undergraduate school helped a little more. But following his father's footsteps into law school was not for him. He found his niche in the financial solitude of accounting.

His early years with Katherine led him out of the shadows and into a mottled light of semi-confidence. She brought out the buried boy in him, the one who spilled his tea and didn't care. Then Justin and all his exuberance helped, too.

The judicial rectitude and Anglican sobriety of his father's ways slowly fell from him. He bounded ahead as his CPA and investment business expanded. The growing stock market of the 1990s made him look smart, and when he doubled down on the "this time it's different" dot-com economy of the later '90s, he felt like a prodigy.

But then, with the sudden turn in the market, the shadows of self-doubt began to creep back in. Since his father's death the year before and his mother's retreat into dementia, he had taken over management of his parents' finances. In a year's time he had let their estate shrink from twelve million dollars to eight. His own portfolio had declined by an even greater percentage, to a little less than a million.

He had to turn things around. He was determined. He was obsessed.

But what about Justin? Sam wanted something better for the boy. He wanted to reach across the distance, to know and to love his son in a way that his own father never had. He would reach toward Justin and fall back, reach and fall back. Ambition's call kept getting in the way.

Sam's mind made another random bounce, this time a couple of years back.

"Mom, have you seen Henry?"

It would have been a Sunday morning. Katherine and Sam were deeply nested in the bed. Justin was about nine, Gracie still a pup, but a big one. Sunday mornings were Sam and Katherine's only time to sleep in. But this wasn't going to be one of those Sundays.

"Henry?" Katherine turned toward Sam, who had remained unmoved, curled under the covers and pretending not to hear.

"Mom, I was playing with him in my bedroom and he got loose and Gracie chased him in here."

She perked. She hated that gerbil. "In here?"

"He could have come up here — climbed right up this bedpost — and gotten under the covers. He likes it nice and warm. Have you felt anything wiggly, Mom?"

"Oh God."

"Gracie, come on, girl! Up on the bed! He patted the bed and Gracie leaped. "Let's sniff him out!"

Katherine pushed up on one elbow. "Justin, for God's sake."

Sam felt a lunge of weight at the end of the bed and those hand-size paws walking between them, stepping on Katherine, then him, Katherine again.

"That's it! That-a-girl! Find Henry, Gracie. Sic 'em!"

Soon Gracie was sniffing right in Katherine's face, then Sam's, then licking.

"Gracie! Please!" She was laughing, but not for long.

"There he is! There's Henry! There's the lump!" Justin grabbed at an imaginary spot above the covers — the back of Katherine's thighs — and she was convinced the critter was indeed in bed with her and heading toward dangerous territory. She screamed and jumped to a sitting position, swatting the covers, and Gracie started barking.

"Oh God, Sam! Catch him!"

By the time Sam turned toward the action, she had sprung from the bed, hopped twice, and slammed the bathroom door behind her. "I'm not coming out till somebody catches that furry little rat!"

Justin sat on the bed, in his mother's empty spot. "Well, that worked pretty good," he said. "Got her up, didn't it?"

"Good job, buddy," his father said, smiling. "You fooled me, too."

"But Henry really did get loose, Dad. I think he went in the kitchen. Can you help me find him?"

"Yeah. Let me go to the bathroom first." Sam went over and knocked on the bathroom door. "Kath? The coast is clear. It was just a ploy to get you up."

He heard her rustling. "Dammit," she said, and flushed the commode. "I could have slept another hour."

A few minutes later, when Sam and Katherine ambled sleepily into the kitchen in pajamas, bathrobes and house shoes, Justin was kneeling on the floor, looking behind the refrigerator with his flashlight. Gracie was looking, too, and wagging. Her nose was in the crack of space between the wall and the refrigerator, just above Justin's curly head.

"Yep, Henry's back there all right," the boy said. "I can see him eating something."

"God, I hope it's not a wire," Sam said.

"Looks like it might be an old pancake," Justin said.

"We need to do something," Katherine said to Sam. "You, actually. I'm not getting within a mile of that little beast."

"We need to drink some coffee first is what we need to do," Sam said.

"Sam, please. This is an emergency. What if he really *is* eating the refrigerator?"

"Right, Dad — an emergency," Justin said, holding the flashlight higher to get a better angle. "He could come racing out of there at any minute and Gracie might bite him."

Katherine poured her coffee and a cup for Sam, edging herself as far away from the refrigerator as possible. She and Sam had talked about this peculiar fear of hers before. Yes, she knew she was a coward when it came to small rodents. She could handle just about anything — even slicing and dicing rats in a biology lab — but not this. It was one of the few girlie things about her.

"I can probably get him out with a mop handle," Sam said.

Justin pulled away from the refrigerator and shined the flashlight into his father's eyes. "No, Dad! You might hurt him!"

Sam blinked and took a sip of coffee. "Then we've got to figure some way to coax him out of there," he said. "Peanut butter?"

"He's already got pancakes," Katherine said. "If I were Henry, I'd stick with the pancakes. There might be enough food back there to keep him alive for years."

"You got a better idea?"

"I don't know," she said. "What about some kind of negative feedback?"

Katherine stepped to her side and opened the cabinet under the sink. "This oughta do it." She held up a can of Raid.

"Mom, that might kill Henry."

"I don't think so. Just a squirt is all. It'll make him uncomfortable enough to get out of there." She handed the insecticide to Sam.

"I don't know about this, Kath," Sam said. "What about just moving the refrigerator? That's the obvious solution."

"He might get under the wheels," Justin said. "You'd squash him."

"True enough," Sam said. "Maybe the spray, then. What could it hurt? Just a squirt or two." He moved toward the refrigerator. "Justin, you be ready to catch him if he comes running out."

"OK, Dad."

Bending, his head against the wall, Sam fired the opening volley. As a fog of poison spread over Henry, the gerbil scratched his ears and rubbed his nose with his front paws.

"I think we're at least making him uncomfortable," Sam said. With half his lips pressed again the wall, his voice was smeared.

"Yeah, maybe," Justin said.

Gracie, who had been sniffing toward Henry, sneezed.

"Let me try a little bit more."

A second, longer spray was getting the gerbil to move. Because of the pantry wall on the other side of the refrigerator, Henry had no other place to go. He moved a few steps toward them, then stopped. Ahead of him were a flashlight, three sets of eyes and a big black snuffling nose.

The next push of the button on the can got a few more steps out of the gerbil, and a few more with the fourth spray. Finally Sam realized that only a continuous spray — over the gerbil's head and behind him — kept his movement constant. By the time Henry moved out into the daylight of the kitchen, he was drenched.

Henry acted drunk. He was swaying. His little beady eyes were closing. Justin didn't try to pick him up, and Gracie kept her distance.

"I think he's sick, Mom. Too much spray."

"He'll be all right," she said in her most affirming diagnostician's voice. She remained as far across the room as possible. "Henry just needs a little air."

And with that Henry fell over on his side, his paws twitched madly, and he went still.

"Oh hell," Katherine said.

"CALL NINE-ONE-ONE!" Justin screamed. "We've gotta do mouth-to-mouth!" He was looking directly at his mother.

"No way," she said. "Sam?"

"You do it," he said. "You're the medical expert."

"I can bag him, I suppose."

She rushed into the bedroom, went into her closet and came out with an oxygen bag. She moved quickly back to the kitchen.

When she put the facemask down over Henry, it entirely covered the critter in a cave of plastic. Sam and Katherine knew it was a lost cause, but they thought the gesture, symbolic though it was, might make Justin feel like they had at least tried. She squeezed the bag, pushing air out. It blew back Henry's fur like a hair dryer. He didn't respond.

"It's not looking good," Katherine said. She lifted the mask off the body.

"You think he's already dead, Mom?"

"Looks like it."

Gracie sniffed him, then pawed him. No response.

"You killed my gerbil, Dad!"

"It was an accident, Justin. I didn't mean to kill Henry."

"You know," Katherine said, "Henry's actually not much bigger than a roach."

"We should have thought of that," Sam said.

"Can we get another one?" Justin asked.

"Sure, honey." Katherine went over and hugged him. "Henry can be replaced."

"Can we go to the pet store today?"

"Dad can take you," she said. "I've got rounds this afternoon."

"Gee, thanks," Sam said.

"Can I go to Toady's, Mom?"

"I think it's a little early, honey. Don't you think we ought to bury Henry?"

"Gracie'll just dig him up. She digs a lot."

"True. What about the park?"

"That might work. I'll go get the shovel."

"Justin," Katherine said, "you need to get out of your pajamas and into your play clothes. Sam? Are you gonna help with the burial?"

"Let me finish my coffee first."

"I'm gonna go watch cartoons." Justin and Gracie left the room.

Katherine got a Ziploc sandwich bag from the kitchen drawer and handed it to her husband. "Sam, Henry needs to be refrigerated."

Sam took the bag and picked up the gerbil. "May you rest in peace, Henry." He dropped Henry into the bag and closed it with a slide of his fingers. "Should he go in the crisper? He might stay fresher that way."

Justin was safely out of the room, and Katherine felt free to laugh. "Yeah, the crisper, why not."

It had been almost half an hour since Justin had gone back to the treatment area. His baseball cap was on the seat next to Sam. He picked it up and began mindlessly pulling the cloth edge back and forth between his thumb and forefinger. He liked to feel the bumps in the back where the plastic catch fastened.

Twins, the cap said in fat red baseball cursive. Dust was still on the back of it where Justin had fallen.

Then, suddenly, something definitely wasn't right. This time Sam was sure he heard it. The receptionist, too. A shuffling of feet and a growing murmur of urgent voices was coming from the treatment area, and she was looking in that direction.

When the tower that was Samuel Patrick Moore stood, everyone in the waiting room looked over. The magazine fell from his lap.

Maybe it was Justin, maybe it wasn't.

To hell with it. Sam was going back there.

FOUR

"Teething," Katherine said to the mom, pointing toward Esperanza's swollen gums. "*Los dientes.*" Katherine made upward motions with her index finger to indicate the buds of teeth sprouting through.

"*Si,*" said Mrs. Zepeda, nodding vigorously.

With Esperanza balanced in one big arm, Katherine stood, and when those six hefty feet of her went up along with her broad, stethoscope-draped shoulders, authority came with her. She reached into the cabinet with her free hand and took out a sample of teething medicine. She opened the bottle, upturned it on her finger, and dabbed the liquid on the child's raw gums.

More nodding, more smiles — except for Esperanza, whose sobs at least were lessening. Katherine took a Kleenex and worked on the baby's tears and drool and runny nose.

"As needed for pain," Katherine said as she underlined the instructions on the label with her pen. Mrs. Zepeda's Hershey eyes went from brown to blank. What was that in Spanish? Usually Katherine's non-English-speaking parents brought an older child or friend to interpret for them, but not this time.

She knew Mrs. Zepeda to be a first-time mom, and guessed that her mother and grandmother were probably still in Mexico. They would have known what to do, would have probably had a home remedy handy, and Esperanza would never have had to suffer this long, nor would Mrs. Zepeda have had to take time from her workday at the dry-cleaners to come in. It takes a village, but this village was across the border. It was the cost of cultural disconnect.

Katherine began some exaggerated boo-hooing, pretending to rub the tears with her fist and turning down her mouth in mock pain. *"Si?"* Then she picked up the bottle and pretended to apply the medicine. *"Si?"*

Little Esperanza thought the pantomime was hilarious. It halted her tears and brought a nubby, drooling grin to her face.

Katherine bent and kissed her chubby patient, touched a dark, fine curl next to the little girl's ear, straightened the pink bow in her hair and smiled to Mrs. Zepeda. Katherine handed the baby back to her, along with the teething medicine. *"Gracias, senora."*

"La medica," said the mom, bowing as she stood. *"Muchisimas gracias."*

Without knocking, startling everyone, Jonesie pushed open the door to Exam Room Two, leaning in half his long frame and interrupting her for the second time this morning, this time in person. His face was all wrong. "It's Sam again. Line one. Emergency."

The word "emergency" always got a stomach-burning surge of chemicals from Katherine. She stood up from the swivel stool, turned away from Esperanza and her mother, and in three steps was reaching for the phone on the wall. Jonesie waited for her to pick it up. He had to know what was going on.

It didn't take long. Her face cringed. "Dear God," she said into the receiver. She inhaled her words.

In less than a minute she and Jonesie were running down the hall toward the back door. "Sam couldn't tell me much," she said. Her words were bouncing and breathless, and her brown mop of hair was a jumble. "I could hear the ambulance coming. In the background. Way off."

Jonesie sprinted ahead on gaunt gazelle legs, the pants of his green scrubs rustling. He rushed into her office for her purse, then pushed it into her gut as she rammed through the back door of the clinic.

They were running across the parking lot. "Sam was at the dentist's office?" he asked.

"Yeah. Out front. Ready to flag down the ambulance."

"So something happened to Justin at the dentist's office?"

"Yeah. Something terrible. I don't know."

He got to the Volvo ahead of her and pulled open the door just after she unlocked it with the key fob. She lunged into the car.

"County General, I'm sure," she said. She brushed in the tails of her lab coat and reached across for the seatbelt. "I'm sure that's where they're headed."

"I'll find out, give you a call." He placed a sympathetic touch to her shoulder, then pushed the car door closed. His eyes were shaded, set back in the caves of his thin face, darkened with care and fear. She started the car.

"Thanks, Jonesie." He stepped away as she bumped the station wagon into reverse and whipped it out toward the driveway. With a spurt of gravel she shifted into forward and bounded into traffic.

FIVE

Katherine was running, and County General's ER receptionist saw her just in time. She pushed the unlock button only a second before Katherine hit the swinging door to the patient area with a full-body slam. The door bounced against the wall.

She knew her way around. Katherine's first job after Johns Hopkins was chief resident of pediatrics at County. These were her people. This was her home.

Justin was easy to find – Trauma One, the biggest and best-equipped room, and the worst place to be in any ER. People who were brought here got the most attention because they needed it.

A crowd was around him, and Katherine had to wedge herself up to the gurney's bedside. A churn of gloved hands surrounded him – white sleeves, blue sleeves, reaching, pushing, adjusting IVs, drawing blood. They had cut off his baseball jersey and dotted his chest with taped wires. The breathing tube, taped to his mouth, covered almost half his face. The tube was attached to a ventilator.

She leaned her head close to his ear. "Justin? It's Mom." Her voice had lost its commanding presence. She spoke in a broken whisper.

Her fingers rested in his spongy nest of dark curls. Her thumb was stroking his forehead. Louder: "Justie? Can you hear me?"

Nothing, no reaction.

Still louder: "Justin honey?"

He was hidden under a swarm of tubes and wires and hands. Technology had taken most of the boy away, but the dirt of the game - the joy of it - was still on him, in his hair, ground into a scrape on his forearm, packed into his fingernails.

OK, she said to herself, breathing as best she could, struggling to right herself inside. *OK. Unconscious. We can deal with this.*

She bent close to his ear again. "Honey, I'm here and we've got lots of doctors helping you. Do you hear me? I'm gonna make sure we make you better. It's gonna be all right."

Katherine had to firm up inside, get her medical bearings and be there for him. Help get him stabilized. Monitor him. Find out what was going on.

It clicked in, the other channel in her. He needed that - Katherine the doctor - more than a mother.

"Tom?" she asked, "Where do we stand here?" Tom Berger, one of the familiar faces around her, was chief of emergency medicine.

"We're gettin' there," he said. "Stable."

"Yeah," said the cardiologist. Arnie Decker was bent over the EKG tape, studying the seismic output from Justin's heart. "I'm liking what I'm seeing. You'd hardly have known he coded."

"It's the epi," Tom said. "Friggin' amazing stuff."

"He coded in the ambulance?" Katherine asked. "Shit, Arnie. Shit."

"I know, Kath. Paddles, epinephrine. It's a miracle he's alive. You've got one hell of a fighter here."

"This is so much worse than I thought." Her breath wanted to fly from her chest, but she pulled it back.

She had talked briefly to Jonesie during her desperate drive in to the hospital. He confirmed the ambulance's destination and reinforced to her the critical nature of the situation, which he had found out from the dentist's office.

Katherine had found out nothing from Sam. He was in one of the plastic chairs off by himself in the ER waiting room, bent like an eroded mountain, staring at the floor between his knees. When he couldn't find his voice after her first question, she touched his shoulder and sprinted toward the trauma room.

Katherine took her stethoscope from the wide pocket of her lab coat, hovered her long frame over her son and had a listen herself. His heartbeat was clear and firm, regular, steady. She stepped back.

"The damage, Tom," Katherine said. "Neuro. Can you tell anything yet?"

"Not much," Tom said. "We don't know what happened at the dentist's office, how long he wasn't breathing."

"Based on what I can tell," the cardiologist said, "what happened in the ambulance wasn't significant. The paddles snapped him right back."

"I've got Goldstein on the way," Tom said. Abe Goldstein was director of pediatric neurology at Children's Hospital next door.

She put her hand on Tom's upper arm. "Damn it, Tom, you're bound to have some idea. What's the damage to the brain?"

Tom Berger was shorter than Katherine by four or five inches. He was trim – runner trim – and he did all the right things except use Rogaine or sleep enough. He was Katherine's age, pushing forty, but he was pushing back a lot harder than she was.

Katherine was determined to find his eyes and the truth in them. She held his arm and refused to let his eyes escape.

"The damage, Tom. The damage."

"Doesn't look good."

"What."

"I don't know what all. Let's wait for Abe, let him take over, CAT scan, whatever. He's the best."

"Reflexes? Pupils?" she asked.

"Very little response, Katherine. Very little."

No, she was saying with the shaking of her head. *This can't be. No!*

She had to see for herself. She had to have the facts. "Let me borrow your penlight, Tom."

She was still standing next to the gurney, opposite Justin's shoulder. She didn't look back at Tom. She held out her hand and he placed the flashlight there as if it were an operating room instrument.

She pushed apart the boy's eyelids with her thumb and index finger. His eyelashes were threads of silk, his eyelids a sheen of cotton cloth.

She had always loved the softness of the brown of his eyes, their speckles of light, their touch of gold. All that was gone. His eyes were almost still and perfectly blank.

"Damn it."

The other one. The same.

"God fucking damn it."

She looked up. "Where the hell's Goldstein? Did somebody call him?"

"He's been called, Dr. Warren, twice," said Kelli Litton, the chief trauma RN. "He was in the middle of a consult, but he should be on his way by now."

"Shit. Call him again."

"No need," Dr. Goldstein said, coming up behind her and putting an arm around her shoulder.

"Abe," she said. She returned the touch.

"When I heard it was Justin, I got loose as soon as I could." Katherine stepped aside as he moved into place beside the gurney. "Let's see what we have here."

Goldstein — a pudge of a guy, short and balding — began examining Justin, occasionally arching the gray fur of his eyebrows over his owl-round glasses. He reached into his lab coat pocket and came out with a Tootsie Roll. He looked at it quizzically, then put it back in his pocket and found the penlight. He did as Katherine had done, waving the small beam of light across the dark glass of Justin's eyes. He took out a rubber hammer and began to tap at Justin's joints.

"So, what the hell happened here."

"We're working on pulling the story together," Tom said. "We've got a nurse talking to the EMTs, the dentist."

"What have we pieced together so far?" Abe asked.

"I can get you started." Katherine said. "Justin was playing in a Little League game this morning, and Sam called me from the baseball field. I was at the peeds clinic. Justin was waiting to go up to bat when he got hit by a foul ball."

"Yes," Abe said. "Here." He gently touched the edges of the red bruise beside Justin's nose. The boy's lips were bumpy, the eye socket was blackened.

"Brian Singleton was there," she said. "Saw it all. I talked to him, too."

"The nephrologist?" Arnie asked.

"That's him," Katherine said. "He was in the bleachers, got down to Justin almost immediately. Anyway, he told me Justin's helmet flew off and the back of his head hit the ground pretty hard. Justin was knocked silly, unconscious for a bit."

"Less than a minute? Two minutes? What?" Goldstein asked.

"Less than a minute," she said.

"Something else is going on here," Goldstein said. "What the hell else happened?"

"The dentist's office," Katherine said. "Sam said Justin stopped breathing in the dentist's office. He took Justin there because he loosened a front tooth when the ball hit him."

"Shit," Goldstein said, taking in a large sigh through his overlapping gray mustaches. He was repeating the test with his penlight. "Do we know how long the boy wasn't breathing? Shit."

"I'm going to go to the waiting room and talk to Sam," Tom said.

A few minutes later Brian Singleton, in the summer shorts and Polo shirt of this morning, came into Trauma One.

"ER called my service a while ago," he said as he came up to the gurney. He stood beside Katherine, put an arm around her. "I can't believe this. I came straight here as soon as I heard." He looked down at Justin and shook his head in disbelief. "This isn't the same boy I saw at the ball field. He wanted to get back in the game. He was next up to bat."

"Brian," Katherine said. "I'm glad you're here. We need to go over again what happened at the baseball field."

"Certainly," he said, speaking up so that all the surrounding doctors and nurses could hear him. "What surprises me, first of all, is that I observed absolutely nothing I'd consider a truly traumatic injury this morning. Like I told you on the phone, Kath, Justin couldn't have been unconscious for more than a minute. I'd say maybe thirty seconds."

"You checked his pupils then," she said. She especially wanted the whole story repeated for Goldstein, who was standing beside her and listening intently.

"Justin was already getting up by the time I got around the backstop, and he was able to walk with help to the bench. His pupils seemed normal - equal, reactive. I asked him where he was, and he answered me instantly and clearly - thought it was a stupid question, by the way," Brian added with a smile.

"Disorientation? Dizziness? Anything?" Goldstein asked.

"Absolutely nothing out of the ordinary."

Goldstein had lifted Justin's head from the pillow. "I can feel a little swelling back here."

"Yeah. I noted that, too."

"Helmet flew away," Katherine repeated.

"Yeah, " Brian said. "As he fell backward."

Goldstein still had his hand cupped under Justin's head. "Hardly anything back here. Minor swelling."

Tom walked back into the group of doctors standing beside the boy. "Sam's calming down some. Based on what he said, I'm starting to think that all the major problems were caused from the incident at the dentist's office."

"Did you get any more details?" Katherine asked.

"He's not real sure what happened. He said he was in the reception area, reading a magazine, and he heard all this commotion down the hall. He went up to the receptionist to find out what was going on, and the woman was real evasive. So Sam just turned around and walked back into the treatment area. That's where he saw Justin in the chair, lips blue, unconscious, a couple of techs around him, the dentist, all working on him."

"Dear God," Katherine said.

Berger continued: "Justin must have suffered some kind of drug reaction, or something went wrong from the injury, maybe a delayed reaction, a blood clot, I don't know. That's what I'm piecing together. He'd apparently been left alone in the room while the Novocain and the gas were taking effect. At least that was what one of the dental techs told Sam. That must have been when Justin quit breathing."

"Left him alone?" Arnie asked. "What the hell? For how long?"

"I'm not aware of Justin having any drug sensitivities," Katherine said. "He's been almost perfectly healthy all his life. Even his teeth. No cavities. I'm not sure he's ever had Novocain."

"So we can assume there was a period of anoxia in the dentist's chair," Goldstein said, "but we don't know how long it lasted."

"He coded once on the way in the ambulance," Arnie said for Goldstein's benefit. "The EMTs had to jolt him pretty good. So the anoxia would have had to have been pretty significant."

"What do you think, Abe?" Katherine asked. "What kind of damage are we looking at?"

"I want a CAT scan, that's what I think. I want an EEG, eventually an MRI, every fucking test we've got."

"Brain swelling?" she asked. "Can you tell anything from the bump on the back of his head?"

"Intracranial hematoma, maybe. Yeah. Which means we've got two things going on at once, possibly, along with maybe a clot. This and the possibility of an anaphylactic reaction, which I agree with Tom might be the chief culprit."

"That dentist," Berger said to no one in particular. "I want to talk to the fucker."

"We're up shit creek, aren't we, Abe," Katherine said. Tears were collecting in her eyes.

The neurologist had gone back for a third look into Justin's vacant eyes. He didn't respond.

"We are," she said.

He didn't respond.

SIX

Katherine was in Trauma One, alone now, leaning toward the window with her hands on the windowsill and looking out onto a parking lot. Her back was to the door. She didn't feel Sam's presence. She didn't turn.

"Kath?"

Stainless-steel shelves and sinks and cabinets multiplied the bright light in the room. Monitors and IV poles were crowded into a corner. On the linoleum floor was a scattering of tape and gauze and empty packages of alcohol wipes, a plastic glove or two, the typical refuse of an emergency.

"Katherine?"

Sam walked across the room. She didn't turn until he touched her shoulder.

"Kath? Where's Justin? Is he OK?"

He looked into her face. She wasn't there.

"It's gotta be the swelling," she said.

"Kath, what are you . . ."

"Brian said that when the baseball hit Justin, he fell back hard and hit the back of his head. Helmet flew away. That's got to be it."

"Kath, where's Justin? The nurse said it was all right for me to come back, that he was in Trauma One. Kath?"

She turned back to the window. "The unconsciousness, Sam, lasting like this, this deep, or what appears to be...swelling, that's it, but we didn't know, couldn't know, no symptoms, see, at first, between the time he got hit and when you drove him to the dentist, and Justin didn't know what he was supposed to be feeling, and you didn't sense anything was wrong, and the dentist never thought, and there was your main problem, right there. Maybe a clot at that point, too. A possibility, or maybe like this gradual swelling that hits critical mass. The rest of it, other possibilities, some say probability, the Novocain, well, I don't know, probably not the cause, the *underlying* cause, but it was the injury showing itself at that moment and who wouldn't be confused as to the cause? Why not this coincidence?"

She turned back toward him. She was still far away, and she continued. "And, assuming there really *was* some kind of anaphylactic reaction, his brain was deprived of oxygen probably not as long as they think — when something like that happens, time just almost grinds to a halt and you think things last for a lot longer than they really do, somebody not breathing like that, it's happened to me, you know, these dire situations."

"Katherine, please. Please listen to me."

"I have no doubt that his heart *did* stop for a minute, of course, but for not really more than a minute. A blip was all. That's incontrovertible. In the ambulance, for sure. But what is probably going on, what's *really* going on, the brain swelling, like cutting off circulation, you go numb inside just like the way your arm goes to sleep when you sleep wrong, and that's something we can do something about. Goldstein will. That's what he'll figure out, piece together, I'm starting to see that. We'll give it a little time, relax Justin with some medication, back off and that's it. Wait. Assist his breathing with the vent. A few hours, maybe a day, maybe three, and he'll come around, Sam. He'll come around."

He took her upper arms in his hands and squeezed a little. He was almost shaking her, trying to jar her loose from a freight train of facts and conjectures and hope.

"Kath. Listen to me, please. Where's Justin?"

At last her focus gathered in his direction, but not enough to see the urgency and frustration in his creased face.

"CAT scan. Abe took him down the hall for a CAT scan. They ought to be back any minute."

"Abe?"

"Abe. Abe Goldstein. Pediatric neurologist. One of the best anywhere, Sam. I can't remember if you've met him or not. I've known him forever, see him when I can, on rounds, and he and Justin were pals when Justin was little and used to come up here with me. Abe's got a hell of a reputation. He . . ."

"OK. So Justin's OK."

"Yes, honey. I guess. I mean . . ."

The tears had begun as a glistening on the panes of her eyes, gathered quickly and now began to drip. No noise, no quaking came with them. Just water, just a nuisance, and she wiped at them with the back of her hand. She was a doctor, for God's sake. She had no use for tears.

She turned away from him again, to the window, to nothing. She was showing him too much. He shouldn't know her level of fear, and she didn't want to know it herself.

"Kath?"

"Yes?"

"Kath, are you all right?" Once again he put his hand on her shoulder, this time on top, but she didn't turn.

"That's gotta be it, Sam, and that explains why it looks so much worse than it is. Don't you see?"

She used the back of her hand again, pushing the water out of the way.

"Yes. Maybe. I don't know. Katherine, you're not making a lot of sense."

"Abe'll confirm all this with the CAT, I'm sure. He'll see the swelling, get a fix on it, get an idea how long it'll be before Justin comes around."

"Kath? I'm so confused."

"That's it, Sam. The swelling. That's gotta be it."

SEVEN

The CAT was taking longer than it should have — almost an hour had gone by. Katherine and Sam, standing by the window in the empty trauma room, drank from the Styrofoam cups of coffee a nurse had brought them. Katherine was collecting herself, working hard to right herself, clear her mind and drill down toward the truth.

When things got tough and the pressure climbed — a bleeder in the abdominal cavity, a frantic phone call in the night — you parsed the situation into manageable bits, and then you dealt with them. The goal, always, was to make the next right decision. One at a time, in small steps, you did the next right thing.

If you had the facts, you had control. Then you could move forward.

The facts. One, two, three; hammering out the facts, as much precision as possible. That's where Sam and Katherine spent their days and made their living — she with her medical practice, he with his accounting firm — blood pressure, blood values; net gain, net loss. One hard number at a time, they made the world make sense.

Solid evidence nourished them. A reinforced bottom line supported them. They framed their worlds with the steel of facts. And now it was time for Katherine to regain this reliable world, and for Sam to do his best to help.

"What we want to know is what's wrong with him physically, Sam. That's the first thing. If we can figure out the cause — the reason for the coma — that will determine our treatment protocol."

"OK, I get that, Kath. But are we making any progress?"

"Not much," she said. "Not yet. But we'll get there. With people like Abe, with the finest minds and best equipment that medical science has to offer, I swear to you, Sam, we'll get there. We'll figure this thing out."

Katherine's breathing slowed and her words relaxed. She would start over.

"OK then, one more time, Sam. I know you told Tom a lot of this out in the waiting room, but let's do it again — every small thing you can remember about getting Justin from the game to the dentist, and what you saw when you went back there at the dentist's office. The littlest thing. Everything."

"OK. Everything."

Sam began to pace. Katherine leaned back against the wall next to the window. The coffee — it was her third cup — provided a reassuring warmth to her hand and to her lips. She shouldn't have needed warmth on a short-sleeve day like this one, but she did.

"In the car on the way to the dentist's," Katherine said. "Disorientation? Listlessness? Did Justin show signs of anything out of the ordinary?"

"Nothing, Kath. I've been wracking my brain since I talked to Dr. Berger earlier, and I'm not coming up with anything. Justie was his usual talkative self. We talked about the Rangers, about his own team, about his chances of being a pitcher, maybe catcher; he hates right field. So we talked about some of the famous fielders in baseball. There've been a lot of them, you know, and I told him I didn't see any reason why he couldn't be that good, and of course he loved that. We went over some of the great plays he's made lately."

Katherine was there, almost. She could hear the boy's jubilant enthusiasm and bouncing optimism. She had to smile as Sam continued.

"He was starting to feel good, not complaining about his cut lip, saying he was hoping we could go right back to the game if the dentist was fast enough. He said he was going to ask that dentist to make it snappy. His teammates were counting on him!"

That was Justin. They were both smiling now. His self-confidence was bountiful. Sam, especially, made sure of that.

Justin was a baseball connoisseur. When Sam's father was still alive, Justin often went with his grandparents to their skybox at the Texas Rangers' stadium. Justin was a favorite of the prominent guests of his grandfather. Justin gave those congressmen and jurists and business executives the lowdown on every player.

"I'm not hearing anything unusual, Sam," Katherine said "It sounds like he was absolutely normal."

"He kept looking in the rearview mirror to see what kind of shiner he was getting."

Katherine smiled again. " That's my boy."

"And he was his same old self at the dentist's, too. He wouldn't let me go back to the treatment area when they called his name. Big, tough guy. No babying. Anyway, I was in the waiting room maybe thirty minutes, reading a magazine, and this feeling of unease came over me. It was the strangest thing. That's before I heard any of the commotion back there."

"You felt Justin was in danger?"

"Something wasn't right. I don't know. But I didn't do anything about it. I wish I'd gone back to the treatment area right then, maybe alerted somebody, something, but I would have felt like some kind of fool if nothing was wrong, and Justin would have had a fit."

She did not reply immediately. Her look at him was hard. "I guess."

"You guess?" Anger rose in him. "What do you mean, you guess? I . . ."

She put her hand out and placed it on his shoulder. "Sam. No. I don't mean to question . . ."

"Kath, I did everything I could. I did. I did. So you would have gone back there right then?"

"No, Sam. I'm not saying that. I would have probably done the same thing. Waited."

After a couple of deep breaths his anger slackened enough for him to continue. Getting to the facts and helping

Justin was so much more important to Sam than any bruises to his ego. "Maybe ten more minutes is how long it was, Kath. Something like that. Then I was sure I heard something, and that's when I went back there. I just got up and went back there. I stopped at the receptionist's but she was evasive and so I just pushed on back there. Fuck her.

"Everything was so confused, Kath. The nurses, the dentist, they were hurrying in and out of his room. I had just a second to see Justin before they pulled me away. I remember his arms were limp, hanging over the side of the chair."

"And his lips, Sam. Were his lips blue?"

"Yes, I think so, but they were hard to see. They had an oxygen mask over his face and I could hardly see his face at all. It came off for a second. That's when the receptionist started pulling me away.

"She kept pulling at me. That's about all I remember, that and yelling at her to call nine-one-one."

"That was the right thing."

"I was screaming, Kath, screaming, everything I had, pushing that woman down the hall toward the phone. 'Call nine-one-one! Call nine-one-one!' I didn't stop. I was screaming. I didn't care. Shit, I finally just pushed her aside, went behind her desk and called the number myself."

"Good God, Sam." She reached over and touched his arm. Its muscles were hard and twitching. "You did the right thing."

"I don't know. I . . ." His eyes were locked on that moment, aimed out into the room. "It's hard to remember. The receptionist was trying to help me, calm me down. She got me some water. She wanted me out of there. They wouldn't let me get back to see Justin again so that's when the receptionist led me outside, in front of the building, and she kept telling me that everything was going to be all right. And pretty soon I heard the ambulance. That's when I called Jonesie."

"So it didn't take long for the ambulance."

"Hardly anytime. And they didn't mess around when they got there. They went fast. They did everything fast. They brought him out on the stretcher, I told them who I was, that I wanted to sit back there in the ambulance with him but they said there wasn't room. So I said I'd follow them, they said let's go, and we were on the road in no time.

"And then oh my God, Kath. Oh my God. I could hardly keep up with the guy, even in the Lexus. He was up on sidewalks, left lanes, barreling through red light after red light, pushing, pushing, and I was laying on my horn. Headlights, hazard lights. I kept up with the guy, but just barely."

"Justin's heart stopped on the way," Katherine said. "That's what Tom told me. They had to really push it."

"I know. Dr. Berger told me that, too. They used the paddles."

"Those guys, the EMTs, they're heroes, Sam. They saved him."

The chills came through him and across him. "I know."

Katherine heard a gurney coming and rushed out into the hall. She went to it, took up a position between Dr. Goldstein and a nurse, and helped roll the bed back into Trauma One. A nurse and a tech from Radiology were pushing on the other side, one also pulling the ventilator, the other an IV pole. Sam backed out of the way as the bed rolled in.

"What took so long?" Katherine asked Goldstein.

"The scan. I didn't like what we were getting."

"What you were seeing? The quality of the scan? What, Abe?"

"Both."

"Swelling, right? You saw swelling?"

"It's hard to tell."

"What do you mean?"

"I mean it's hard to tell, Katherine. I need to spend some time with the scans. The pictures were cloudy, diffuse, which is often the case right after something like this. I've got some colleagues I want to show these to. One in Toronto. There's a guy in Tokyo. Some others. I can email the scans, hear back from the docs in less than a day. Maybe they can see something I can't see, but what I think we'll have to do is wait, twenty-four hours, forty-eight, then try again with the CT. By then we'll have an MRI, too."

"I was hoping for something simple, Abe, something definitive."

"So was I. The trauma, the anoxia — one or the other, one simple cause. Get a better idea of the extent of this thing."

"Yeah."

Goldstein gave her the best, most sympathetic look he could manage and put an arm around her shoulder. "Through a glass darkly, I'm afraid. I'm sorry, Katherine."

A nurse helped situate the bed, locked its wheels, arranged the ventilator and the IV, checked them, rehooked Justin to the BP and other monitors with a mishmash of mechanical tones as each came back online, checked his urine output, and tucked in the sheet around his chest and under his arms, which she placed alongside his torso. He was in a hospital gown now, and his baseball clothes were in a plastic bag on a shelf under the gurney.

Katherine introduced Sam to Abe. Yes, they'd met at a couple of Medical Society dinners, but neither remembered the other. Sam was a social dunderhead, and so was Goldstein. They both relied on their wives to do the heavy lifting on social occasions.

Sam wasn't paying much attention anyway. He watched as the nurse worked around his son. An ache was building in him, sorrow and a new level of fear. So much, so fast, so bad.

"So what's next, Dr. Goldstein?" Sam asked absently, not looking up.

"We're going to send him up to surgery, get a trach established - a small incision in his throat. We'll insert an airway and attach the ventilator to it, extubate - ah, remove the airway he's got now. That won't take long. I've got him a room at Children's ICU. When we're ready they'll send over a crew to take him over there, get him situated, then they'll call me." Goldstein turned to Katherine. "I'm going up to my office to study the scans."

"OK," Katherine said.

Tom Berger came in the room. "I've got the dentist on the way over here."

"Good," she said. "Abe, can you hang on a minute and help us quiz this guy?"

"Sure. Be glad to."

"I'll set us up in the conference room," Tom said.

"No reason not to go ahead and send Justin to surgery," Goldstein said.

"I'll go with him," Sam said.

"That's fine, Sam," Goldstein said. "It'll be a few minutes before they come down to get him."

As the nurse finished her work with the boy and departed, Sam found his chance to move in close to Justin. Katherine escorted the doctors out of the room, and at last Sam was alone with his son.

He touched Justin's bare shoulder and let his hand slide down the long, smooth, unbunched muscles of the boy's arm. Sam stopped at the hand, picked it up, held it in both of his. Justin's limp fingers were Sam's, thick and blunt.

Sam bent to Justin's hand, lifted it to his lips, touched it to his cheek and rubbed the knuckles across his lips. Back and forth, back and forth, but not a twitch of movement answered back from the boy. Every muscle in Sam's face, long and small, was breaking. His eyes, turned down, were heavy with a backup of tears.

"A lot more tests we can do, Sam," Katherine said, coming back to the room and standing by the door. "A lot more."

He didn't look up.

The facts, he was thinking. *One connected to the next connected to the next, and with that chain of facts they will throw him a lifeline and pull him out of this mess.*

But wait. What facts. Somebody show me some facts. Nobody around here knows a fucking thing.

There was only one real fact so far. His child was in terrible trouble.

EIGHT

When the dentist walked into the conference room, Katherine stood. She wanted him to feel her full presence. She was four inches taller and forty pounds heavier.

"Dr. Shields," she said with the firmness of a judge, offering her hand and possessing his in a shake as sure as her voice, "I'm Katherine Warren, Justin's mother." His hand seemed to cringe in hers, and she felt a film of dampness.

He appeared frail next to her and much too young. He released his hand from her imposing grip and looked across the room and its phalanx of medically dressed people sitting at a long table. In his left hand he carried a cellophane-crinkling pot of yellow mums, which he had picked up from the hospital gift shop on his way in.

"You're..." he said, taking in her white coat and the authority in her tightened face.

"I'm Justin's mother."

"I thought...His name is Justin Moore. And . . . the gentleman who brought him to my office? Mr. Moore?"

"His father. He's with Justin now. We asked you here to meet with our team to..."

"A meeting? What kind of meeting is this? Who are all these people? I came to see the boy, to go over with a Dr. Berger what happened in my office. I feel so badly about what happened."

Tom said: "I'm Dr. Berger. Yes, I have some questions, and so does the rest of Justin's medical team. You won't be able to see the boy. He is in very serious condition, as I'm sure you know. We need to figure out how he got that way."

"In serious condition? I thought the boy would have come around by now. Stable. Stabilizing. I...when he left in the ambulance, he seemed . . ."

"A few questions, sir," Tom repeated.

"Of course. I want to help, but if this turns into some kind of inquisition . . ." Maybe the mums had been a bad idea. He set them on the table and reluctantly took a seat.

Katherine introduced her colleagues, who remained seated. Each nodded gravely at his name. The dentist's eyes, heavy and protruding behind gold-framed glasses, blinked defensively.

"Abraham Goldstein, peeds neuro," she said, pointing to each as she went around the table. "Arnold Decker, cardiology; Brian Singleton, nephrology; Tom Berger, chief of the ER; Kelli Litton, trauma RN." She took her seat across the table from Shields. Her tone hardened. "I'm a pediatrician. If you had read Justin's records, you would know that."

"We appreciate you coming in so quickly, Dr. Shields," Kelli said, working to calm the waters and get the group on task. "What you tell us can be of enormous help in our assessment of Justin's condition and how we treat him." A yellow legal pad was in front of her, and she began writing as she talked.

"I canceled all my appointments for the rest of the day," he said. "I couldn't work. None of us could. Justin gave us quite a scare. We've all been so traumatized."

"I'm sure you have," Katherine said. She felt her jaw grind on the words.

"The neurological damage appears to be extensive," Goldstein said, cutting to the point. His padded exterior hid layers of muscle and gristle. He was a cuddly grandfather with his young patients, but he could turn his mind into a fist when the occasion called for it. "We need to know what happened."

"It's vital that we pinpoint the length of anoxia," the cardiologist said.

Dr. Shields's receding chin receded farther. It seemed to shiver just a bit. "I, ah...I had no idea. He was breathing normally when the EMTs arrived. Pulse, heartbeat normal."

"That was certainly not his condition by the time he got to my ER," Berger said with a distant rumble in his voice.

"Was he conscious when he left your office?" Goldstein asked.

Shields ignored him. "Something must have happened in the ambulance. Something beyond my control."

"You're damn straight something happened in the ambulance," Berger continued. "The boy arrested. A healthy 10-year-old boy arrested."

The dentist swallowed hard and stiffened in his chair.

Before Dr. Shields arrived, Katherine explained to the group that her family had yet to visit him. He'd taken over from their longtime dentist, who'd recently retired.

"You're how old, sir?" Kelli asked. "How long have you been practicing?"

"I'm 26," he said. "Just...I've been out of dental school about a year."

Kelli continued writing. "I see."

Shields seemed to regroup somewhat. "Let me remind you that this was my first time to treat the boy."

"We're aware of that," Goldstein said. "We're assuming his records were thoroughly reviewed before you began treatment."

"Yes. Of course."

"Actually, Abe, to be fair, there was no contraindication for Novocain," Katherine said, "if that's indeed the cause here. When I talked to our old family dentist an hour or so ago, he said he didn't remember ever administering either Novocain or nitrous oxide to Justin. Justin never had a cavity, not a thing wrong, ever. Just cleaning, fluoride treatments, checkups."

"I talked to Fred as well," Shields said. "He told me the same thing."

"So it's your opinion that the boy suffered an anaphylactic reaction to the Novocain?" Berger asked.

"Possibly, yes," the dentist said. "Although I understand from talking to you and to Ms. Litton over the phone earlier that there was a possible head trauma involved. I wish I'd known. Perhaps I would have been more careful with the anesthetic."

"Whaddaya mean?" Goldstein asked. "You couldn't see the mark on his face? The loose tooth, which was the goddamn reason he was there? Isn't it reasonable to assume, sir..." His voice went up a notch about every third word.

"Hold it, Abe. Hold it," Singleton said, reaching out with a gesture of restraint. "This is not helping."

"We're not here to lay blame," Decker added, turning toward Shields. "We need to find out what happened. We may never know the *reason*."

"Agreed," Goldstein said, backing off a bit. "How long was he out, not breathing. That's what we've got to know, Dr. Shields. How many minutes."

"That's hard to say," Shields said.

"And why would that be?" Katherine asked. Each word arched into an accusation.

He tried to ignore her. He turned toward Goldstein. "My techs and I had been called away to another patient. We were in the midst of another procedure across the hall."

"And you left my son alone," Katherine said.

Shields turned back toward her, reluctantly. "Not that long. A few minutes at most. We needed to let the medication take effect."

"And you left him alone," she repeated. Her voice began to sink. Her body began to slump. All of her anger was suddenly retreating into fear.

"There was no reason to..."

"And you left him alone." She had gone all the way down to a whisper. The facts were overpowering her.

Goldstein took up the slack. His words were sharpening into lawyerly precision. "The length, sir. We need to know the number of minutes that elapsed in which the boy's breathing could have been occluded."

"Two or three, max. I wasn't gone that long. He wouldn't have stopped breathing for the entire time we were absent."

"Based on the damage done, I'd say it was longer than you're guessing," Goldstein said.

"I understand from one of your techs," Kelli said, "that his lips were blue when she finally got back to him."

"Maybe four," Shields said. "I suppose it could have been four minutes."

"Or five minutes?" Goldstein asked. "Could the reaction to the Novocain have swollen his throat closed for maybe five minutes?"

"Maybe...I...as soon as we got there, we all went to work exactly as we have rehearsed. Karen turned up the oxygen on the boy. Jan retrieved the anaphylaxis kit, drew the epi, we got an airway established, began compressions. He responded almost immediately."

"Six minutes? Seven?" Goldstein couldn't let up. His anger was slicing the air.

"I don't think..." Shields began again.

"Eight? Nine?" Each of Goldstein's words was jarring. "Just how fucking long did you let this boy strangle on his own vomit? How long had his heart stopped?"

Shields was breathing hard, his guppy eyes blinking frantically. He stood. As he turned toward the door he said, "I've told you all I know. That's it. I'm done. I think I need a lawyer."

"You bet your sweet ass you need a lawyer!" Goldstein bellowed as the dentist closed the door behind him. He stood halfway up and leaned toward the departing man. "A God damn criminal defense attorney!"

Shields was gone. Goldstein's roar echoed into the silence of the closed room. Left behind were the happy yellow blooms in their festive cellophane wrapping.

Katherine leaned over the sink in the doctors' lounge. The cold water ran in a whining gush below her, whirling toward the drain. Her hands grasped both sides of the sink, her weight leaned down her arms, her eyes were closed, her head hung down. She needed to wash her face, to take a breath, to try to re-collect herself. But she couldn't move.

Justin's condition was worse - much worse - than she had been able to see clearly at first. Fear and denial had been keeping it hidden, and then came the dentist.

The other doctors had seen it, surely, especially Goldstein. But she couldn't. The stakes were too high for her. Motherhood was blocking her medical perception.

God, the possibilities. Three minutes. Four minutes. Five minutes. The cutoff of oxygen. The deepest kind of damage. The dire possibilities.

God, God, God. If she could have just been there with Justin, she could have done something. *Dear God.*

"Dr. Warren?"

Katherine looked up at the mirror. Kelli was by the door behind her, watching her. "I came to see if you were OK." Kelli let the door close.

Katherine didn't reply.

Kelli Litton was short and sharp and always revved, three steps ahead of the docs when the shit storms hit the ER. One hand holding a pair of hemostats, the other with a syringe, lactate bag under her arm, barking out the orders through her paper mask. When Katherine was chief resident of pediatrics, followed by a couple of years as an attending, she'd spent plenty of time in the ER, and Kelli had been at her side. Their bond ran deep.

When Katherine looked at the mirror, she saw that her tears were back, soundless as before. Her eyelashes were clotted with them. Her nose was beginning to run again.

Kelli came closer. She reached out with an arm around Katherine's waist.

"I put my son's life in the hands of that guy, Kelli."

The nurse didn't reply.

"I did that, Kelli. That little prick. That weasely little son of a bitch. I did that. I let this happen."

"Yes. It happened. But..."

"I can't undo it. I can't go back. I don't..."

"Deep breaths," Kelli said in a whisper. "That's all I know to tell you, sweetie."

"I'm trying, Kelli."

"Justin needs you. It's time to go forward. You can do this."

Katherine dampened a paper towel under the swirl of water and began to work on her face. "I can do this," she said to the haggard image in the mirror. "I can do this."

NINE

"Sunny Sam," Katherine used to call him. "Sunny" for short. "My good old, big old boy."

When Katherine saw him for the first time that day at the Johns Hopkins cafeteria, she thought of him as a kind of lighthouse. She was in her second year of med school and he was working on his MBA. God knows he was tall enough. His shy, toothy smile was bright enough. Her eyes followed him across the room, and when he sat by himself with his tray in front of him, she picked up her coffee and went over.

"Hi, I'm Katherine."

He looked up from his three cheeseburgers and five cartons of milk, blinked at her astonishing, charmingly impertinent greeting, and smiled that first, biggest smile. "Sam," he said.

She heard the bare hint of two syllables in the pronunciation of his name. "Sa-um," she exaggerated. "That sounds like home. Where you from?"

"Texas."

"Me, too."

"Fort Worth."

"Me, too!" she said, then added in a playfully exaggerated Texas accent, "Well ain't that somethin'!"

That was a start, enough to inch open the door of a very well barricaded young man. The rest of it took awhile.

That iron door of his needed lots of oiling, but soon enough she had him wide open. Before he knew what hit him, he was gone and he was glad. Her, too.

In six months they had an apartment together where daily, almost, despite an overlay of books and papers and sweat and tests, they made room for each other on that compact bed. Her big, big boy gave her all the depth she craved, filling her with his liquid light.

Although they were from the same town, they discovered they had grown up on opposite sides of the tracks – Katherine with her grandmother in a little house in a fading neighborhood; Sam with prominent parents on an estate. One side, public schools and scholarships; the other, Exeter and Harvard. The tracks between them might as well have been a wall.

They hammered it down. In a year, they were married. In another, a baby. The tripled light came pouring in. Sam was her beacon, and she was his, both tall, both bright. Welcome home.

Katherine loved the struggle of their careers, and at first Sam loved it, too. Once back in Fort Worth she had her 18-hour days at County General, and he was almost as busy with his newly hatched CPA practice. Soon enough, the baby balancing act started – sitters, day-care, grandmothers; diapers, bottles, midnight wailings. Katherine did what she could in child raising, and he did the rest. His career came second, and that was OK. It was all for the greater good.

Actually, it was OK until it wasn't OK, and he wasn't sure when that day arrived. It came sometime after she moved from the hospital to her barrio clinic. While she was out saving the world, he was at home trying to save their personal little piece of it—the most important piece, he believed – the boy, their financial wellbeing, their future. All he knew for sure was that one day he could no longer ignore that burning inside him, that drip, drip, acid drip of resentment. She was never home, never doing her share. She was missing their life together. And sometimes, alone, deep in his bitterness, he wondered if she cared.

He was sitting in the OR waiting room, off by himself, looking down at his folded hands. They said it would be an hour or so until the tracheotomy was complete. He looked at his watch. Minute by minute the time was going by, waiting upon waiting.

It was supposed to have been his turn to work today, her turn to stay home. That had been their agreement – every other Saturday – but at the last minute she had gone in to cover for her partner, Lydia, who was still complaining of morning sickness months after she should have.

Katherine should have been there at the baseball game. She could have intervened in the dentist's office. She would have known what to do. She put an idiot like himself in the middle of it, and look what happened.

TEN

Two techs from Children's ICU, plus Kelli and Katherine, pushed Justin's gurney and his attached technology out of Trauma One, through a back door of the ER and down the hall to an elevator. Sam followed.

It had been a couple of hours since the interview with the dentist. After Justin's tracheotomy was completed, the doctors had held him for observation in the ER to make sure his condition was stable enough for the ten-minute journey to the hospital next door.

The elevator took them down to a walkway that tunneled under the street from County General and came up into the new Children's Medical Center. It took some effort to get all the wheels across the ridged floor at the base of the elevator doors.

Jonesie was waiting for them downstairs when the doors separated. His smile was small and concerned, and all the sharpness was gone out of the bones in his face. "Kath?" he asked, and she knew there were several parts to that question. Was she all right? Anything hopeful about Justin's condition? Was there anything – *anything* – he could do to help? He stepped out of the way of the gurney as they pushed it forward.

"Nothing," she said to those unspoken questions. "Nothing definitive from the tests."

As he came up to her she stepped forward into his soft embrace. She needed his gentle hands around her. Away from the clinic they were free to indulge in the intimacy of their years of friendship, which went all the way back to County General.

"God, Kath," he said against her ear. "God."

Jonesie pulled away and looked down at Justin. He touched the boy's pale cheek with the back of his fingers. "My little beasty boy." It was one of a hundred pet names he had for his surrogate nephew.

"His heart is back to normal, at least," she said. "The cardiologist is feeling good about things."

"That's something. That's good."

Katherine knew Jonesie was holding back. She suspected he'd been talking by phone to some of the ER nurses – his old pals – and he was fully aware of the seriousness of the situation. With Justin, the heart was nothing now. The brain was everything.

The medics turned the gurney toward the opposite end of the hallway and re-formed the flotilla of equipment around it. In front of them was an underlit passageway ribbed with pipes and wires, tunneling under the street. It was a long way ahead through the gray light. Katherine couldn't see the end of it.

"Yeah, the heart is stable, at least," Katherine said absently, maybe to Jonesie, maybe to nobody. "Not even a blip in three, four hours. However long we've been here."

"Five hours," Kelli said. "Closer to six."

Six hours? To Katherine it was one blank, dark stab of time, a concentric moment that pulled her and the rest of her world down into its tight curvature. She had no idea where the bottom was, but she feared they had a long way to fall before it found them.

She looked back from her place at the front of the procession. Justin was being pushed feet-first and Sam was at the head of the bed, holding the metal rail, looking down into the still swirls of Justin's hair. Sam had fallen into a troubled silence, and Katherine could see a deepening smudge of age and despair in the bowls of his basset eyes. The beacon was shutting down.

"Abe — Abe Goldstein — peeds neuro — he's the primary now," she continued with Jonesie. "He's studying the scans, seeing what . . ."

"I know Goldstein; everybody does," Jonesie said. "Hell of a reputation."

"The best."

"Have you guys pinpointed a cause?" he asked.

"The cause." She looked down the hall and into its dissolve of distance. "Everything hangs on that."

"Yeah?"

It was as if a second soundtrack had been running in her mind for the last several hours, a loop, and now she switched over to it. Jonesie had the medical background to absorb it easily.

"What we keep going over — Abe, the consultants — the debate we've entered . . . Anaphylaxis, certainly, the dentist, reaction to the Novocain, the gas, whatever. The weight of evidence is shifting us in that direction. I'll go with that. But underneath, subtly influencing things, maybe pivotal, maybe, the injury from the baseball and especially when he fell backwards and slammed his head against the ground, suffered some kind of mild concussion, maybe a clot. If that's the case — even half the reason — we've got something treatable."

"I think . . ." Jonesie began, but her tape wouldn't stop.

"Mostly time. Forty-eight, seventy-two hours. Inner-cranial swelling, possibly, give it time to ease off, reduce pressure, get blood back in there, bring the light back in there. That's what we want. Abe said . . . . That's . . ."

How many times had she cycled through this now, inside herself and out? Who was she trying to convince with her stumbling logic and babble of possibilities?

They walked in silence for a while. A wheel on one of the IV stands was wobbling as it bumped along. Science stumbled.

"Katherine?" came a rolling voice from behind them.

She looked back, and so did the others. They stopped.

A rotund little man with a stiffened leg and a cane came hobbling up to them. It was Father Red, headmaster of St. Alban's. He was breathless when he finally reached them.

"Katherine," he said again, and hugged her, then shook hands with Sam and nodded toward Jonesie and the others.

The kids called him Friar Tuck, and he was the kind of man who got a kick out of it. There was only a hint around his ears of the reason for his first nickname — a gray rust of tonsured hair — a freckled scalp and a bulldog neck choked in his clerical collar. Justin loved him, was always telling his parents the corny jokes that Father Red told them daily at Morning Prayer.

From his countless visits to hospitals and his own medical background, Father Red knew that this much equipment and staff concentrated on one boy was not good. He looked down at Justin and touched his shoulder. He asked if he could say a prayer, and Katherine said of course.

"No reason to hold things up," he said. "I can make this a mobile prayer."

As they restarted the procession, the priest reached out, keeping one hand on Justin's shoulder and the other holding open his black, leather-bound, hand-worn Book of Common Prayer.

"Lord Jesus Christ, good shepherd of the sheep," he read in a stately chant, "you gather the lambs in your arms and carry them in your bosom: We commend to your loving care this child, Justin. Relieve his pain, guard him from all danger, restore to him your gifts of gladness and strength, and raise him up to a life of service to you. Hear us, we pray, for your dear name's sake. Amen."

Katherine tried hard to bring the prayer inside her, but so much was already going on in there — a circular shield of ideas and speculation and fears and guilt surrounding a solid core of rationalism. Religion hadn't been important to her since childhood, and they were not a church-going family now. She and Sam figured Justin got plenty of religion at the daily chapel services at school, which let them off the hook on Sunday mornings. Sundays were their family days, so precious and few.

The priest came back to her, taking Katherine's opposite shoulder in his arm. This draped hug was a reach for him.

"Another time, when things are a little quieter, Katherine, we'll do a better job. I've got a lot more tricks up my sleeve — actually not *my* sleeve, but you know what I mean."

She smiled. "If you know of any rabbits in any hats, let me know."

"I will. Promise. I'll be back. And I want to talk to you and Sam," he said. "You need prayers, too."

"Sure."

"Meanwhile I'll put Justin on the prayer list at church, and at the school. We'll pray for him at chapel services every day. He'll be in my own prayers, too."

"I appreciate this so much, Father."

"Meanwhile I'm going to get out of your way. I know this is a critical time medically. Call me any time."

"I will. Thank you."

He turned back toward the way he came, and they continued.

In the pauses of conversation, the wheels clacked and bumped, and the ventilator sighed. It gave people time to visit their private fears, but nobody wanted to stay there long.

"How bad was it at the clinic after I left?" Katherine asked Jonesie.

"Not terrible."

"Bad, in other words."

"Yeah, Kath. Waiting room was full. I told 'em you were called away in an emergency, we didn't have backup available, they'd have to go to the ER, or wait till Monday. We had a few parents that pitched a fit."

"Figures."

"Nobody was that bad off. Nothing that couldn't wait. Couple of URI's, pink eye, checkups. I did what I could. I hate to turn 'em away."

"I hate it, too," Katherine said.

Silence returned. She thought she could see the end of the passageway, but all the walls were gray. It could have been more distance.

ELEVEN

"On three," said the nurse. "One, two . . ." and "three" was smeared into the effort of the four of them, who lifted Justin on the gurney's sheet, up and over, to the ICU bed. They pulled the sheet out from under him, covered his bare legs, pulled down the skirt of his gown, lifted his head to center it on the pillow and tucked the light blanket around him.

"There you go, sweetheart," said the same nurse to Justin. "Now let's get all your tubes and wires where they belong."

Maggie was her name. Katherine couldn't remember her. Maybe they'd worked together, maybe not. When one of her clinic kids came into the ICU, Katherine was always preoccupied.

"Intensive" was the operative word here. A kid's in real trouble. Monitoring was everything. Katherine would have a lot on her mind, mostly the lineup of new tests and whatever results had already come in.

Katherine liked the way Maggie talked to Justin as she worked to arrange his IV tubes, the Foley, the oxygen monitor. The nurses at Children's — guys, young women, all of them — had a deep well of motherhood in them. They also had iron strings for nerves, but the hardness was padded with remarkable patience. That's what it took to deal with children in pain, Katherine knew, to handle their outrage and whining

boredom, their sense of entitlement and injustice. You wanted
to throttle them as you swaddled them.

Docs like Katherine came in, smiled, ordered the
shots and more tests, left. It was the nurses who got to hang
around, inflict more pain, wipe up the shit and the tears.

But this time Katherine would be hanging around,
too. Justin was going to be her only case for a while, maybe a
long while. Maybe she hadn't yet grasped how deep the ordeal
was going to be. These were just the first few steps on the gray,
long way of uncertainty.

But all that was for later. Not now. She needed to see
Goldstein again. She wanted a better look at those scans.
Maybe she could see something he couldn't. Doubtful, but
maybe.

Justin's room, like the others on the ICU wing, was
half windows facing the hall, designed so the nurses could
keep a constant watch on the patients (besides being present
ninety percent of the time). His room was across from the
nurses' station. The worst-off patients got this place of
proximity, where more eyes could be on them. Was that why
Justin was there? Or maybe it was because Katherine was on
staff at the hospital and a member of its board. Only the best
for the doc's kid. Or the most care for the one who needed it
most.

Again she tried hard not to go beyond the present
moment. Too much to do, too dangerous to go there, the
boundless gray light of the future. Sam was going there, she
feared. There was nothing much he could do to help,

nothing to hold him back, no place else to go but into the tight circles of fear that had bored through the heart of his interior.

He stood across the room, watching the transfer to the bed, watching Justin, the nurses. The lighthouse had dimmed to almost nothing. He was a cumulus heap of darkness on the horizon.

As soon as Justin had been tended to, and after Katherine went over some instructions for the nurse, she walked across the hall to their private family waiting room with its small kitchen, a phone and a decent window that looked out over trees and walks and a playground. Marcie and Brian Singleton had joined Sam and Jonesie.

Marcie came right up to her with tears and a hug. "Miss Midget," Katherine called her, bending to her five-foot-two frame to accept her embrace. Marcie reached up to Katherine on tiptoes.

"This is awful, Kath," she said, her words muffled in Katherine shoulder. "I'm so sorry."

"I guess Brian has been keeping you updated," Katherine said as they moved to a pair of cushioned chairs and a couch. Jonesie had served the others coffee, and he brought a cup to her — double-sugar, double-cream — the usual. They settled in.

"Any changes?" Brian asked.

"Nothing," Katherine said. "Abe should be up here a little later with some more test results. Maybe then. But I doubt it. Nothing's changed in Justin that I can see."

Marcie and Brian lived three doors down from Sam and Katherine. In addition to Justin's best friend Todd, Marcie had three younger boys, unlimited energy and an ace maternal attitude. She was constantly bailing Katherine out with help for Justin's over-scheduled life; chauffeuring, fast food dinners, overnights. Sometimes Katherine thought Marcie did more mothering of Justin than Katherine herself did. Katherine stayed in Marcie's debt — deep in debt — so much that she thought Sam wanted to declare her bankruptcy.

"Todd's called every kid he knows to tell them about Justin," Marcie said. "All the kids on the team, half of St. Alban's, and half their mothers have called the house. My phone's been going non-stop."

Brian added: "He wants to round up every kid on the Twins and visit Justin *en masse*, give him the game ball even though they lost by something like twenty-seven runs this morning. I'm trying to discourage that."

"Good," Katherine said. "Tell Toady I'm sorry, but Justie's not up for visitors now."

"I understand," Marcie said.

"Is he the one who called Father Red?"

"Actually I did, Katherine."

"I'm glad. He met us in the hallway a little while ago. It was so good of him."

"The boys love that guy," Brian said.

Marcie pushed a partial swath of fire-blonde hair off her face. "Todd feels bad about what happened with the foul ball he hit, Kath. He wants to do something."

"Todd was the one who hit the foul?" Katherine asked. "I didn't realize . . ."

"He feels so guilty, Katherine," Marcie said.

"I probably should call him," Katherine said. "Kids are little sponges of guilt. We can't let him . . ."

"You've got enough on your plate, Kath," Sam said with a slight rumble.

"That's right," Marcie said, nervously sensing the tension. "More than enough. We'll talk to him. Brian and I can handle it."

After they asked for the third time if there was anything more they could do, Katherine suggested that Todd could feed Gracie. The Singletons had duplicates of the Moores' house keys and the code to their burglar alarm, and Todd knew every corner of their house.

"Maybe Todd could take Gracie on a few walks, too," Katherine added. "I think it's going to be a while before we'll be at home much, and the dog's going to get lonely."

"Excellent idea," Marcie said. "That's how Toady can help. Sure. He'll love doing that."

Marcie collected the foam cup from her husband and headed to the trash at the back of the room.

"Are you sure now, Kath, there's nothing else we can help you with?"

"I'm sure, Marcie. Really. You guys should go home. I don't know who you've got babysitting now, but I bet she's near meltdown."

"It's my mom," Marcie said. "And you're probably right."

Brian stood, and so did Sam and Katherine. They all walked to the door together.

"Call us if anything changes," Brian said. "We can be here in fifteen minutes."

"I will."

"If you need anything," Marcie said. "Anything, Kath."

"Yes."

She gave Katherine another hug, and they held it for a moment. "Anything," she whispered against her shoulder.

The sun was going down and the light was lessening in the waiting room. Sam was across the hall, sitting alone with Justin. Katherine sat in an armchair, her chin resting on her hand, staring. Jonesie was on the couch across from her, his long arms resting like twists of vines on the top of the cushions. There was silence, but it didn't last long. With Jonesie, it never did.

"Kath, you're gonna hate me."

"What."

"You're really gonna hate me. And I was just trying to help."

"What, dammit. What have you done?"

"I called Granny."

"Oh God, Jonesie. You didn't. Tell me you didn't."

"I told you you'd hate me."

"OK, you're right, I hate you. She's going to want to come down here, help out, pitch in. God, that's all I need."

Jonesie said sheepishly, "Actually, she's on her way, Kath. Or almost. She said she'd be here as soon as her shift was over tonight at the nursing home."

"Damn it. Didn't you try to talk her out of it, Jonesie? She's too old to handle any of this."

"I did. I tried, Kath. I underplayed everything as best I could, told her you had everything under control, and you know what she said? 'I'm on my way,' and she hung up on me and wouldn't answer when I tried to call back."

Katherine's grandmother, despite being a year or two over eighty, wasn't a resident of the nursing home. She worked there, currently serving on the three-eleven shift as a sitter for a lonely, rich old woman. Granny was a Licensed Vocational Nurse.

"She has no business being on the road that late," Katherine said. "It'll be midnight when she gets here. This is such a crappy part of town."

"I'm sorry, Kath."

"Jonesie, for goodness sake, I'm not mad at you," she said. "Granny'll probably be all right. As bad as this situation is with Justin, she'll be able to handle it. She can handle damn near anything."

Another small patch of silence intervened. Katherine drifted off and returned.

"Jonesie, aren't you getting tired? You've had a long day."

"I'm staying. Till hell freezes over, as long as I don't have to be at the clinic, I'm here to stay."

"You're an idiot."

"I'm family, Kath. Same thing."

She stood, went to the door, came back to him, trying to shake him off. He was giving her that look, the one close friends give each other, a kind of soul inspection, mentally undressing you down to the core to see if you're hiding anything, or hiding *from* anything. She could feel the blue of his eyes come through her. As she stood there, she wanted to squeeze herself shut, cover her most private, recessed self and not let him in – not anybody, not even herself.

"What, Jonesie. What are you thinking. I can tell you're thinking something."

She was expecting one of those brutal heart-to-hearts of his, the same kind she was known to turn on him, about T-cell counts and viral loads and taking care of himself. She braced for it: that she hadn't opened up sufficiently to him, come to terms with things, hadn't let go of her doctor's instinct to control the situation and given that control over to the dispassionate others who would do a far better job at it anyway. That she wasn't coming anywhere close to recognizing how bad this situation was, how deep in the ditch they were, how long this uncertainty could go on.

But what he did was worse. He came up to her, put his willowy hand against her cheek, then his face where his hand had been. His whisper was as delicate as his touch.

"I'm going to go, Kath," he said. "I'm going to your house and check on things, get the mail, give Gracie a scratch."

"OK."

"I'm going to get the pillows off your bed. I'm not having you and Sam using these hideous slabs of foam they call pillows here. You need signs of home."

"OK."

"Can you think of anything else? Anything from Justie's room?"

She shook her head no.

Jonesie knew her best, better than Sam knew her, sometimes better than she knew herself; he knew her fears and weaknesses, the troubles in her marriage, how much she weighed, her shoe size, her dress size, her passwords; he went shopping with her and always told her really, really truly if she looked fat in something. And this same friend believed things were so bad now that she didn't dare be nudged toward the truth. That no matter what kind of tower of strength she'd been in the past, no matter how many chests she'd cracked and medical boards she'd aced and diagnostic mysteries she'd solved and all-nighters she'd pulled, she couldn't take this. This – what the blankness of Justin's eyes was saying – was too much for Katherine Warren, M.D. This was too much for anyone.

That bad. It was that bad. And not saying it out loud made it that much more true.

They moved apart, but she kept a hand on his upper arm. She couldn't let go yet.

She tried to answer him, but it wasn't going well inside. She couldn't find her voice. She shook her head no, that she didn't need anything else from home, except that she needed everything. She needed yesterday back, she needed time reversed, she needed the universe righted and repaired.

As she shook her head she realized that everything was shaking inside, that the muscles that held the self in place were twitching, and that these were the first tremors, the first small signs of warning that lead to the convulsion of a life and the breaking of a heart.

But not now. No breaking now. Hell, no.

You can do this, Dr. Warren. You can do this.

TWELVE

Standing outside the front entrance of Fort Worth Children's Medical Center, looking into the remnants of the late-evening sunset, everything for Sam was new and wrong. The parking garage, the streets. Where was the other hospital? The ER entrance where he had come in? The parking lot? Sam had gone into one world and come out into another. He was paralyzed.

He wanted to move his Lexus SUV from County General to the parking garage at Children's. He thought it might be safer. He wanted to move Katherine's Volvo, too.

Remember the basement passageway? That had been a long distance. Katherine said they went under the street. Then the elevator up to Children's ICU. One turn. Another turn. Get Justin situated in his new room. Wait. The little waiting room. Wait. Back to Justin's room. Wait some more.

He told Katherine he was going to the hospital cafeteria. She was with Justin. Did she want him to bring her anything? She didn't want anything.

He was empty but he wasn't hungry. It was something to do. It was a place to go. And the cars were a mission to accomplish. If there was something to do, do it.

He had followed the signs to the cafeteria. He went down another hall from Justin's room, a different elevator, down. A different lobby. A new door.

No. He'd move the cars first, then maybe he'd eat something.

He was standing at the bottom of the front steps of Children's Medical, a brick-floored plaza leading out to a lawn and gardens, a fountain and live oaks. He was a bewildered giant, lost inside and out. He couldn't move.

Nothing was forming inside, nothing was coming together, everything was out of order. Sam didn't know why – why now – but he was going to cry. And after everything else, after his world had come undone and after holding himself in check through it all – but he was going to cry. Right here on these stupid steps, for all the world to see.

Sam struggled to close off his throat. He put his fist to his mouth and closed his eyes and bent and bore down. People walked around him and kept their distance.

He wasn't going to fall apart. No he wasn't. He swayed but he didn't fall.

THIRTEEN

Katherine stood at the doorway of Justin's ICU room. Sam, who had just returned from re-parking the cars and stopping at the cafeteria, was in a straight-back chair close to the head of the bed. He was bent over, his forearms on his knees, looking down at his finger-locked hands. The last of the evening light had left the room and a fluorescent fixture behind the bed had taken over.

Six feet four of gentle thickness and thinning hair and sagging eyes, and now something at Sam's center was sagging, too. Katherine had seen the new slump in him earlier in the day, and she had seen it grow. It was growing still. Everything about him was falling; each empty minute of waiting seemed to add another small measure to the weight he was carrying. A future of darkening possibilities, she imagined, was accumulating in him.

For more than a year things had not been going well for Sam. First, he had been trying to expand his accounting business into a boutique financial firm, offering investment management and estate planning along with traditional income tax services. For a while it had worked well, but then, in March of 2000, much of the air fluttered out of the dot-com bubble in one big, stinking whirlwind of flatulence. He'd lost some clients, and others were angry and threatening to leave.

Along with the Nasdaq, his confidence had lurched downward. His financial worth was his self-worth. And thanks to his education, he could count the ways. He could measure the loss of esteem as well as his own net worth and that of his mother's, watch it all tick downward by the week and by the month. The numbers that he had always held dear had turned on him.

Sam quantified everything. It was his nature, and it was his job; that's what accountants did. You were never standing still, he'd tell his clients. Sweating, sleeping, it didn't matter – you were either moving toward your goal or away.

If you were in debt and still spending, you were digging yourself into a ditch. Saving, investing, you were firming a foundation and getting the first and strongest walls up, building a structure that let in the light and turned away the wind.

No structure was invulnerable, of course, but a roof was better than a hole in the ground. When the rains came, the smart guy watched the beating drama through his picture window, sitting by the fire; the dumb guy watched his hole fill up until he was ass-deep in mud.

Now something much worse had hit him and his family, and on a perfectly sunny Saturday, too. Clouds piled on clouds, weight upon weight—in him, around him. The pounding water hadn't stopped. The trees were bowing and the leaves were awhirl. It didn't look like the walls were going to hold, and he'd worked so hard on them. It was a financial crisis times ten thousand, an equation that didn't equate.

What could Katherine do to help? For the last year he'd been talking to her about their financial setback and his plan for a way forward. She'd tried to listen, to care, but she came home every day with a brain and heart near empty, or else she missed the evenings entirely because of her innumerable committee and board meetings, or hospital emergencies. Numbers, unless attached to a body and its functioning, meant little to her.

Besides, there was Justin. She tried to save her meager evening leftovers of mind and spirit for him. Hearing about his day and helping a little with his homework were about all she could manage.

Now this. A fear beyond all fears had come to be, and she who was supposed to know so much was running out of ideas. Nothing was more uncertain than the brain and its galaxy of working parts. How deep did Justin's darkness go? How many points of starlight had been extinguished forever? How black was this night going to become?

Sam's wasn't the only structure with the roof torn off and the walls tilting. They were all three tumbling back and back and down, unprotected. The rivers were out of their banks and their world had become an unruly sea. Solid ground was a thing of the past. The only thing above them was the emptying, darkening night.

An empty seat was next to Sam, and Katherine walked quietly in from the doorway and sat. She put a hand on his rounded shoulder, touching the stretched knit of his shirt. He didn't look up. He spoke toward his hands. "Any news?"

"No," she said. "I haven't been able to talk to Abe yet."

While Sam was gone she'd called down to Goldstein's office, but he was out, probably on rounds. He'd promised to come by the room, and she figured he was on his way. Meanwhile she'd been in the nurses' station going over Justin's chart, reading it from the top down, the bottom up and the middle outward.

"Is Jonesie back?" Sam asked.

"Not yet."

"I hope everything's OK at home."

"I'm sure it is. Jonesie would have called. He's been such a great help to us, Sam."

"Yes. Yes he has."

Katherine had come to believe that Sam, in a weird way, saw Jonesie as a competitor. Although her relationship with Jonesie was totally platonic, their friendship was intense and intimate, and she spent most of her time with him because of their work proximity, plus occasional weekend shopping trips. She couldn't blame Sam for his jealousy, but she needed an outlet, and Sam could be so remote, lost in his office upstairs and his financial obsessions when he wasn't with Justin. She wished he would apply his calculator mind to their relationship and see what she was seeing – one plus one made two separate lives. She wanted one plus one to add up to a bigger whole, the way it was long ago, but she felt just too spent to get around to having the Big Talk. It had become easier to keep their separate lives separate on the weekends, too, and "easier" was something Katherine always seemed to gravitate to considering her long, draining days.

She brought her hand down to her lap and folded one hand into the other. She looked over at the small body in the long bed, resting at the bottom of a canyon of machines, each looking down on him with digital blinks, steady drips, and sighing shoves of air. A nurse with the look of a weathered mother who wore a teddy bear smock was among the monitors, writing down numbers on a clipboard.

Katherine was trying hard to keep the future at bay. She had been an MD for a dozen years; her training insisted that she stay grounded. You don't go anywhere – to despair, to hope. You stay put with the facts. You remain in the present. You cling to the evidence. It wasn't much different from Sam's philosophy.

Reason, numbers, tests and more tests. There lay the hope, if there was to be any. There lay a measure of control in a wind-whipped situation. There, with facts, was how you found each toehold, and with plenty of ropes and steady patience you could climb the sheer wall of worry, eventually into the light.

That had always worked before, through her most difficult cases. But how do you stay grounded if there *is* no ground?

"Changes?" Katherine asked the nurse.

"None," she replied. "Nothing."

She offered Katherine the clipboard, but Katherine shook her head no. "That's all right."

Katherine looked at Justin again. She wanted a blink, a wiggle in a finger, anything. He was as still as ice.

Life was there. Some small warmth of color, a beat of blood, processes. She could see that. Breath and nourishment were being forced on him, but his body was well enough to accept them and use them and keep going.

The body was there, but where was the boy in him?

Gone, yes, but for good? There was no evidence for that, she believed. Not yet. He was sheeted over with dark ice, winter-still, but what the doctors didn't know yet was how thick it was, how hard it was going to be to warm it and crack it and allow the boy to reemerge.

Just resting, yes? That's where he was. Hiding, recovering, preparing to bound back into his old pestering, puppyish, chattering, questioning, whining, jubilant self. He was curled and quiet down there behind the lidded eyes. Waiting, the way she and Sam were waiting.

Then, soon – maybe soon – Katherine hoped soon – a bath of warming blood would re-enter the desiccated cells of his brain, refurbish them, reinflate them, reignite them, and her full-blooded boy would be back.

Close call, Justie. We were really worried there for a while.

And there went Katherine. In less than a minute she had lifted off into hope. Gone, unmoored from her numbers, and so easily.

She couldn't. No. She simply could not afford to do that. She had to fight it. Taking flight gave room to fall, and that wasn't what Justin needed. Presence of mind was what he needed. *Her* mind. *Here. Now.*

She sat back down next to Sam. "The hardest part," she said. "By far the hardest part."

"Waiting, you mean." He still hadn't looked up.

She put her hand on his shoulder. "Yeah."

She closed her eyes for a moment, and the elongated basement hallway of a few hours ago was back. She was alone in her mental picture, pushing the gurney by herself, just beginning, just her and the emptied boy. The gray at the end got grayer. The end was nowhere near.

Katherine looked up and Dr. Goldstein was standing on the other side of Justin's bed, peering over his glasses that had been pushed to the midpoint of his glob of a nose. He was adjusting the drip on a bag of glucose. Karen and another nurse were beside him.

Katherine's consciousness had diffused into the weary gray distance of the hallway, but it had not dipped into the inkwell of sleep. She snapped back into focus. Sam came to attention just as fast. She put her hand on Sam's thigh and pushed herself up.

"All settled in, it looks like," Abe said to no one in particular, concentrating on the controls of the IV bag.

"We are," Katherine said. "Settled and quiet."

Goldstein turned to her. "Have you noticed any changes in him, Katherine?"

"No," she said.

His eyes fell back to the open chart in his hands. Then the clipboard of hourly numbers. Then he closed the chart over the clipboard and handed the unruly matter over to Karen.

Dr. Goldstein pried up Justin's eyelids and waved the penlight across the glaze. He put the light back in his inky front pocket, reached for the stethoscope in the side pocket of his lab coat and had a listen at Justin's chest. He listened to the carotid. He closed his eyes when he listened, cocked his head outward, wrinkled his gray bush of a moustache, but his expression did not change. He stepped back, put a cupped hand to his forehead, and settled into a forgetful sigh.

Katherine wondered if he were going somewhere with it. Did his long breath carry him into a longer thought, a piece of a theory, a preliminary arrangement of data toward the pattern of an assumption? Or did the sigh simply help take him down to his seat across from them? He sat, crossed his arms and leaned back.

Something was there, she was convinced. He wasn't looking at them but at the neural wall within himself, the circling, smudgy blackboard of it, and the figures there. The topography of an initial diagnosis. She was sure of it.

"Diffuse cerebral edema," he said. "That's all the hell I've got."

"That's nothing, Abe," Katherine said. "Absolutely nothing."

"It ain't worth spit is what it is," he said. "From every angle, every snapshot of his brain, all we've got is one gray oval. It's like the weather guy tellin' you it's cloudy outside. Well, no shit. Tell me somethin' I don't know."

When Abe was Abe - in hallway meetings with other docs, in office conversations with people who knew him and whom he trusted, and now, with a fellow hospital board member and longtime colleague - he let his Louisiana roots show. She liked that. She liked the clarity of it, the honesty, the bareness of it, stripped of the softness and care and proper English that normal patients and their families found reassuring.

"General swelling of the brain," she said for Sam's benefit. "Diffuse cerebral edema. It didn't take a CT to find that out. It's what a coma looks like."

"Pea soup," Abe continued. "Exactly what's expected, I'm afraid."

"Any other theories out there?" Katherine asked.

"I've emailed the scans to all my go-to guys. Not all have responded - time zones and all that - but the ones who have can't find shit either. Can't find one remarkable thing about it. No clues to the cause, the prognosis. And they all said what I already knew: The only thing we can do is wait, see what develops after this goddamn fog lifts."

"Couldn't that be considered good?" Sam asked. "I mean, that nothing horrible showed up? Nothing that makes you want to give up hope this soon?"

Goldstein looked up, as if he'd forgotten that Katherine had a husband with her, a civilian, and now he might have to adjust his communication levels, turn down the technical volume and the blunt-force, home-grown language of the swamps.

"We can't consider it either good or bad, Sam," Goldstein said. "It's the brain's normal reaction to an insult...an injury. The brain throws up a sort of protective barrier, this swelling, attempting to heal itself." He looked at Katherine "That dumb-ass dentist? The baseball? How much each contributed? We can't tell yet."

"But *you* have a theory, don't you?" she asked. "A gut hunch?"

"Well, Katherine..."

"And the other people you've talked to. Them, too."

"It's much too early, Katherine."

She could feel him withdrawing, equivocating, beginning the dodgy dance that all her fellow docs learned early in their careers. She knew she shouldn't, but she pressed him even more.

"All your experience, Abe. I know you. I know how you operate, just like the rest of us. You have a working hypothesis, which you acquired the first minute you saw Justin."

"I'm just not prepared to venture a guess this early in the game, Katherine. Honestly."

He's holding back, she was thinking. *No doubt.*

She should have known what a bad sign this was, but she didn't push it any further. She realized, as the conversation went on, that she had to be as much a patient as a colleague – a stand-in for her son – and as such was now getting the kid-glove treatment, at least when they got down to essentials. Not the as-one-doc-to-another, between-you-and-me-this-guy-is-toast treatment.

Or then again, she wondered, did he honestly not know?

No, he knew. And a large part of her didn't really want to know what he suspected. She really *was* a patient. And she was so weary.

"The EEG has been of little help either," Dr. Goldstein continued. "Just what we'd expect, an encephalopathic picture" – he turned toward Sam – "what the swelling does to the electrical patterns of the brain. The monitoring of Justin's brain wave is indicating lots of slowing and disorganization, typical of this condition. There's a marked loss of the normal, faster rhythms."

"And so now what?" Sam asked.

"Waiting," Goldstein said. "Just like I told you earlier. Twenty-four, forty-eight hours. Let things settle out. Meanwhile, an MRI, other tests. Get a better indication of which direction this thing is going."

The conversation paused. Abe had run out of things to say, and so had they. In the absence of words, the noise of the machines came forward, especially the rhythmic pressure of the ventilator: inhale, exhale, pull, push, whish, whoosh, and on, and in. The pause was an invitation for the neurologist to retreat again into the sanctum of himself, back to whatever maps and thoughts and data were talking to him, surrounding him on that internal blackboard of his.

Nothing. Once again he wasn't ready to reveal so much as a breath of speculation.

"Any questions?" he finally asked.

She nodded no and wanted to scream, *Are you kidding? ARE YOU FUCKING KIDDING ME?*

Do I have a child at all? Does he have a life? A soul? A future? But all she said was, "You've got to be bone-tired, Abe. It's long past suppertime."

Sam stood along with Abe. Katherine joined them at the foot of the bed.

"I somehow always seem to find a meal now and again," he said with a smile, putting one hand on his generous mound of a belly. "I manage."

"Don't we all," she said as she touched her cheek to the gray splinters of his mustache and patted his back. Hugs bewildered him, but he managed. "You're a dear friend, Abe. We are so grateful for all your time, this tremendous effort."

They separated, and Sam stepped in to shake his hand.

"Nonsense," Abe said. "I haven't done anything yet." They started movinging toward the door together. "Sometimes it's good for me to step back, though, to sleep on things, see what I might trip over in the darkness. The mind has a strange way of working things out in dreams. I'm a big believer in rest."

"I find tax breaks in my sleep," Sam said.

"For God's sake, find me one too," Abe said. They were both smiling.

In the hall they let Dr. Goldstein amble free of them. Katherine watched him slip back into his inner workings as his walk lost purpose. She wasn't sure he had enough presence of mind to find the elevator, but just past it he looked up, corrected course and pushed the button.

He was their hope, and he seemed as lost in Justin's fog as Justin was.

FOURTEEN

"Goldstein's holding back."

Jonesie leaned forward on the waiting-room couch. "Holding what back, Kath."

"His hunch," she said from the armchair across from him. "His initial diagnosis, which I believe is not good, not good at all. In fact I think it's probably something dire."

"Maybe, maybe not," Jonesie said, narrowing his blond, bare wisps of eyebrows.

It was just after ten p.m. He had returned from their house after checking on the dog and going through the mail. He brought back as many small comforts as he could carry – pillows, the family quilt that Granny had made years ago, junk food. He'd made sandwiches, then stopped at a 7-Eleven for two huge bags of potato chips, sugared Cokes, fried pies, Nutter Butters. He knew all her favorites. She was going to need all the comfort she could get. They'd work on the pounds later.

Katherine scarffed down a ham sandwich while Jonesie took food across the hall to Justin's room, where Sam was taking a shift. When he returned they started on the cookies—Jonesie nibbled, Katherine wolfed. She was drinking a can of Coke along with her coffee. She called it hot and cold running caffeine.

Jonesie continued: "You told me earlier that Goldstein said it was too early to know anything for sure. Why not take him at his word, Kath?"

"Yeah, I know, I know."

"And what if he *is* holding back? Isn't it for the best that the worst-case crap stays unspoken until it can't be avoided? He doesn't want to cause you guys any unnecessary harm, in case his preliminary hunch is wrong – and that's presuming he even *has* a hunch."

"I guess. Maybe. But I want to know, Jonesie. Even if we *are* in deep shit – which I strongly suspect we are – I want to know."

"Of course you do, Kath. Like every doctor I've ever worked with, you're a raging control freak. Bad news is better than no news."

"Yes. Always."

Jonesie had brought a framed five-by-ten from Katherine's dresser at home. It was a picture of Gracie with a baseball in her mouth and Justin running after her, both toward the camera. Justin was nine. He called the game keep-away baseball, and they played it in the park across the street from the house. Justin would bat the ball, the Lab would retrieve it, wouldn't give it back. The chase was on.

Jonesie believed it was important that the nurses and others see the whole of whom they were working with, to remind them of the loss, to show them the distance the boy had fallen, to get them to want to try a little harder to bring him back. He walked quietly into the darkened room and put the picture on Justin's nightstand next to his baseball glove and Twins cap, which Sam had brought in from the SUV.

"Justie'll want that glove first thing when he wakes up," Sam said with a whisper, as if Justin were sleeping. "He likes to slip his hand in, pound his fist into it to loosen up the leather. It'll give him something to do while he waits to get the hell out of here."

"Yeah, Sam," Jonesie said. He whispered, too. If it helped Sam to think of the coma as a form of sleep, then he would support the illusion. Anything to help.

Jonesie and Katherine, each with a refill of coffee, stood by the windows in the waiting room, sighed and sagged and let the silence develop. Her lab coat and scrubs were the worse for wear, and so was the rest of her. Her face was damaged with deeper lines and new blotches. Her hair, which was never in great shape anyway, appeared grabbed and twisted.

She looked down onto a lighted forest; it was the hospital's parklike area at the front and sides of the building — sidewalks and benches, gardens and a playground — all lighted from below, which made a moonlit dream of leaves. She had been on the subcommittee that had approved the landscaping plan, then fought for it in the budget meetings. She wanted peace and beauty to surround the children. It was what they deserved, she insisted, a beckoning back into life, as close as a walk to the window.

"Did you talk to Lydia?" she asked.

"I did," Jonesie said. Katherine noticed the wiggle of a chill on his neck at the mention of her name.

"Well . . . ?"

"The Psycho Lesbian Bitch From Hell sends her sympathies."

"Well isn't that sweet," Katherine said.

Lydia Rojas was the physician who helped out at the clinic part-time. A city cop named Inez was her partner; a turkey baster was the father of a child Lydia was scheduled to deliver in two weeks.

Lydia's office style was a continuing problem for them. She was a stickler for details, and she wanted the intake and chart filing just so. Jonesie and Katherine were slobs in that department. They believed in giving as much time as they could to each patient; the administrative details were far down their list of priorities. Lydia was always looking for ways to push the patients through the mill more efficiently.

"What did you tell her?" Katherine asked. She walked to the couch.

"Actually, to be fair, when I called I didn't know how bad off Justin was. I just said it didn't sound good, I expected that you wouldn't be able to come in Monday and I wondered if she would be available to pitch in for a couple of days. She didn't sound too enthusiastic about the idea. And actually, she seemed genuinely concerned about Justin. Maybe the motherhood thing is softening her a bit."

"I guess I'm gonna have to call her tomorrow, fill her in, tell her I'm gonna be out for quite a few days, probably."

"I'll call," Jonesie said. "You've got enough to worry about, Kath."

"OK. Sure. But I guess I'd better talk to Hugh," Katherine said. (Hugh Gentling was administrator of the county medical system.) "He's gonna have to pull a pediatric resident out of County rotation to fill in for me after Lydia bows out."

"Shit. You know how I love breaking in fresh residents."

"You'll do fine, Jonesie. You'll keep the place running, maybe stop those apple-cheeked docs from killing anybody."

"Oh God. And if the Queen Bitch *docs* come in for a few days, I can just see her popping out her kid on my watch. I might have to deliver the hideous little beast."

"Jonesie, for God's sake."

"It could happen, Kath. Irony of ironies. Then I might have a baby lesbian named after me, right? So let's see. A name..."

"How in the hell are you going to turn Kirby Jones . . . ?"

"Kirbette? Whadya think?"

"You know, actually, it has a nice ring to it. Darling name, in fact. Kirbette. I like it."

"God, I might even have to be a godfag or something."

It was Katherine's first laugh of this whole awful day. It came from a deep place, sweeping outward, accompanied by a brash display of teeth. She laughed with authority, the way she did everything else.

"You must have called my service, Jonesie. I haven't gotten a page all day."

"I did. I told them to hold back anything they could, divert calls to the hospital. I thought I'd let you decide tomorrow what you wanted to do about it."

At off-hours, calls to the clinic went to Katherine's medical answering service. They'd screen the calls, send people to the emergency room if something was urgent, asked them to hold off to the next day if they could, or paged her if it was something they thought she should hear about. Duty nurses at Children's used the service to report things she should know about her hospital patients.

Her pager didn't go off every night, but sometimes it beeped her awake two or three times in a night. Sam had learned to sleep through it. Once every couple of weeks or so she was called into the hospital for a young patient in crisis. Two a.m. seemed to be prime time for those sorts of calls. When Sam woke up alone in the bed, he didn't think of it as anything unusual.

"I don't know what I'm going to do about the calls," she said. "And my hospital patients. I can probably slip away from my watch here, check on my kids. Rounds don't take all that long."

"I wish you'd turn everything over to somebody else," Jonesie said. He came over to the couch and sat beside her, draping his *Swan Lake* arm around her shoulder. "Kath, I'm worried about you. Your shoulders are broad, honey," he said with a pat of his hand, "but you can't keep holding up the whole world. Are you listening to me, Superdoc?"

"Yeah, yeah, I'm listening."

She stared away, and the endless, windowless hallway came back again. Her new future. One patient, one path. Take a step, take another, take a hundred.

After a period of silence and another freshening of coffee, they returned to their original seating in the waiting room, Katherine in one of the padded armchairs, Jonesie on the facing couch.

"What about Sam?" Jonesie asked. "Is he like you, wants to know the truth no matter what?"

"No. Absolutely not."

"You'd think he'd be as much of a controlaholic as you are, Kath."

"I know. The accountant, everything on a grid, every dollar of income and outgo projected out to death and beyond, best case, worst case.

"But this, Jonesie. This is different. This is so much beyond his well-constructed little world. I can feel his fear radiating across the room."

"I can feel it too," Jonesie said. "Such a big man, but he seems so fragile."

"I don't know what kind of reserves he's got. A lot of things have been wearing him down lately. I'm thinking about his business."

"Have you guys talked, Kath? The real deep stuff, I mean. Get his worst fears out in the open. Yours, too."

"Not really. Not much."

"You need to, Kath. Listen, if you want me to, I'll go in and watch Justin, relieve Sam, let you two sit in here and talk."

"Not yet. Not now. Sam's not ready, and neither am I. Too much has gone on, too fast. We've both been knocked off our feet, and I feel like we're both just barely standing."

"Whatever you think. But I'm not liking this."

"It's too early, Jonesie. It hasn't even been twenty-four hours. Wait till we have something to work with, some solid news."

"I guess."

"You guess?"

"I'm just saying, Kath...I don't necessarily mean the biggest thing, here, Justin, what to do. I mean all the other stuff."

"The distance thing, you mean."

"Yeah. You know, you and Sam. Work and kid, kid and work, and how you two have lost touch. You've kept saying — promising me — you were going to bring it up with him, get to work on it."

"I know."

Jonesie and Katherine did lots of talking during their workdays — whenever a break in the action occurred, and always at the end of the day as they worked together on the charts. They'd occasionally get down and dirty with their feelings. They called them Oprah Moments.

"Like two ships sinking in the night," she'd say of the disrepair of her marriage. Jonesie's response was always "glub, glub." Often they'd reverse things then, talk about the trail of tears that was *his* pitiful love life, when another one of his boy-meets-boy Internet relationships went cold before the sheets dried.

"You guys are going to need each other more than ever," he said. "This is the kind of thing that can pull a marriage apart."

"Please, Jonesie, *please.* Let's not go there now. I can't . . ."

He could feel a rise of anger in her voice. He had pushed too hard, gone too far. "You're right. I'm sorry."

He got up, sat on the padded arm of her chair and put his cheek against the top of her head. She wanted to cry, but she didn't have the strength.

FIFTEEN

Katherine's cell phone let out a businesslike chirp. She looked at the screen. "Oh God." She touched the button. "Hi, Mom."

"Katherine? Where are you? What's going on? I got a message on my cell from Granny, something about Justin and the dentist or something. I was going to call you right back but Lord what a day this has been. You know how things can get on Saturdays for me. Everybody and their cousin wants to look at houses on Saturdays."

Jonesie looked at Katherine, put the back of his hand to his forehead and flopped his head back with a woe-is-you gesture. Katherine nodded with an exasperated shake of her head. "Mom, it's . . ."

Faye Jean resumed on the crest of her next breath: "I was trying to get away, honey, earlier this evening, to just take out a minute and call you. I'd locked the house — you know, one of those open houses I seem to always get stuck with on weekends — and I was walking down the front walk and here came the sweetest little couple, just dying to see the house — you know I just love to help out kids like that, hard-workin', responsible. The house was just precious, just perfect for them, and they wanted to see it so bad, so I led 'em through it as quick as I could and they had so many questions — it's obvious they'd been doin' their homework, they knew all about escrow and mortgage insurance and home warranties, and I just couldn't let 'em go away without answering all their questions. I took them to supper at the cafeteria — spur-of-the-moment thing, you know, but I thought the timing was right and hell, for the cost of a couple of meatloaf dinners, I'm thinkin', I can nail 'em."

"Mom, I . . ."

Away she went, and Katherine closed her eyes and settled in for the duration. Jonesie knew where things were going — dozens of times he'd been caught in the same swamp of real estate news when Faye Jean would call Katherine at the clinic. He came over with the coffee pot and poured more into her foam cup. She nodded thanks to him and took a sip. *Might as well do something with my lips while Mom uses up her breath.*

"Honey, I wouldn't be surprised at all if they didn't call me tomorrow with an offer. That girl was so excited and I could tell the boy was tryin' to signal her not to look too eager, you know, that they needed to make a low-ball offer and test the waters and what all — it was obvious he'd been coached by somebody pretty savvy, so I don't expect the negotiations to go smooth, but if that sweet little wife of his wants that house, she'll wear him down and she'll do most of the work for me."

"Mom, Justin's in the hospital," she finally inserted into her mother's chain link of words. Not much got through the barrier, but that did.

"Oh my God!" Her words were the usual blur, not the late-night slur. Faye Jean could hit the Maker's Mark pretty hard at the end of her long days of commerce, and although Katherine could hear the tumbling clicks of ice against glass, her mother's condition didn't seem to have deteriorated too badly. At least not yet. "Do you need me to fly up there, Katherine? I don't think I can get a flight out tonight, but maybe first thing tomorrow. I can sit with him, stay up all night, no problem, do it all the time, you know, TV shopping — some of the best stuff they've got, what the general public doesn't get a crack at, is on Home Shopping after midnight. I got the cutest little — well, they're not really that little, really kind of big and flashy — gold earrings about two weeks ago, I think it's been. Sixteen bucks. Not genuine solid gold, of course — they tell you that before you call in — but, I mean, who can tell? I dare you to tell the difference, Katherine. Even directly in a good, strong light and all, shoot, I can't see any difference, but then again maybe it's time to get my glasses changed."

"Mom?"

"Yes, honey."

"You need to get some rest. We're fine here. I don't think this is going to be that bad."

"Are you sure, honey?"

"I'm sure, Mom."

"I don't see how a dentist and the hospital are connected."

"Mom, it's a long, complicated story, but we've got a handle on it. Promise."

"You're sure you're OK, honey?"

"Yes, Mom. Yes. I'm sure."

Katherine knew her mother didn't really want to fly in from Houston. Dissuading her was easy. It must have been eleven by then.

"You give that boy a big ol' kiss for me, OK?"

"I will, Mom."

"A big, big kiss."

"Yes, Mom."

"He's gonna be just fine. I'll get Justin on the prayer list, get our prayer squadron at Living Word to put our sweet little boy right up there at the top. He'll be good as new before you know it. Jesus never fails."

The ice clicked again and the liquid burbled through her lips. She'd hit the bottom of her drink. "Call me if you need me, honey," she said.

"OK, Mom. I will. Goodnight, then."

"Goodnight, sweetie."

SIXTEEN

Katherine felt a familiar hand on her forearm. "Hey, honeybun," the old voice said.

"Granny?" she asked with a smear of lips as she pulled herself upright. Katherine had been resting her head on the crook of her arm, which was lying on the edge of Justin's hospital bed. Her face had been smudged into the sheets. She leaned back on the straight-back chair, then pushed up from it and stood — the old medical heave-ho, another interruption of sleep and a move she'd been well versed in since her intern days.

"Katie, honey," Granny said as she moved into her granddaughter's bending embrace.

Katherine looked above the old woman's snowy curls to the clock on the wall. "It's two in the morning, Granny," she said in a sleep-crackled voice. "Where . . . ?"

"I know, I know," Granny said. "I sorta got lost on my way from the nursing home."

There wasn't a lot to her, five feet and an inch or two of mostly bones and gristle. She was easy to hug, like a loose bag of groceries, and Katherine hung on for dear life. Granny wasn't letting go of Katherine, either. That's just how you did a Granny hug: Make it count.

"Hey, Granny," Sam whispered from behind her. He'd been in the chair on the other side of the bed, arms crossed, slumped back into a doze. As he walked toward her,

Granny unlocked her hold on Katherine and turned to him, slapped him on the back and clutched him around the waist. "You big old thing," she said.

"Boy oh boy, we've needed you, Granny," he said.

"Well here I am, honey," she said, talking into his shirt. She didn't come up much above the bottom of his chest. "I'm right here."

Katherine looked again at the clock on the wall. She and Sam hadn't been asleep that long. Jonesie had gone home sometime after midnight.

Granny left Sam and went over to Justin. A fluorescent backlight from behind his bed made it easy to see him. She put her splotchy hand on his forehead and began rubbing through his eyebrow with the side of her thumb.

"Justie, can you hear me? Your old Great-Granny's here. I've come to take care of you, baby."

Granny's voice was a sweet, low rasp. That voice was part of the firm but easy way she touched people, and she touched everyone who got close enough. The habit came from her life as a private-duty nurse of old people. Stubborn, scared, half-dead, needy as babies, they required the constant, reassuring presence of hands. Granny's were the best.

"This boy's filthy," she said, taking a hand down one of his arms. "Get me soap and a basin, Katie. We gotta get him cleaned up."

"Don't you want . . . ?" Katherine began.

"No great-grandson a mine is gonna look like he just come out of the henhouse."

"The nurses'll do that in the morning, Granny," Sam said.

"Not as good as I will," she said to him. "Get me a washrag, a towel and a fresh gown, too."

Sam knew how to handle Granny. "Yes, ma'am," he said.

Katherine found a plastic basin and some liquid soap in the bathroom. As she filled the basin with warm water, Sam went to the nurses' station for the rest of the supplies.

"Playing baseball?" Granny asked, raising her voice to reach Katherine over the water's flow. "That's what Jonesie told me." Katherine guessed her grandmother's voice probably reached out of the room and to the end of the hall as well. Granny had learned how to deal with distance growing up on her family's seven hundred acres outside Pampa in the Texas Panhandle. If you wanted to reach a man on a tractor, you developed a voice that could carry. Grandpa used to say that that voice of hers was big enough to carry wood. (It helped with her mostly stone-deaf patients, too.)

Katherine turned off the tap in the bathroom and walked carefully back into the room with the water. "That's where he got the mark on his cheek," she said.

"Knocked him cold?" Granny asked.

Katherine set the basin on the nightstand beside her. "It's complicated, Granny. Yeah, it was a foul ball that hit him and knocked him out for a second, but something worse happened at the dentist's office afterwards when Sam took him in to get a loose tooth fixed. We think he had a bad .

reaction to the pain medicine; that stopped his breathing and put him in the coma."

Granny ruffled the water with her fingers to get the liquid soap to suds up and to make sure of the proper warmth. She glared at the ventilator tube attached to the hole in Justin's throat. "I hate dentists," she said.

Sam came in with his supplies plus the nursing shift supervisor, who lumbered in behind him. Middle-of-the-night sponge baths were highly irregular.

"Dr. Warren?" she asked. "What's . . ." She was a hundred pounds heavier and almost as tall as Katherine.

"Sharon, this is my grandmother," Katherine said.

Granny didn't look up. She folded the covers down to Justin's ankles. "I'll hold him up if you'll get that gown off, Katie," she said. "Hi, honey," she said to the nurse. "You here to help?"

She laughed. "Well, I suppose I am, Mrs . . . ."

"Call me Granny."

"OK, Granny."

Katherine sent a knowing smile at Sharon, and Sharon returned a twinkle of resignation. Order was established that quickly. Granny was in charge.

Justin's head eased back limply as Katherine lifted him, and Sam reached into Justin's brown curls to keep his head from falling back too far. Sharon unhooked the IV tubes so they could pull the sleeves of the old gown free, then she reinserted them like plugs in a socket. Granny eased Justin gently back to the bed and returned the covers up to his chest.

She started with his face, washing across his forehead with the cloth, as lightly as a butterfly over his closed eyes, a little firmer over his dark, soft eyebrows. Granny was very careful over the bruised cheek, touching it like a kiss, daubing at it.

She rinsed and rubbed, rinsed and rubbed — mouth, nose, ears, neck — especially the back of the neck, a prime collection point for boy dirt. Same with the hands and those awful fingernails.

She smiled as she worked. To Granny, dirt on a boy was evidence of joy. That's the way they were supposed to get, and then it was your job to get them clean so they could have the pleasure of doing it all over again. That was her attitude when Justin spent part of every summer with her at her little house on the north side of town, helping her with the tomato garden, mowing the yard with the push mower, then taking a deep bath and settling down with her to watch pro wrestling on television. In the afternoons they'd walk to his mother's clinic, which was only three blocks away.

"Granny just now drove in from her job at Autumn Lodge," Katherine told Sharon, who took the basin of already-dingy water in her beefy hands and carried it back to the bathroom for fresh water and new soap. "She's an LVN."

"Practical nurse is what I always called it," Granny said. "You just do what needs doin'."

"Now I see where the medical profession comes from," Sharon said from the bathroom. "It must run in the family."

"Granny raised me," Katherine said. "Yeah, I come by   it   honestly."

"If you got off at eleven, Granny," Sam said, "you must have been pretty lost."

"Lord, I think I may have gone all the way to Dallas," she said. "You go in one of those little stores and it's always an A-rab in there, they don't know which way anything is. I shouldn'ta listened to 'em.   Shoulda followed my own instincts."

"Sorry about all that dirt on the boy," the nurse said, coming back into the room. "Baths aren't a priority during critical care situation."

"Honey, you don't need to apologize to me," Granny said. "I know how busy y'all can get in a place like this." She started in again on the grime of Justin's hands.

"You're handling the boy like you know what you're doing," Sharon said.

"I've been in the nursin' business off and on for sixty years," she said. "You learn a few things along the way."

Katherine's first decade of life had been a disaster. Her parents' marriage turned into something like a redneck version of *The Days of Wine and Roses*, which Katherine and Jonesie had renamed *The Days of Beer and Carnations*. Granny saw a need and stepped in as Faye Jean's relationship with Katherine's father went from bad to worse to occasional gunfire. She welcomed the girl into her little home, molded her, got her heart going in the right direction. Katherine had lived with Granny full time from the age of ten until she left for her undergraduate work at Austin College.

Katherine's years with Granny had been one long struggle to grow out of her awkward isolation. In elementary school she had been almost as tall as her teachers. In high school she aligned herself with the nerds of the science lab. And throughout those years she carried with her the embarrassment of her mother's tacky life and a gnawing need to dilute the dismal residue that her mother had left behind.

But she also had Granny. Her worn, golden light had been enough. With Granny's no-nonsense, muscular support, Katherine found her way out and up, and here she was.

Granny soaked one of Justin's hands in the basin while she worked on the other, then got the nail clippers from her purse and scraped out the dirt the best she could.

"It's gonna take at least three more baths to get this boy up to snuff," she said. "We're gonna wash his hair next time, clip his fingernails and soak 'em some more. Maybe four baths, but we'll get there."

She began working down and up the contours of Justin's body. She kept him mostly covered as she worked. "He could catch his death in all this air conditioning," she said to no one in particular.

Granny brought the warm washcloth up his arm, across his shoulder, down his chest, all of it boy-smooth, supple, hormonally untouched. Justin was a month away from his eleventh birthday. She scrubbed across his middle and down his legs. She was careful with the catheter, got extra soap there, figured it needed it, boys being boys. She worked his feet over good.

Sam helped Katherine pull Justin to his side while Granny went down his back, the back of his legs, the recesses. "Same bottom as I remember when he was little," she said.

"Kinda hard to forget a bottom," Katherine said. "You stare at it enough, all those diaper-changings."

"Yeah," she said with a smile.

Granny pulled away and Sam handed her a towel. Granny dried Justin's back and then they let him lie flat. She continued rubbing him with the towel as they put the new gown on him and reworked the IV connections. Granny fluffed his pillow when they lifted him. Sharon took the basin, washcloth and towels away, and Granny and Katherine worked to get Justin better situated in the bed. Granny added pillows to prop up each arm. She brought the covers up to his chin, smoothed them out and tucked them in around his shoulders and down his sides.

"That's better," she said, touching the uninjured side of his face with the back of her fingers. "Much better, skeeter. Granny's got you all fixed up."

Granny let her hand linger on his face. She kept a longing look on him. Katherine put her big hand on the worn hand that touched him.

Granny looked over at her granddaughter, and her silver-rimmed glasses flashed in the fluorescent light. "Appears we got us a long row to hoe here, Katie," she said.

"Yeah, Granny," Katherine said. "I'm afraid it's gonna be pretty tough."

She brought their prayerful hands inward and let them rest on Justin's chest, over his heart. The ventilator shoved and pulled, shoved and pulled. For the moment it was the only sound, and it was huge.

Part Two
Tuesday-Monday
May 15-21, 2001

SEVENTEEN

Katherine, Sam, Justin. Three lives had been churning along, and now three lives had stopped. The waiting had gone on for three days. Nothing but waiting.

Hours upon hours, tests upon tests, and nothing changed. Three whirling minds, weighed down under the crush of emptiness, sputtered, then slowed, and for moments, stopped.

Justin was still, and remained so. He was frozen in a solid dark. Nothing had changed with him since Saturday.

Sam paced inside and out. He walked from Justin's ICU room to the little waiting room across the hall. He walked back. He walked downstairs to the hospital cafeteria. He walked back.

He tried to walk into the future, but there was hardly a future anymore. At least not a good one. The bad one, no. He was never going to go there.

The present was pacing and waiting. He was already there too much.

That left the past, where there were bad things and good things. What he needed were the good things, and so that's where he went. And the best of the good memories, the very best one, was a deep, quiet pool . . . .

Gardening had always been the common ground between Sam and his mother. From his earliest memory he'd been helping her turn their two-acre estate into a flowering showplace.

The back yard dropped in terraces to a creek bed, and each level had its season and a palette. Water — circulated with pumps — fell down the stairsteps of gardens, meandered among boulders and collected in quiet pools. Abundance was his mother's philosophy. Joy was the result. Their home, a grand Southern colonial with fluted columns and rooms upon rooms, was often on charity garden tours in the spring, and old ladies in Sunday pastels would come to cluck with awe.

Although he loved quail hunting with his father, it was for only a couple of months in the fall; most of the time his dad was in court or studying his cases and fashioning his rulings. Gardening with his mother became Sam's passion.

He was good at hauling and digging. He learned the arts of seeding and pruning. The best part was planning and wandering, discovering and uncovering.

"Sammy, we need more daffodils."

"The big ones, Mama. What about King Alfreds. Naturalized. I was reading about it."

"Under the oaks?"

"Yeah, but not too much shade. On the outer edges is best. In drifts, like in a forest."

"Let's do it, Sammy."

Then Sam was grown, and he was a father, and now in his favorite memory he was standing at the top of the hill at the back of his childhood home, beside the garden gate. The St. Augustine was perfectly trimmed and as lush as he could remember. The spring daffodils had gone to brown stalks, and now the daisies were coming out, the first dahlias, and roses and roses, bushes high and low, white and yellow and a rainbow of reds. The smell was brilliant, a sweet confusion. The water tumbled and burbled. From his vantage point at the top of the hill he could see a bouquet of orange and white and red koi fish lolling in the deepest pond, serene, suspended in stillness. They were underwater roses.

Justin was three years old. Sam's mother was kneeling beside him at the edge of the pool, one hand around his waist to keep him safe. Justin knelt, too, holding out his little hand to the water. The fish came up to him and lipped the food pellets from his half-submerged palm. They tickled his hand and he laughed every time.

He named the fish, and she would help. "See that one, Justie? That big, big orange one? I call him Justin."

"Let's give Justin some more food, Memaw. He looks hungry."

Katherine was the same. Certain memories were a blessing – rare, still moments in a churning life.

Justin had always loved coming to Granny's little house near the clinic. Katherine would bring him as often as she could.

When he was five, they would have picnics. Granny made the sandwiches, and the boy helped. He got peanut butter in the jelly jar and jelly in the peanut butter jar. Granny didn't mind.

They'd go to the far back of the yard, next to the vegetable garden. A weeping willow, almost as big as Granny's house and twice as tall, made a huge stretch of shade. Granny spread the blanket beneath it. Justin handed out the sandwiches. Katherine told him how she used to come there, too, when she was young.

They ended every picnic lying down on the blanket on their backs, the three of them lined up, looking up into the billowing strings of leaves swaying in the wind. It was a waterfall of leaves. It was full of cooling shadows.

"I see the sparrows," Justin said. "They're in their nest."

"They're a family," Granny said.

The little nest was way, way up. A pair of sparrows was bringing bugs to their babies.

"Look how the nest is rocking, Mom," Justin said.

"It must be fun," his mother replied. "Like being in a little boat on a great big ocean. Rocking and rocking."

"I want to go there," Justin said. "Like those little birds, I want to go way, way up there."

"You can," Granny said. "Just close your eyes, honey, and go."

EIGHTEEN

"Kath?"

"Hey, Sam."

It was Tuesday morning, day four of the hospital vigil. Sam came padding across the ICU's family waiting room in his socks, heading to the mini-kitchen in the back corner. "Coffee's ready," she said from her place on the couch.

"Good."

His clothes looked as slept in as Katherine's scrubs. His untucked knit shirt slouched on him, with one side of the collar up, one down. His khaki slacks were wrinkled up, down and sideways. One sock was pushed down to the top of his foot.

He returned with his coffee and sat in the armchair across from her. His hair had gone to a deep brown from its unwashed oil. It had a flat side and an upended side, and the middle was a confusion of limp curls. His eyes were wrinkled almost closed. His bristled face slumped.

"Did you need any coffee? I forgot to ask."

"I'm OK, Sam."

"How long have you been up?"

"I never really went to sleep."

"I did, finally. Maybe an hour. Have you ever heard Granny snore? It's something else."

"Are you kidding? I grew up with that snore, Sam. She snores like a truck driver."

They smiled. It was a fortifying moment, and then it was over.

He looked at his watch; it was seven-thirty. She'd worked through five cups of coffee since she'd been sitting there.

"Another hour and a half," Sam said, still looking at his watch.

Goldstein had promised a meeting with them at nine this morning. She'd spent all day Monday at Justin's bedside, monitoring the numerous neurological tests that had been ordered. She watched every blip of the machines, every sigh of the testers, every unmoved moment of her son. She went over the new scans with Dr. Goldstein; she could see no changes, and he said nothing.

"Abe'll be on time," she said. "For the important stuff he always is. In fact I bet he's in his office now, pulling things together. A lot of test results to consider."

"What's he going to say, Kath?" Sam turned a searchlight look at her. She knew what he wanted – any possible scrap of hope to put in his pitiful little pile of odds and ends.

How many times had he asked her this? Just as before, she had nothing for him. She'd been in the middle of every procedure they'd done on Justin since he arrived. Sam had grilled her after each test, and each time she'd given him the same answer. "I don't know," she'd said then, she said now.

Was he buying that? Katherine wasn't sure. If he knew her internal debate, she could do damage.

She was of two minds because she was two people – a mother and a physician. If Sam or Granny heard the viewpoint of the mother in her, they would hear hope, or at least the absence of despair. That side of her clung to the idea that it was still too early to know anything. The scans were cloudy, indicating swelling, which pointed to the possibility that the swelling could go down and some kind of normalcy would emerge. That would engender hope, which would set them up for what she feared was the truth, which was what the physician side of her was saying: that if there were swelling it would have gone down by now, that the damage to his brain was deep and lasting, and that Justin very well could be beyond recovery. That's what she'd taken from what she could make of the tests. Her reason and experience and inferences were clear.

But what if the physician side of her was wrong? Neurology was not her area. Her own worst fears could be talking to her — not her reason — and if she let that out she could be infecting Sam with unnecessary suffering. God knows he'd been through enough.

The right thing to do, she decided, was to carry the burden silently, and that she must continue to do so until the meeting with Goldstein. If there was bad news, let him be the one to bring it. Let him be the bad guy. Let him burst the bubble.

The endless hallway came up in her mind again. She pushed the gurney forward into the gray future. She was alone. There was nothing else to do.

Sam answered his own question. "More waiting then, probably. That's what I think he'll say, Kath. Inconclusive. Inconclusive. It's Dr. Goldstein's favorite word."

"Yeah, Sam. You're probably right. Get ready for that."

"Weeks? Months? How long will we have to wait?"

"I don't know, Sam. I suppose it could be a long time. Yeah."

"It already seems like forever, and we're only on the fourth day."

Katherine got up for more coffee. Her head was abuzz, but that was OK. It had the familiar ring of her caffeine-rattled days as an intern and resident.

"I'm trying to prepare myself, Kath. Yesterday, all night last night, preparing, going over things, getting ready. For the worst."

"That's probably good."

But what he said surprised her. It wasn't the worst.

"Months of rehab. That's what I think we might be facing. Granny and I were talking about it yesterday when you went home to clean up. That it could be months before Justin's fully recovered, that it will take a tremendous effort from all of us — money, time, just plain physical work — to get him back on his feet and his brain functioning again."

"Maybe, Sam. I suppose, yeah, maybe."

"Rebuilding the neural pathways. That's what one of the residents was telling me yesterday, one of the neurologists. He said that that's what they do with stroke victims. Physical, mental, all these exercises, getting everything working together again. The neural pathways."

"It's like teaching piano, Sam. By rote, by exercises, you retrain the brain as if it were a muscle. In many ways that's what it is. The mind and body all one thing."

"Exactly. I'm ready to cut back my work hours, Kath, whatever it takes to help Justin through this. I'm going to be there every day. If we have to, we'll turn half the house into a gym, home-school him, bring in therapists, whatever it takes. We've got the money. I can borrow it from my mother if we need to. Even if our insurance pays for none of it, we can still do the right thing."

"Yes, Sam. But . . ." She wanted to pull him away from this rehab idea, gently. But how?

"And then of course the news could be a lot better than that." His words came faster, heated by a sudden reinforcement of hope. "Goldstein's hidden it from us so far because he wants to be sure, he doesn't want to give us false hope, so he puts on this poker face while the encouraging data come in. Doctors do that all the time, don't they, Kath?"

"Yes. Sometimes." Katherine could feel herself being drawn in by Sam's brightening conjecture. There was just enough logic in it to get her hooked.

"Goldstein will tell us this as soon as he's sure the data are incontrovertible. He'll say the scans are showing new life, rejuvenation, the astounding way kids leap and grow and bounce back. And in no time Justin'll come bounding out of that bed in there. That's my dream, Kath. Two weeks, a month — maybe not near as much rehab as I think in my worst moments — and away we go."

Sam looked up. Hope had fully invaded him and sprung him open, and a kind of wet light spilled out of his brown eyes. His words began to sprint.

"To hell with our budget, Kath, our schedules, everything. You can take a leave of absence. Me, I don't know, I was thinking I could get Rawlins to take over most of my clients, maybe all of them.

"And when Justin comes out of this, away we go, wherever he wants. OK? Promise? Disney World. Hawaii."

"If . . ."

"To hell with our jobs. Screw everything. OK? Just for a little while?"

"Well, you know, Sam . . ."

"Justin's always talking about wanting to be a surfer dude in Hawaii."

"I vote for Hawaii." She couldn't help it. Hope overwhelmed her. Suddenly she was gulping it down by the lungfuls, like a drowning woman breaking the surface.

"Wherever Justin wants to go," he continued. "Take Toady. Sure, Hawaii."

"A surprise. No asking him, Sam. OK? Keep it a surprise." Tears of imagined joy began to fall.

"Yeah, surprise him. Tell him we're flying to Houston, let's say, then driving to Galveston. That way we could pack the swimsuits and such, and he wouldn't be suspicious. Then tell him the truth once we're in the air."

She put her hand up to her face and caught the tears just in time. "Yeah. Oops, I think the airline made a mistake. Look at these tickets, Justie — they don't say Houston, they say Honolulu!"

They were both running full-throttle now, as if their bare feet were slapping the foamy sand at the edge of the waves.

"Surfing, definitely," Sam said. "Lessons. Hell, we'll all take lessons."

"Snorkeling."

"For sure. And the smell, Kath. That's what I tell Justin when we talk about it. As soon as you step off the plane, the air is a flower shop."

"Where was that place y'all stayed?"

"The best. Dad went all out that summer. I was sixteen. Man. The Royal Hawaiian. A big pink elephant of a place."

"Other islands, too. Right?"

"Absolutely. Maui. It's much more beautiful than Oahu. Yeah, we'd *have* to go to Maui."

"Maui. OK."

It was only a minute or two, a perfumed minute. She inhaled. She couldn't stop herself. She let that cold, cold place of science sink away in her, and the flowers took over.

The barking. The yelling. Christmas morning, not quite six months ago. Katherine remembered.

"Oh, cool, Mom!" Jumping on their bed, two feet, four paws. "Thanks, Dad!" More barking.

Katherine pulled her face out of the pillow and looked over at him. "Merry Christmas, Justin."

The main gift tucked under the Christmas tree was a skateboard — a fancy one, Tony Hawk something or other. Fancy as in fast. "Can we go try it out?"

It could have been Hawaii. It should have been.

Up they went, no coffee, bathrobes, into a chilled, unmoving morning with enough dawn in the east to be classified as a hint. They went out the side door, under the porte-cochere where the driveway curved and dipped.

Justin set the board down and let it start rolling. Then, in a hop, he was aboard and streaming, bent and balanced like a surfer on a wave, the cloth belt of his bathrobe flapping behind him. Gracie barked and ran beside him. He'd done lots of practicing on Todd's board. This was nothing.

The ride didn't last long — just long enough for him to turn back to see if his parents were watching, and to smile triumphantly. Everything stopped at the asphalt-roughened street. He hopped off.

"Awesome, Mom! Now it's your turn."

"Are you kidding, Just? I never even mastered roller skates, honey."

"Nothin' to it, Mom. Step up on it, bend your knees, hold your hands out for balance. Like this." As he explained, he demonstrated each step standing on the concrete.

He went to her and lifted her arms. She made a flapping motion and added a goofy grin.

"No, Mom. You'll feel like flying, but you won't."

"Like this?" she asked him as she stepped up on the board, one arm on Justin's shoulder. "I'm not so sure about this."

"That's it, Mom. You've got it. Now roll!"

He stepped away. The skateboard took off, but her center of gravity — which was considerable — stayed put. In two seconds the skateboard had gone on without her and she was left perpendicular to the ground. One more tenth of a second and she and the ground were one. She landed with a thud of breath.

"Mom, are you all right?"

She remembered, first, what looked like ten thousand blinking white and yellow Christmas tree lights — then that concerned voice of Justin's and a patch of gray sky. She tried to answer him, to reassure him, but nothing came out. Nothing came in, either. Her lungs were stunned.

"Mom?"

"Kath?"

"Arf?"

A leftover breath exited at last, along with a word. "Shit."

Justin rushed up to her, reached down and took an offered hand. Sam came, too, and took the other arm. "I think she's all right, Dad. She said shit."

"I heard."

They pulled. Katherine came to her feet with an overarching moan.

"That's what they call a wipeout, Mom. Yours was pretty awesome."

She stumbled over to the brick wall and leaned against it. She bent toward a breath that was hard to reach. "Holy *shit*, Justin. It's a lot harder... than it looks."

"You're not gettin' me on that thing," Sam said. "No way."

"Mom's not afraid of anything," Justin said.

"I am now."

Her pager went off. Katherine reached into her pocket. Goldstein already? Sam's every muscle watched her.

"Three-West," she said, looking down at the digital readout.

"Not Justin? Anything to do with Justin?"

"I don't think so, Sam." She retrieved her cell phone and dialed the number of the nurses' station. Three-West was the ward opposite theirs, on the other side of the building.

"Yeah, Margie," Katherine said. She listened for two or three minutes. "I'm practically across the hall, be there in half a sec."

She folded the phone. "Another kid, Sam."

"They don't know what's going on over here with us?"

"Apparently not. Margie thought I was on rounds."

"Somebody else can't . . . ?"

"Doesn't sound like a big deal. Ten minutes max. Monique's one of my kids. Plenty of time before the meeting."

"Ten minutes? You promise?" He didn't look happy.

She went to a mirror beside the coffee pot and ran her fingers through her displaced pile of hair, which was as lopsided as Sam's. She tried not to notice her puffball eyes.

"Ten minutes, I'm sure. Fifteen max, Sam."

Katherine Warren, M.D., suffered from an overabundance of empathy. If somebody called, she answered. If they were hurting, she was going to fix it, or call for help if that's what it took. She was constantly being pulled into one drama after another. She took her white coat off the hook on the back of the door, jammed her arms through and headed down the hall.

"Don't forget the patient you've already got!" Sam called out.

A disheveled blond girl, with purple stars tattooed to the backs of both hands, was standing by the nurses' station when Katherine came around the corner. Brandi was as much a patient as her own daughter. She'd had Monique when she was 15, and when she'd brought the infant in for well-baby care Katherine had treated the mother for a nasty cold. Two kids for the price of one.

"Dr. Warren? I'm so glad I found you. The nurse said you might be here."

"Brandi honey." They hugged. "What's going on?"

"Monique. Can you come see her? She's just not right. I brought her in to the ER yesterday morning and they said they think something's like wrong with her blood."

Brandi continued with her story as they walked together to a room down the hall. As soon as Katherine saw the two-year-old in the crib bed, she knew. The baby was listless and her coloring — usually a beautiful bronze combination of her African-American father and Anglo mother — was a yellowish vanilla.

"They've checked Monique's liver function?" Katherine asked.

"I don't know. A lot of tests. Nobody will tell me anything."

"Dr. Humphries? She hasn't been by?" Mary Humphries was the pediatric resident on call.

"She came by for a second but I was downstairs. That was yesterday evening."

"Damn it." Katherine stroked the baby's spongy blond hair. "Let me go see what I can find out."

At the nurses' station Katherine put on her half-rims and went over the Donovan chart. As she suspected, liver failure looked like the direction things were going. Monique's blood had been drawn and an extensive panel of tests had been ordered, but the results were not among the paperwork. She asked Margie about it, and the nurse said they had a call in to the lab but nothing had shown up yet.

"Was there a stat request made?" Katherine asked.

"I don't think so," Margie said.

"Why the hell not? Why hasn't anybody called down to the lab again? What's wrong with you people?"

"I'm sorry, Dr. Warren. This is Dr. Humphries' patient and we didn't . . ."

"Shit. Hand me the phone. I can't believe . . ."

And down she went, into the bureaucratic bowels of the hospital. Twenty minutes. Thirty. Three phone calls. Five. Sometimes you've got to push hard on the enema bag to get things moving, and Katherine knew how to do that. In forty-five minutes she had Humphries there, the lab results, a liver guy to read them and a three-way discussion on what to do about it.

That's when she bowed out. She'd done her part.

She took a nervous glance at her watch. She had to get back to Justin.

NINETEEN

When Katherine walked into Justin's room a few minutes later, Abe Goldstein was bent over the boy, checking his pupils with the flick of his penlight. A nurse was standing beside him, adjusting monitors. Granny sat quietly on the other side of the bed.

"Abe?" she asked. She looked over at Sam, who was sitting in one of the chairs by the bed opposite the doctor. "Sorry I'm late." Sam averted his eyes. He was clenched all over. She could feel the anger radiating from him, seeping through his knotted muscles.

"You're not late, Katherine." Goldstein didn't look up. "I'm early. Wanted to take one more look at Justin before we had our talk."

He repeated the light test on the other eye and took in a long breath. She thought she saw the slightest shrug of despair as he clipped the light back to the front pocket of his lab coat.

"Here?" she asked. "Your office?"

He turned. "Let's go to the family room."

"I'll stay, keep an eye on my boy," Granny said. "Y'all go talk." Katherine nodded her thanks.

They moved across the hall and shut the door. Sam and Katherine sat next to each other on the couch. Goldstein sat in one of the wing chairs opposite them.

Justin's chart, already half a foot thick, was resting on the thigh of one crossed leg as Dr. Goldstein leafed back through it. He paused at points, looked up over his wire-rims, pinched at the wrinkles on his high forehead, stroked his moustache, wrote something.

"Let's start with what we know."

He began to read from the chart in his syrupy Louisiana accent. "Diffuse hypoxic-ischemic insult to the brain." He looked up at Sam. "The diagnosis. Essentially it means what happened from the reaction to the pain medication at the dentist's office, which was the anaphylactic shock – massive and immediate swelling in the airway, cutting off oxygen, stopping the heart and strangulating the brain."

Slowly, carefully, steadily, Goldstein began building his case. But Sam interrupted.

"And the baseball," Sam said. He might as well have blurted it, the way it came into the conversation, shoving things aside. Sam was going to make sure his hope was heard. He had a case to make, too, and already seemed to sense that he was going to have to work hard to make it.

Goldstein looked down at his paperwork again, but he wasn't reading. He was looking for a place for his eyes to go. "Yes. The baseball."

"We can fix that. Kath? Right?" Sam looked at Katherine as he spoke, then back to Abe. "The baseball — the injury from that, concussion, hitting the back of his head, out for a second, that's what Katherine said was what he could recover from." Sam's words became faster, louder, as his bubble of hope expanded. "You know, like an internal bruise. Some rest, some time, then all the rehab — it comes back.

The neural pathways. Justin is coming back. Kath and I've been talking about all the rehab that's probably ahead."

"The baseball," Goldstein repeated. He looked up, but his focus was not on either of them. It floated across the room. "The baseball."

"Abe, Sam is convinced . . ." Katherine was going to help Sam state his case. It was something the mother part of her wanted to believe, too. She'd pushed it with Goldstein earlier without much success, but she was willing to give it another try. Sam needed her. Hope needed her.

Abe said, "Katherine . . . this . . ." He cleared his throat, gathering resolve, and turned his focus back to Sam. "It's true, generally, when a trauma has occurred. You're right, Sam. Katherine's right. Car accidents, for instance. The swelling in the brain — the main cause of the problem in such cases, when the head strikes the windshield, for instance — will gradually go down. People in these situations often come out of comas, and after a period of rehabilitation, they can oftentimes be as good as new."

As Sam took in a long breath, he closed his eyes. He had to listen. His world was based on facts, and he had to let them in. He looked at Dr. Goldstein. "But Justin . . ." Carefully, very carefully, he began to open the door that Goldstein needed him to open. "You're trying to say that Justin's injury wasn't . . ."

"In this case, Sam, I'm afraid, after three days of extensive testing and consultation, it's becoming apparent that the baseball was not the chief culprit here, like we were hoping at first. In fact I'm pretty sure the initial injury was not a factor. All the bad stuff happened in the dentist's office."

"That's not good."

"No, Sam. I'm sorry. Not good."

"Then . . ."

Goldstein closed the chart. He took off his glasses and leaned forward. "By inches, Sam" — and he looked over at Katherine, too — "ever since Justin came into the hospital on Saturday, he has been losing this battle."

"Losing?" Sam had hardly enough breath to say the word. What freshness of color he had in his face was disappearing.

"We've done everything we can do, run every test — twice, three times — and by inches Justin's brain function has been deteriorating. It was terrible when he came in, and now it's worse. The brain injury was catastrophic."

Neither Sam nor Katherine took a breath, much less spoke.

"Right now he's on automatic pilot, Sam. The brainstem is functioning, keeping his heart beating with the help of the vent. We can get some reaction when we push ice water against his eardrum."

Sam looked quizzical.

"It's a standard neuro test, Sam," Goldstein said. "We use a syringe, squirt the cold water into the ear. Normally this causes the eyes to move, but in Justin's case, not much."

Sam's head dropped, and he was speaking toward the floor. His words were short of breath. "I don't get it, I don't understand. I thought . . . I always had the idea that time was on our side here. He's getting worse? He's getting worse?"

"You see . . ."

"Neural pathways," Sam continued. "One of the residents yesterday. He was talking about neural pathways, retraining, exercises . . ."

"As in a stroke. That's right, Sam, but Justin's case is much different. The injury to his brain is much more severe. Widespread. Global."

A silence took hold among them, an unsteady silence of fear and clipped breaths. Goldstein inserted another throat clearing and tried again. "There are many levels of unconsciousness. Think of it like steps going down to a basement, Sam. Anesthesiologists, for instance, can take a patient down and down, three steps, five steps.

"Your son has gone deep, Sam, many more steps further down than any anesthetic could take someone without threatening his life, much worse than from the kind of stroke that people can recover from. And after three days of observation, I can be ninety-nine percent certain that his level of consciousness is very unlikely to ever rise again.

"Justin is one or two steps up from the bottom of the stairs, and there is no way back. Science knows of no way back."

Katherine was reeling. Ambushed. The news was a fist in the gut to her as much as it was to Sam. She'd been right there with all the tests, and she hadn't seen this coming?

She'd lost her clinical equilibrium. She'd been fighting off hope, shooing it away as if it were a gnat, trying to ignore it. She should have been trying to kill it.

Somehow Sam was still making words, gasping words. "God. God. Will he die?"

A muscle began to twitch in the corner of one of Dr. Goldstein's eyes, but he continued. He reached out and put his hand on Sam's shaking knee. "I don't know, Sam." He brought his hand back and tried to rub his twitching eye into quiet, and that produced a tossing sea of wrinkles.

Goldstein sighed. He looked away. "Justin is somewhere in that murky area we call the persistent vegetative state." He sighed again. "I've never heard of a patient recovering from a point this far down." He sighed. "Recovery is highly unlikely."

"But . . ."

Katherine watched the last of the color fade out of Sam. A glistening came from his pores, a start of tears in his eyes. Hope — the color of hope, a low blush of enriched blood, a thing as real as oxygen — had drained from him, and a damp pallor was coming in to take its place.

Katherine took Sam's hand. She reached her other hand across and added it to the clasp. She tried to breathe, but nothing much was coming in or going out.

She closed her eyes. Inside — all over inside — was a spillage of wiggling darkness, the upside-down of everything.

"You'll both need some time," Abe said

"Yes," Katherine said, surprising herself with a voice.

The old man stood, and so did Katherine. His arms reached for her, and she leaned into him. His arms enclosed her, and she didn't want to leave. "I'm sorry, Katherine," he said. "I'm so sorry."

"Yes," she said again, in that same voice that hardly had a life.

"Sam," he said, holding her shoulders and pulling back to look at the heaped man on the couch.

Sam didn't move. His head was hanging, and he didn't even try to tighten the muscles in his neck.

"Sam, I'm sorry." Abe took one hand from his embrace of Katherine and put it on Sam's mound of shoulder.

"Some time," Abe said to Katherine. "We need more time. I want to rerun all the tests, triple-check everything, then we'll talk again, as much as you need. I'm not ready to be absolutely definitive about PVS."

"OK."

He looked at her, but she was looking at the floor. "Katherine. Sam. If this situation is going where I think it's going, we have some big decisions ahead."

TWENTY

Sam and Katherine were doing their best to hold things together when Granny came into the family room. She had been with Justin, waiting for word, and when she saw Dr. Goldstein leave, she decided it was time to find out what was going on. She sat where Abe had been sitting. Sam and Katherine remained on the couch. Granny waited for them to speak.

Sam had Southern culture on his side, the expectation of boys to be men and men to stay men. Bunch up the abs and take it full force — whatever — the blows of a bully or the sudden punch of grief or loss or disappointment; nothing shows, not even the loss of air; all the muscles — of the eyes, the heart — go dry and stand fast.

Katherine was maybe even better at holding back. She'd trained like a boxer for these kinds of battles. The traumas that rolled into the Johns Hopkins ER from the Baltimore front lines came in at a pummeling frequency around midnight on Saturdays, and fresh interns like her learned to take it. Wall off the heart and keep your brain lively and clear. Be prepared for anything. Reach into the red-bubbling chest cavity, peel back the crisp skin, push the forceps in for the misshapen slug of a bullet; do the next right thing for the patient. The next right thing, again and again and again. Emotion was a luxury item you couldn't afford.

Katherine didn't yet know what the next right thing was going to be. She was going to have to reach deep to find the right words to describe Justin's condition in a way that brought Granny gently down to reality. She could feel Granny's pointed, mother hawk eyes on her, looking for the truth.

Katherine was reeling inside. Particles of thought blurred by. How was she going to form something coherent from the whirling pieces?

Sam just wanted to keep the door locked. That was the main thing. Man the barricades. Don't let it in. It had gotten too close. Don't let it in.

Then, fast, at once, it broke down the door and leaped at his face.

Sam's first cry was something like a pup's yelp. From his place next to Katherine on the couch he bent and brought his fist to his mouth, but it was too late. The cries coughed through his hand and trembled across his great bulk.

Katherine grabbed his shoulders. She held him as best she could, but there was no holding back the full throat of grief. It choked him and flooded him and bellowed out.

Granny came to him and helped Katherine hold him, crying with him, and tears came from them all as Sam delivered the truth of Justin's condition — the whole ragged truth of their grief — in the language of animals.

TWENTY-ONE

If there was anything to contradict Goldstein's grim prognosis, Katherine was determined to find it. She went to the Internet for additional depth in neurology. She went over Justin's records, researched journals and consulted colleagues. Over the next several days she summoned up the same kind of energy that had propelled her through med school, internship and residency.

Her life became an endless rotation of brain-wrenching days followed by nights of jerky naps. She didn't know if it was day or night unless an uncurtained window showed itself, and whichever it was was always a surprise. She lived off adrenalin, prayed for adrenalin, and what little sleep she got was a dry thing, an unrefreshing blackout. Days and nights were the same gray soup; no real light, no depth to the dark. She pushed and pushed toward the end of the endless hallway.

But one night stuck with her. It was Thursday, wasn't it? Or Friday? It burned into her presence as deep as bone.

Granny and Sam had insisted she try to get a full night's sleep, the first one since the accident. Granny kept up the pressure until Katherine eventually relented, adding the stipulation that she wouldn't have to go home and that they would wake her if anything – the slightest thing — changed.

It was nearing midnight. She was lying on the couch in the family waiting room, two pillows under her head and the old quilt from home covering her, with her hands folded across her stomach and her eyes closed over the darkness. She had taken a sleeping pill, but it wasn't working.

She thought about that quilt, and she remembered when Granny made it. Katherine was a young teenager and Granny was between nursing jobs. She decided to stitch together a quilt the way her mother had done long ago.

Granny wasn't that good at it. There was a lot of cussing. She didn't have the patience.

"Son of a bitch, Katie, this is harder'n it looks," she said.

But she finished it. Over the years it lost a lot of threading, but Katherine just cut off the frayed ends and the quilt kept going. Justin loved its silky feel, and he kept it on his bed throughout his early childhood.

That quilt was home. As ragged as it was, it retained the warmth of family.

When Justin was much younger and the day had come to an end, she'd lie next to him in his bed, both of them safely under that quilt, and tell him about her favorite place in the world when she was a little girl.

"It was at Granny's, wasn't it, Mom. Outside."

"Yep. My favorite place was at the very back corner of her back yard, next to the vegetable garden."

"It was under the willow tree. Right, Mom?"

"Right, Justie. The weeping willow."

"I want to go there, Mom."

"We will, honey. Next summer, I promise. You and I and Granny can have a picnic there."

For her to go beneath that huge, bending tree with its hundreds of green strings hanging to the ground, she told him, she'd push back the branches as if they were curtains. Next to the trunk, inside a green cave of leaves, it felt like the safest place in the world. It was her secret place. She could lie back in the grass and look up through the swaying leaves that sparkled the sun. She'd close her eyes and nobody could find her.

"Could Granny find you, Mom?"

"Granny could find me. But nobody else."

"And you could sleep there if you wanted to. And read books. And dream."

"That's right, honey. The best, the sweetest dreams in the world were there."

"And there were the sparrows, and they had a nest."

"That's right. I'd lie on the ground and watch the nest, and the mama and the papa would bring food to the baby birds, and that nest full of babies would swing gently in the wind." She began to softly sing. "Rock-a-bye birdie in the treetops, when the wind blows the cradle will rock."

"I wish I had a place like that," he said.

"You do, honey. Deep in your mind. You can close your eyes and go there. You can ride the wind, and you can fly."

She rubbed his forehead with her thumb and stroked her fingers into his wayward curls, and in a minute his breath would soften. He was gone.

Now, lying alone on the couch in the hospital that night, she wondered if maybe he had gone to the willow place when he was in the dentist's chair, waiting for the nitrous oxide to take effect. She went to him in an invented memory. She wanted to see him one more time. She wanted to know . . . .

Justin was lying back in the dentist's chair, and he was alone, his head turned toward the wall, the mask over his nose and mouth. He didn't see her come in from the hallway behind him. He didn't notice her settle into the depths of him as quietly as the breath of a ghost. He didn't stir.

She was very quiet, very still, closely attentive. The gas was just coming into him, a cool breath of juniper and pine, and soon she was floating, too. She was airborne, riding the currents that swept up from his cranial mountain ranges.

It was a marvel of a trip. She was a swirl of amazement — his enlightened brain, this glowing globe, this aurora world crackling and flashing among its succulent cells even as the dentist's gas began to lull it. Just look. His brain was lighting up in extravaganzas of microscopic neon.

The dentist came in, then a tech, a mumble of voices. It didn't matter. His eyes were closed. The shot of Novocain to the gums that the doctor gave him was no more than a pinch. Justin didn't try to say anything. They left, and that was better.

The floating was fun. Remember the Tilt-a-Whirl at the State Fair? Sometimes, on the widest turns, the best spins, it was as if you could be flung into the sky. Your guts went one way, you went another, and the whole of you lifted into lightness.

Now Katherine felt the pinch in his throat as if it were her own. It wasn't that bad. He could pull for breath but the floating was so nice. He could try harder to come back, but it didn't matter. The ride was spinning and spinning.

Something was turning off the faucet to his world, but he didn't know it, and he hardly cared. He was going down, and she was going with him. The boy didn't know why, and it didn't matter to him. He was going down. The gas answered all his needs and overwhelmed the need to struggle.

With the final, slow turn of the handle, his throat swelled shut and the breath went out of his blood. Throngs of twinkling neurons faded from his brain's sky - millions a minute — a billion — billions — and soon the shelter of the self was gone. His home beneath the willow tree wrinkled into paper-dry wisps of leaves, which fell away in a torrential whirl.

Now the night sky in him was bare. His cortex was frozen sand. There was no one left to leave tracks across it; not even God could live there. A heartbeat echoed in the hollow dark, an empty wind of breath was forced in and out, but there was no one there to hear it. He was gone, and she was alone within his emptiness.

That easily, that quickly, a world died.

Justin?

She couldn't believe it. Was he really gone? She was walking across the icy moonscape that he had become. *Justin?* *Justin?* She couldn't keep from calling out to him.

Her mind knew, but her heart wouldn't allow it. Her physician self could imagine the suffocation of Justin's brain, the resounding silence that was left of it. But she could not keep from calling. She was his mother. She had to find him. He had to be there somewhere among the ruins.

Justin?

This cold rock of broken cells was uninhabitable. Nobody was coming back to it. The emptiness was plain to see.

Justin?

She called and called. She couldn't help it.

Justin?

Hope is insane.

"Justin?"

She came thrashing out of her sleep, yelling out his name

"JUSTIN!"

Sam ran across the hall from Justin's room. In less than a minute he had taken her dampened hand and was trying to reassure her. He was leaning over her.

"You're having a bad dream, Kath," he whispered.

She sat up on the couch, blinking, returning. "It wasn't a dream, Sam," she said. "I don't think it was a dream."

TWENTY-TWO

For all of them, the days became a jumble, a backward and forward of time, a tumble and toss of memories and visitors and interruptions and hope and dread.

The tests of Justin's brain function were repeated, double-checked, triple-checked. Dr. Goldstein came into the room, out of the room; alone, with residents, with equipment, with colleagues, with nurses, with interns; scans and tests and more tests. Katherine was on the computer in the nurses' station, then down to Abe's office, on the phone in the waiting room, night and day and night, following the details of each test and studying hard to understand them and their implications.

After Sam gave voice to the truth of Justin's condition with his guttural cry from the heart, he fell back into something like a trance, and people walked around him, mostly, and touched his shoulder if they were close enough. Todd's parents came by. Father Red twice. Jonesie came every day, straight from work. They didn't allow any children to see Justin. It would have been too much for them.

Granny bathed the boy daily, fluffed his pillows and combed his hair with her fingers. She couldn't keep her hands off him. Every time she walked by he got a soft little toe pinch, an ear hug with her fingers, a kiss on his forehead. Hers was a ministry of hands. To have and to hold, to pray and to caress, to lift up and to bury. The hands — stringy with blue veins and scraggly with old bones, blotched and freckled — said it all. No sermons necessary.

But Justin's daily baths were becoming a disappointment to her. The water didn't change color like it used to. Granny had finally gotten beyond the last layer of dirt on the boy. Now she was working on fresh skin, and it wasn't much of a challenge.

In compensation she tended the garden of flowers that lined the shelves and filled the corners of the room. She watered them and pinched off the bad leaves and pulled out the stray blooms that nodded toward brown. The get-well cards came in by the stacks, and on a second shelf she propped open a line of them into a gathering of hope and encouragement. A thousand prayers and a hundred blossoms gathered around the deep well of silence that was lying in the bed.

Conversations with family and friends were hardly more than fragments. Words bobbed to the surface, formed into patterns, dispersed. Nobody asked Katherine about the details of the conversation she and Sam had had with Dr. Goldstein on Tuesday. Nobody asked Sam. They knew enough. And they also knew that they didn't want to know more. They tiptoed around the truth, careful not to wake it. They whispered around Justin, as if someone were there. They were heading toward a future no one wanted to see, and so they didn't see it.

"We'll wait it out," Sam said to Katherine one morning in the family waiting room. He was reviving. A little bit of hope had pulled him out of his emotional paralysis. "More tests. We'll see."

"Yes," Katherine said.

"More time. That's what we need. There could be something."

"Yes," she said, a little bit softer, with a little less conviction.

"It's just too early to know anything for sure. It's way too early. Right, Kath?"

"Yes," she said, and she was down to a whisper.

Dr. Goldstein was in the ICU nurses' station, sitting at the desk in the back, holding open Justin's records at a page not too deep into the folder. His elbow was crooked on the top of the desk, and his head was resting on his folded-down fingers.

"Anything, Abe?" Katherine asked. She was standing at the door.

He didn't answer.

She waited.

He didn't answer. He didn't move.

By the time he looked up to see where the voice had come from, she had moved off. She didn't really want to know. He didn't really want to tell her.

"I bet you haven't even noticed all the rain we've been gettin'," Granny was saying. Katherine was on the opposite side of Justin's bed from Sam and Granny. It was early Thursday morning, Day Six.

"I thought I heard some thunder last night," Sam said.

"Not much," Granny said. "A good rain last night, though, slow and soaking. My tomatoes needed it."

Katherine didn't remember any thunder. A soft rain was nothing she could have heard over the noise of the medical machines.

It wasn't that way in the old days, when she lived with Granny. The weather was always welcome in that little house. Bad, good, it didn't matter. She and her grandmother were open to whatever came by, storms and sunshine, cold and blankets of heat, whipped up and gentle. Mostly the windows were up and the weather had an open invitation. You always knew where you stood with the weather. Granny made sure of that.

Katherine went to the window and parted the heavy curtains. She looked out on the back of another building. There was a row of dumpsters in a concrete alley. There were puddles of dirty water. She let the curtain fall back.

"Sam, what are you thinking?" Katherine asked him. "You haven't said much lately."

They were in the waiting room, Thursday midday. Granny had joined them while Jonesie watched Justin. It took several minutes for Sam to recognize Katherine's question and access his voice.

A thickness separated him from the world. He was having a hard time putting a thought together and making it go. His scaffolding of facts — what helped him climb high and see the big picture — had collapsed days ago. There weren't many pictures anymore.

"I don't know what to think, Kath. I guess I'm just waiting like everybody else."

"Yeah. The tests. Tests and more tests."

"It's all we've got, Kath. The only hope." A straw. He grasped it.

"I guess you're right."

"Is there something else?"

"Sam, no, not at this point. Nothing else. I haven't talked to Abe since Tuesday, with you, except in passing."

The waiting room was quiet for a while. Granny was drinking coffee and eating one of the cookies Jonesie had brought.

"How long can this go on, Kath?" Sam asked. "All this waiting. This terrible waiting, test after test. How long can Justin hold out in this state?"

"Sam, I don't know what to say. Nobody knows. Years, I suppose. Justin could live in this state of suspended animation for a lifetime."

"He'd stay in the hospital?" Granny asked.

"A nursing facility," Katherine said. "Something like a nursing home. He wouldn't need so much close attention from the medical people."

"There's where the rehab would be, I guess," Sam said. "Retraining the brain."

"We talked about that a little with Dr. Goldstein on Tuesday, Granny," Katherine said. "In Justin's case, that's probably not going to do much good, the kind of training they do when someone's had a stroke."

Granny ignored her granddaughter's negative spin. "I can help, honey. I'll stay with him night and day if I have to, exercise his arms, his legs, read to him, work with him. Whatever it takes. If I can do it with the old folks, I can do it with Justie." Another straw, another grasp.

"Granny, I don't think . . ." Katherine wanted to rein them in, keep them in the vicinity of reality.

Granny suggested they start reading to Justin now — "You never know what they can hear" — and Sam said he could bring some books from home.

"Remember what Dr. Goldstein said, Kath?" Sam asked. "Remember? He said it was unlikely that Justin could ever recover from the coma. He didn't say impossible. *Unlikely.*"

"Yes, Sam," she answered. "'Highly unlikely' I think is what he said."

It was already too late, Katherine realized. Hope, the thief of reason, was loose in the room, wending its way among them, enticing them, calling to them, pushing, pulling. It frightened her. She had seen hope take over the parents of some of her patients and cause days of unnecessary suffering by delaying a decision that was inevitable.

But was she supposed to fight it? She'd be the bad guy if she did (doctors often were, she knew), and besides, Katherine had a big, big stake in the outcome here, too. She was as vulnerable to hope as any of them.

Her immediate future, for a moment, rose from the fog: Within herself and out, she was in for the fight of her life. The burden of truth was going to fall on her shoulders. She was going to have to guide them to a place that she hadn't fully grasped herself and where she didn't want to go.

Highly unlikely. Highly unlikely.

Nobody seemed to have heard it.

TWENTY-THREE

Jonesie sat across from her. They were in the family room, Katherine in an armchair, Jonesie on the couch. Sam was at the other end of the couch.

It was late in the afternoon on Thursday, and Jonesie had just come in from his day at the clinic. The silence had grown to at least ten minutes, but nobody seemed uncomfortable with it. It was easy for Jonesie to study Katherine; she was gone and unaware.

She was hardly trying with her appearance. She hadn't used any makeup in at least three days, and her hair didn't look like it had been washed in that long, either. Her eyes rested on dark pads. The upper lids hung heavy and bunched up into something that looked to him like those atrociously tacky balloon shades that were all the rage. And her eyebrows: They were growing together into what appeared to be something positively Slovakian.

But what could he do short of wrestling her to the floor and attacking her with tweezers? A good nail-buffing wouldn't hurt, either, and some fine lotion on those overwashed hands. While he was at it, the right base could lighten those eyes and brighten those cheeks. He'd have to pin her to the floor with his knees while he worked on her. God, he was thinking, if someone didn't do a beauty intervention on her soon she was going to end up looking like a very tall and well-fed Mother Teresa.

He smiled inside, but he didn't let it show. Before, she would have laughingly accepted his teasing, welcomed something to cut the tension. Now, she was too far gone. He couldn't reach her. He didn't try.

The hospital elevator arrived, and Katherine and Jonesie stepped in. He had convinced her that they needed to take a break outdoors. As they stood on opposite sides of the elevator, leaning back against the shiny silver walls, Katherine zeroed in on the bulge in Jonesie's front pocket. It was behind the nametag on his scrubs. Hers was a greedy look, and he saw it.

"No, Kath, no," Jonesie hissed as the doors opened on the ground floor. "I absolutely forbid it."

"I want one, Jonesie. I need one. I deserve one." Her tone shifted into mock pleading. "Just one little, measly little ciggy-boo?"

"No, Kath. You can't."

They walked across the soaring atrium that was the lobby of Children's Medical Center. Her whispered words echoed into the patter of a three-story rocky waterfall and its jungle of ivy and ferns. "If I have to beat the crap out of you, Jonesie, I'm going to get one of those cigarettes."

His voice was tempered, too. "Lay one hand on me, bitch, and I'll scratch your eyes out and scream like a girl."

They moved together into a compartment of the revolving door and took tiny steps to get into its rhythm. "I'm willing to risk it," she said.

They took the steps down the hospital's limestone entrance and crossed the bricked plaza. Beyond a garden of newly planted petunias and impatiens and across from the outdoor play area was the stretching shade of an overlapping alleyway of live oaks. They walked to a concrete bench next to one of the trees and sat together. This early evening in May was perfectly warm. The rain was gone, but dampness lingered in the air. Like Jonesie, she was wearing her scrubs. She wore her white coat, too.

"I know these are tough, tough times, Kath." He forked a stork leg over the opposite knee and leaned his head back against the bumpy trunk. "But are you sure it's worth the stink, the hacking, the humiliation of all your patients knowing that you aren't worth a shit at taking your own professional advice?"

"Shut up and gimme a fucking cigarette, Kirby. *Now!*"

He took out the pack. She noticed his buffed nails and tapered fingers, and got her usual little fit of jealousy. Jonesie's hands were what she'd always wished for, instead of the nubby raw paws that were hers. She had a man's ring size, a soapy diamond and cuticles that hadn't been addressed since the turn of the century.

Jonesie held the flame of his butane lighter out to her. Just leaning toward the fire made her mouth tingle and water. As she inhaled, her lungs quivered in recognition of their old friend Nic. In a chemical homecoming, a shimmering lake of endorphins gathered in the echoing caverns of her brain.

"Two years. Can you believe it, Kirb?"

He lit his own cigarette and took in a long drag. "Yeah. You're right. Somewhere right around this date, I think. Two years already?"

Second intake, third. Each time she inhaled, the smoke seemed to go in easier and find a deeper resting place in her. "The ceremonial flushing of our last communal pack. Remember, Jonesie?"

"Well, sort of flushed."

They smiled. For their first few years together at the clinic, she and Jonesie had shared cigarettes — that's when she'd first started keeping a pack in her office bookcase, behind the Physicians Desk Reference. On their most hectic days (all of them, in other words), Katherine or Jonesie would tell the other that he needed to "go look something up." They'd close the door to her office, open a window and take a smoke break. Oftentimes they'd wind up "looking something up" at the same time, especially right after lunch.

They justified the cigarettes by keeping the habit at the office, away from home and weekends, and protected themselves with a cover-up of mints. Then one day, after months of discussion, they made a vow to each other to quit for good and forever.

On an evening after the clinic had closed, they allowed themselves a final puff, then went into the bathroom for the ceremonial flush. She flung the pack in and Jonesie pushed down the handle.

Once around, twice around, sinking, sinking, and then Jonesie screamed operatically, went to his knees and grabbed for the pack on that last downward swirl.

"I can't! I can't!" he kept pleading as he retrieved the package, shook out the water and gingerly carried the cigarettes to the kitchen area to dry them out in the microwave. Two minutes, defrost. The cigarettes, he reported later, were crispy but smokeable.

Katherine was able to stay away from them, however, and from that day forward Jonesie smoked in the parking lot, far away from her. She gained ten pounds — fifteen tops — but at least she felt superior, and she let him know it almost every day. "So how's my favorite nicotine-stained wretch?" she'd ask him. That sort of thing. She was unmerciful, but he could lay it on pretty good himself. "You eat one more donut, missy, and I'm reporting you to Oprah."

In the hospital's park, as she and Jonesie smoked and reminisced, a graceful little breeze came across them, weaved between them, carrying the monologue of a mockingbird and the lapping sound of waves of wind among the oak leaves. The far-off voices of playful children came, too. They fell into a long silence and their separate worlds.

Soon after that first cigarette was stubbed out and the filter deposited into the trash, Katherine's cell phone rang. She looked at the caller ID. Olsen Realty. It had been three days since she'd talked to her mother. She simply had to answer it this time.

"Honey?"

"Hi, Mom."

"I've been tryin' and tryin' to get hold of you, sweetie. How's my boy?"

"It's not good, Mom."

"Oh dear." Katherine could hear her mother shuffling through her purse for a tissue, and then came a somewhat delicate blowing of the nose. "That just doesn't seem right. I don't know if I can bear it. What's the latest?"

Katherine told her about the conversation with Goldstein. She kept out most of the details, but Faye Jean still managed to go straight to the dark drama of the situation.

"Oh my God, my God! That just couldn't be right."

"It is, Mom. I know you don't want to believe it. None of us do. But so many tests have been run, and they're all saying the same thing. We're running out of good options."

"That's just ridiculous."

"Mom, you can't argue with the facts."

"Honey, I've prayed and prayed. Jesus is . . . Darlin', hold the line a minute. I've got another call."

Katherine could hear her mother's cell phone chirping in the background. It stopped. Faye Jean must have called her daughter from the office phone, and now she'd neglected to press the hold button.

Katherine touched the speaker button on her own phone so that Jonesie could hear. In a sugar-glazed singsong, her mother answered the other phone, "Jean Massey, Billy Olsen Realty. How can I hep yew?" Her voice had the contralto force of a sales pitch. It was easy to overhear the conversation.

"Alan, honey . . . Honey, listen . . . I know, I know, termites are serious stuff, especially if the infestation is as bad as you say it is, but . . . what's a few little bitty bugs between friends?"

Katherine soon figured out who Alan was — a building inspector/exterminator. "Alan, sugar, listen to me. Listen. We've just *got* to pass that house. That deal's *got* to go through by the end of the month. I promised my sellers!"

Another pause as Alan worked in a comment.

"I know. Honey, I know. I'll owe you one, OK? Spray 'em, stomp 'em, I don't care. Just get 'em dead enough so we can pass that house!"

Pause again.

"Alan, you dear man." Jean's voice had come down a few decibels, but its glycemic index remained stratospheric. "Yes, yes, I promise. I know. I'll owe you one, honey. Yes, promise. I wouldn't think of using another inspector. I'm always talking you up around here at the office. Yes, yes, I know. And thank you, sweetie. Say hello to that sweet wife of yours . . . Oh, no, honey, she left you? When did that . . . ?"

It sounded like she was about to open a whole new chapter, but, no, she must have remembered that Katherine was waiting.

"Listen, honey. Alan? Honey, I've got to go. Yes, my daughter the doctor's on the other line. I told you, didn't I, about my grandson? Yes, I know, and it's been touch-and-go for a time, but I think we're about to turn a corner. Yes. I'm optimistic. Yes, he's still unconscious but . . ."

And on she went, into every detail she knew about Justin and his predicament, which weren't many. At last, then, with just three more "honeys" and two "goodbyes," Jean extinguished the cell phone and came back to the other line.

"Sorry, honey," she said to Katherine "That son of a bitch is impossible to get away from."

"I'm sure."

Katherine and Jonesie smiled at each other. Jonesie was ready to burst out, but he kept his hand firmly over his mouth.

"So, you were telling me about Justin. Nothing much has changed?"

"Not since I talked to you the other day, Mom."

"I don't know if I can bear it, honey. I just knew he'd be up and about by now."

"Mom, I'm sorry. I know it's not good news, but we're holding up pretty well."

Katherine heard more sniffles into the Kleenex. "Don't you want me to fly in?"

"Stay home and pray, Mom. Really. We're in good hands with Granny. Sam's here, of course, and a lot of friends, and we've got the best medical people anywhere around."

"Honey, I'm gonna pray my little heart out, that's what I'm gonna do. I'm gonna get the whole big bunch at Abundant Life to keep workin' on this, maybe step up the pace. You just think about one big prayer circle down here in Houston putting itself around you and Sam and Justin. Feel the energy, hon. There's no way that Satan can get through that circle of love and take our boy away."

"That's what I need you to do, Mom. Keep praying. That will help us the most."

Katherine and her mother made a formidable couple — Faye Jean Robinson Warren Ellison Somebody Somebody Massey and Dr. Katherine Warren Moore — each six feet tall, although six inches of Jean was a bubble of hair that had been poofed into cotton candy and then sprayed into a reinforced mesh.

Faye Jean was a rock-solid presence. Nothing much about her moved: her Botoxed forehead remained unfurrowed, her painted eyebrows unfallen, her dye-darkened hill of hair locked down in frozen swirls. She kept her maraschino lips continually polished. Her bosoms were permanently pert. She wore a pound of imitation gold.

In normal times Katherine heard from her mother once a month and saw her twice a year. That was more than enough. Katherine had always come in third or fourth place in her mother's list of priorities, behind all those open houses, dinners with her "precious" clients, time at the office to write up contracts, a hundred other phone calls and the real love of her life, Maker's Mark.

But so what? The center of maternal gravity in her life had long ago shifted to Katherine's grandmother, and Justin had done the same in a next-generation sort of way. Mostly Katherine was able to observe her mother's antics from a bemused distance. Mostly. It had taken her years to achieve such an equilibrium, and still she was subject to tumbles into rage and sadness.

If reality wasn't up to snuff for Faye Jean Robinson Warren Ellison Somebody Somebody Massey, she by God changed it. It had been that way since Katherine could remember.

Sometimes it worked. Katherine was thinking of that little house down the street from Granny that her family had started out in. There was her tool-belt daddy and his elbow-walking, Saturday night binges, and her mother often matching him drink for drink and rage for rage. Then one day her mother marched herself right out of that mess, out of her double-wide name (Faye Jean to Jean) and away from her honky-tonk husband, out of the secretarial pool at the Fort Worth defense plant and right up to the top ranking of one of the biggest real estate agencies in Houston. Along the way came four more husbands – two ne'er-do-wells and two rich ones – cleanly fleeced upon their departure (two divorces, one annulment, one coronary); a ranch-style house half a city block long; and a doctor for a daughter who married into a fully pedigreed family. For a mama like Faye Jean, she at last had hit the mother lode.

Jean liked to give her Hallelujah God and prosperity preachers most of the credit — she told Katherine she prayed for the good life and God said sure — but it was her own claws that did most of the work. Those blood-red, perfectly manicured nails stabbed into life and pulled all six feet of her up and over the pile of losers and onto the top of the heap.

When Jean buried her second husband and temporarily lost her battle with the bottle for a second time, Katherine, at ten, moved in with Granny, although she would spend at least a weekend a month with her mother when she lived in Fort Worth and part of every summer in Houston when her mother moved there.

Faye Jean didn't let those days with her daughter go to waste. She tried to drag Katherine up the ladder with her, but the girl didn't make it easy. Faye Jean broke a nail or two on her. Her mother wanted a baton-twirling Cinderella and what she got was an outsized, clumsy science nerd who'd rather autopsy a June bug than go to a tea party.

She pushed Katherine into diets, to the beauty shop, to dance lessons, into some shame-faced blind dates. They had some fire-spitting fights. That's when Katherine gave her the name "Rex," as in Tyrannosaurus rex, the monster that ate her young.

Katherine preferred Granny's care, of course, where she could keep her head in her science books as much as she wanted and be left alone to dream within the willow's secret shade. By the time Katherine graduated from med school,

Jean had moved into a million-dollar house in Houston with hubby number three. No, wait; number five.

Jean's other ship came in when Sam and Katherine got hitched in a grand Episcopal wedding (written up by the society editor). But it wasn't long before Faye Jean's ship began to take on water: Katherine failed to open her own practice and instead worked with the destitute at County General and then moved on to her barrio clinic. Jean called it her "hippie phase," but after ten or so years there was no sign Katherine was moving past it.

Katherine knew that Jean had always felt betrayed by her daughter's decision to live with Granny all those many years ago, and her mother's resentment remained just below the surface. Surely Jean at some point had realized she had neither the ability nor the inclination to be an adequate mother, what with her bouts with the bottle and the shuffling in and out of husbands and careers and religious excesses. (Before real estate had come Mary Kay, Tupperware and Amway; Baptist, Pentecostal and now the Abundant Life Bible Fellowship Church; and husbands Bill "Tiny" Warren, A.C. "Ace" Ellison and Wayne Lee "Bubba Lee" Massey, not counting a couple of conveniently forgotten others.)

But if any guilt or mettlesome self-doubt buzzed about Faye Jean, she made quick work of it the way a lizard takes care of a fly — one quick flick of its sticky tongue. At the center of her self-centeredness was a voracious appetite for the picture-perfect life. Now a smudge had come along that wasn't going to be so easy to tidy up. Her only grandson, stricken.

After the phone call ended, Jonesie said, mimicking Faye Jean's honeyed drawl, "What's a few bugs between friends?"

Katherine laughed. "I knew you'd pick up on that. I knew it."

"It's going in my Faye Jean bio," Jonesie said. He'd come up with the title years ago: *Profiles in Narcissism*. It was one of their running jokes.

"The power of positive bullshit. That's Mom's working creed."

"Faye Jean's got a direct line to God," Jonesie said. "She's convinced she can even coax someone right out of a coma."

Katherine tapped off the ash of her second cigarette. "You're absolutely right, Jonesie. When Mom's life was just a somebody-done-somebody-wrong song, she'd say this must be some kind of terrible mistake. 'I deserve better than this. I *am* better than this.' And, by God, she changed it.

"And that's why she thinks she can pray her grandson right back into health and sell another house before dark. It's just amazing. But somehow it works. People seem to love her, and she can sell 'em the shirt right off their own back."

From the beginning of their friendship she and Jonesie had traded battle stories and compared psychic scars in their respective mother wars. Jonesie's mom (Marzella Jones, also known as Godzella) was a beer-swilling, bass-fishing, tattooed, right-wing nut job. On her pickup was a bumper sticker that said "GOD, GUTS AND GUNS MADE THIS COUNTRY GREAT."

Jonesie was afraid of guns. His weapon of choice? An electric curling iron, on high.

Jonesie handed her a third cigarette. They'd been quiet for a while. The evening light was dimming.

"Are we finally gonna talk, Kath?"

As she pulled the fire from his lighter into the end of her cigarette, a family walked by. Katherine was fully uniformed in scrubs and lab coat, and the mother gave her a tut-tuttting, slight nod of disapproval. Katherine returned with an eyebrow-hardened look that shut the woman down.

"You mean really talk, I guess."

"Yeah, Kath. You know, Goldstein, test results. Where we stand and all that. Where we're headed."

"Yeah. No. I don't know."

"It's not good, Kath. It can't be. Everything you've told me. Goldstein's demeanor. The other docs. Nothing but grim since you guys had the big talk on Tuesday."

"That's the whole story in a nutshell. All the retesting the docs have been doing the last few days — I think it's just been a formality. The verdict is already in, and all the testing is a mere formality to confirm it."

"Persistent vegetative state, you mean."

"Yeah, and with emphasis on the persistent. I don't see how anything can turn this thing around, Jonesie. I've been reading up on it, trying to learn everything I can about Justin's condition. I think we're probably truly, deeply up shit creek. No paddle. A hole in the boat that just keeps getting bigger."

"Yeah." She was coming to the place, finally, that she needed to be, and now that it was here, Jonesie wanted to protect her from it. But he couldn't.

"We'll know soon enough. Our next talk with Abe is just around the corner, I'm sure."

Jonesie waited, and then Katherine continued. She was looking down into the new green grass at her feet. "I haven't had the heart to say it aloud to anybody else, or even to myself, really. But I don't think God is going to come to the rescue this time, even with all that prayer from Mom's church friends." She struggled to finish. "Jonesie, I think we're waiting for a miracle that's not going to happen."

TWENTY-FOUR

Katherine needed memories. She was desperate for them, for the good days, even the average days. When memories came along that bounced her out of the empty waiting of the hospital and into the life and light that used to be, she welcomed them. She cherished them. She followed them.

So when her memory heard Jonesie's familiar greeting of "knock, knock" just outside her office door at the clinic, her mind answered. It was two years ago, late fall.

He stuck his head in. "Yo, Kath."

"Yo back."

"Johnny Escobar is here. He says it's kind of an emergency. He won't tell me what's wrong. Seems pretty antsy."

"All right. Sure. I'll be there in a minute."

When Katherine arrived in Exam Three, the boy was sitting on the papered, cushioned table, swaying his sneakered feet, which were almost touching the floor. His hands were folded in his lap. Hints of a mustache shadowed his upper lip, and a few well-scrubbed pimples dotted his cheeks and jaw line.

"Hola, Johnny," she said.

"Hola, Doctora."

Katherine had been seeing Johnny and his two younger sisters since she opened the clinic five years before. He was eight then, small for his age, sickly, asthmatic. She'd straightened him out medically, and since then he'd caught up with his classmates in growth, then spurted ahead. At thirteen and five-feet-nine, he was a forward — and the best player — on his eighth-grade basketball team.

Johnny's mom and his aunt worked together as housekeepers and came weekly to Katherine's house. Johnny's dad had died years ago in a bar stabbing.

"You doing all right? Still working in your uncle's shop?"

"Yeah."

"School going OK?"

"Honor roll."

"Good boy. Good for you. So what can I do for you, Johnny?"

"I kinda got a problem, I think."

"What's that."

Katherine could hear the tenuous crack in his voice She softened her look and opened herself with a motherly lean toward him, the way she'd learned to coax children out of their fears. He was looking down at his lap, unconsciously pointing out the problem.

"When I pee . . . it really hurts."

"Burning?"

"Yes ma'am."

"Discharge?"

"Huh?"

"You know, does stuff come out — kind of weird-looking runny stuff?"

"Yeah. A little."

"Stand up here and drop your drawers, honey. I need to take a look."

Johnny stood and pulled down his pants and underwear, looking across the room. On the wall was a pharmaceutical company's rendering of a digestive system in need of the company's reflux medicine. Katherine thought of it as a chance to educate her young patients on people's internal engineering. Their main question? Where does the poop come out.

Katherine slipped on a pair of latex gloves, sat on her rolling stool and pushed over to him. She parted the boy's shirttail.

"Well, well, well, this is gonna be an easy diagnosis. Looks like our little Johnny down here has grown up and left home."

"Huh?"

"You know, been where he shouldn't have been."

"What?"

"Screwing around, bucko, and it's bad news. You've got gonorrhea, I'm guessing. Venereal disease. STD. The clap."

"Are you gonna tell my mom?"

She laughed. "No way. Your secret's safe with me, Johnny."

"Am I ruined for life?"

"No, honey, you're not ruined — I can fix you right up with a shot. But I am going to need your help with something."

Katherine got a sample of the discharge with a swab into the boy's urethra. She told him she'd be sending the test to a lab to double-check the diagnosis. But there was no doubt what it was, and she saw no reason to wait on treatment.

"What do I have to do?"

"First thing, keep your pants down, turn and face the exam table."

"OK."

"Then tell me who you got this from. I hope it wasn't a girl from school."

"It wasn't a girlfriend. It was this lady on Jacksboro Highway."

"Let me tell you something, kiddo, that was no lady."

Katherine removed her gloves and went over to the cabinets. As she prepared the injection of antibiotic, Johnny explained that his cousin Joe, who was on leave from the Navy, said he had a special present for Johnny's thirteenth birthday. "You're a man now," his cousin had said. "It comes with certain, you know, privileges."

"Joe drove me over there since I can't drive yet. She lives in this little travel trailer over behind the flea market."

"You remember her name?"

"She says, 'My name's Sugar Pie. You wanna piece?'"

"Hmmm. Guess we'll get the Health Department to pay Miss Sugar Pie a visit. She's gonna get the same present as you're about to get."

Katherine came over to him, pulled up his shirttail again and cleaned a spot on his clinched buttock with an alcohol swipe. "Don't tighten up on me, Johnny. Just relax. In we go."

"Oow! God!"

"Acting like a man, huh? Let me get a Band-Aid on that. You want Bugs Bunny or Porky Pig?"

He wasn't listening. "Man that hurt."

"I don't guess your cousin thought about getting a rubber to go with that birthday present, did he?"

"He got me one, yeah, but it kept falling off. Joe said I was pitiful — said it was like trying to put a sock on your big toe. You know, a lot of sock left over."

Katherine smiled, which the boy didn't see. She put on the Band-Aid. "You'll grow into that Trojan one of these days."

"You really think so?"

"Give it a few years. Yeah. Meanwhile, stay away from people like the pie lady. God gave you two hands, buddy boy. Pick one. Use it."

He smiled as he pulled up his pants and buckled them.

"Listen, pal, I've got some guys I want you to meet. Do you work every afternoon at your uncle's butcher shop?"

"Not during basketball season. I got practice."

"Could you take an afternoon off once a week?"

"Yeah. Maybe. I don't have practice every day."

"Listen, do me a favor. Go sit in the waiting room for a minute. I need to get this sample ready for the lab and then we're gonna walk next door."

"To the firehouse?"

"Yeah."

She handed him a sugarless sucker. "Cherry OK?"

"Si." Big smile. "Thanks."

The fire station had been built the same time as the pediatrics clinic, approved as part of a city-county bond election. Except for its shape — taller and boxier — its cream brick and drab trim were identical to the medical building. It had two big bays for the fire trucks and a side driveway where an ambulance stood at the ready. On this day one of the engines was at county maintenance.

Katherine and Johnny walked across the weedy lawn that adjoined the two buildings. In the shadows of the one empty bay was a small circle of chairs. A half-dozen men and one woman were in them.

Katherine called out to them: "Hey, don't you fire bozos have any flames to put out?"

"Hey, Doc," one of them said.

"Somebody's gonna have to light a fire under your lazy asses if that buzzer ever goes off," Katherine said as she and the boy came into the shadows of the bay. Faces came into focus as the outdoor glare subsided. They were all friendly.

"I got you a new serf here," she said. "Johnny Escobar."

"Hey, John Boy," one of them said.

"Fresh meat," said another.

"Somebody get that kid a broom," Isabella said.

Johnny smiled back shyly, uncertainly.

Katherine and the firefighters had been developing a community outreach program over the last few years, bits at a time. For instance, a firefighter (shortest straw) dressed as Flu Bug worked to distract the kids as they anxiously lined up for flu shots at the annual fall immunization clinic. From there, the kids and their parents were directed to a fire safety demonstration and a tour of the fire trucks. Additionally, the guys were helping with a community garden behind the station and the clinic, and on Saturdays, monthly, Jonesie was using the station's large kitchen for demonstrations of nutritional cooking. He had a Spanish translator and hospital dieticians helping him.

Now Katherine was putting together an informal program for at-risk boys to hang out at the station one afternoon a week, help out, hear a few stories and get an idea of what healthy male camaraderie looked like. "As role models I grant you the guys next door aren't saints," she told Jonesie as they hashed over the plan together, "but they beat the hell out of gang leaders, dope dealers and predatory priests."

One of the men brought up two more folding chairs, and Katherine and Johnny joined the circle.

"So where's my donut," Katherine said. "I brought three dozen donuts this morning and only got one stinking little tiny one out of the deal."

"You're too late, Doc," Chris said. He was the lieutenant in charge of the station, tall guy, National Guard, red-blond, crisp and clean. "Jack and Randy ate the last two an hour ago." Those were his young sons, the Bean In Nose boys.

"Waylon? How many did you eat?"

"Three, Doc. That's all." Waylon was one of the heftier guys and one of two EMTs.

"I counted five," Isabella countered.

"Five my ass," he said.

"That's where they all ended up, too," Ben Ray said. "On that fat ass of yours."

"There's not an ass in this house worth bragging about," Katherine said. "Mine especially."

They laughed, but it was true. "I'm telling you guys, these donuts have got to stop," Katherine said. "I'm talking to myself as much as to you." The guys, including Katherine, took turns bringing in donuts from the shop down the street. It was supposed to be just once a week, but there were lots of special occasions, mostly made up, like National Hispanic Heritage Donut Day.

"So when, Doc," Jorge said. "How about New Year's? Let's get a grip after the last football game on New Year's."

"I vote for Super Bowl," Waylon said.

"New Year's Day," Katherine said. "That's going to be our D-Day. Diet Day."

"Just what kind of misery are you planning for us, Doc?" Chris asked.

"I was thinking of putting Jonesie in charge," she said.

"Oh, God," Waylon said. "Not that skinny bastard."

"Exercise," Katherine said. "Not just a diet. Exercise. I've been talking to him about it. Three times a week. Right here in this bay. Before the clinic opens."

"What can that Richard Simmons dude teach us? " Ben Ray asked. "How to knit?" He almost immediately regretted it. They all knew that Jonesie and the Doc were best buds, and she had no tolerance for intolerance. But Katherine wasn't riled, or at least not too much. In fact she was smiling.

"The guy has ten years of ballet training under his belt," she said, turning toward Ben Ray, a paunchy Anglo with a bulldog neck. "I daresay he could lift your redneck ass over his head and do a triple whammy pirouette. You think you can do that, hot shot?"

This brought on a storm of laughter, and Ben Ray backed off. "OK, OK. I'm in. Exercise with Jonesie."

"What about the rest of you guys?" she asked.

There was a general chorus of grumbling agreement.

"It's settled then," Katherine said. "Bring your tutus."

"And smoking?" Chris asked. "My kids are on me all the time about it. Worse than Linda."

"Smoking," Katherine said thoughtfully. She'd been over to the station plenty of times, begging for cigarettes when she found her PDR stash empty. It was one among her several attempts to quit. "Are we making this thing a little too ambitious?"

"No, Doc," Chris said. "Let's go all the way with this. As soon as the football games are over, no more cigs."

Katherine let out a long groan, and Ben Ray chortled.

"Don't laugh, Benny boy," Katherine said. "No more of that nasty Copenhagen crap, either. Your spittin' days are over, my friend. We're cleaning house. Right, guys?"

Nobody said anything.

"So I'm taking your silence as a yes."

They seconded the motion with an unenthusiastic round of nods.

After a few more wisecracks, they began talking to Johnny about the times he'd be coming in and what he'd be doing. Besides helping wash the trucks, cleaning the equipment and doing the dishes, he and two other boys would be working on CPR and other rescue techniques, such as the fireman's carry.

"Do I get paid?" the boy asked.

"Are you kidding me, kid?" Ben Ray said. "You're a serf. Serf's don't get nothin'."

"I think back in the old days they paid 'em in vodka," Jorge said.

"I'll take vodka," Johnny said with a big smile, and that brought an outburst of laughter.

"Kid, I think you may work out just fine," Ben Ray said.

Summers were the best time for Justin to help out at the clinic. Tax season was good, too. From mid January to mid April his dad was covered in work — by March he was working seven days a week, twelve hours a day. On Saturdays for the last few years, Katherine took the boy to the clinic with her. Also, during the week, Todd's mom would pick up the boys at school and drive them to the clinic. Katherine would bring them home. Maybe it was only a few hours, and usually just once a week, but to Katherine it was enough to give the boys a healthy dose of the real world and maybe stretch their empathy muscles just a bit. Todd's mom heartily approved. Both boys occupied a bubble of privilege, and both moms wanted to keep as much air out of that bubble as possible.

Justin and Toady's job was to entertain the kids in the waiting room, especially the healthy brothers and sisters who were forced to come along because of a lack of babysitters at home. That also included the kids coming in for shots and checkups. The sick ones usually held back, isolated by their earaches, stomach aches, and fevers.

Jonesie showed the boys how to form a reading group, arranging them in a circle on the floor. Justin and Todd took turns reading aloud in English. Sometimes the other kids would read in English or Spanish. Justin brought books from home. His favorite was *Hank the Astronaut*, and he read it almost every time.

Granny came often, too. She'd had the boys help get her old rocking chair in her pickup and drive it over to the clinic. Granny liked the babies, and they loved to be rocked. Justin sometimes helped with rocking duties, too.

"Hey, Toady, do you smell what I smell?"

"Yep. It's coming from that baby in your lap."

"Now what do I do?"

"Give him back to his mom, Justin."

"What do I tell her? I don't think she speaks English."

Todd went over to Jonesie, who was sitting at the receptionist's desk, going over some charts. "Hey, Jonesie, how do you say poopy in Spanish?"

He didn't even look up. "Poopy."

Although Justin was supposed to be helping out at the clinic when he was there, he spent much of his time next door at the firehouse. The guys loved him. Like most of them, he was a nut about sports.

He'd bring over shoeboxes full of baseball and football trading cards, and lay them out on the table in the dining area. He participated in their fantasy football games, and usually came out ahead and raked in their dough. When the guys got into heated discussions on stats, they relied on Justin to settle the arguments.

One afternoon Justin came running into Exam Two. Jonesie was holding a screaming baby on the cushioned exam table while Katherine was taking his temperature rectally.

"Mom! Mom! This kid Victor is throwing up blood in the waiting room!"

Justin went running back and his mom quickly followed. Jonesie handed the baby to its mother and joined the small stampede. Todd was waiting for them, and eight-year-old Victor Puente was wiping his mouth with the back of his hand when the others arrived.

They stood around a dark pink pool on the floor.

"See, Mom?" Justin said. "Blood."

"It's not blood," Todd said. "Blood's not chunky. This is chunky."

"You can have little chunks in blood, can't you, Mom? If it comes from your stomach?"

Katherine turned to the queasy-looking Victor. "Honey, what did you have to drink before you came in here?"

"I was helping my big brother mow the lawn. Then I drank a Big Red."

"There's your culprit," Katherine said. She bent down to the boy and combed her fingers through his hair. "Don't drink your soda pop so fast next time, OK?"

"OK."

Jonesie came in with a mop and the mop bucket.

"I still think it's blood," Justin said.

Jonesie handed him the mop. "Whatever it is, dude, it's all yours," he said.

"Do I have to, Mom?" the boy asked.

"Don't you want to be a doctor?"

"No way, Mom. I'm gonna be a fireman. All you gotta do is sit around and talk. I'm good at talking."

"Whatever, Justin."

"The guys said I was already part of their team. They said all I had to do was grow up, and then they'd make it official."

"Right now you're a janitor, Mister First Responder," Jonesie said. "Start mopping."

The summer before, as the Bush-Gore presidential race began to heat up, the discussions around the firehouse often turned to politics. It was true at home, too, and family dinners at Sam's parents' were often heated as well.

Sam's father, U.S. District Judge Leo Moore, was alive then. He was an Old Money, fire-breathing conservative. Sam had absorbed his father's politics, and he was backing Bush, too.

Katherine had grown up with Granny's view of things, and they were both supporting Gore. Granny was from Old Sweat, having grown up on that Texas Panhandle farm during the Dust Bowl. She was a Roosevelt Democrat.

Leo's father had done well in the oil business, and Leo had practiced oil and gas law before being appointed to the bench. He had been a friend of the elder George Bush since the early '60s, and they continued to chat occasionally.

Justin had met George W. several times at Ranger games, and sat with him in his suite once, discussing problems with the lineup. Bush listened attentively and amusedly, offered his own opinions, and presented the boy with a baseball signed by Nolan Ryan.

"I don't care what you say, Mom, I'm votin' for Dubya," Justin declared.

"That's my boy!" Leo had said, smiling victoriously.

"You're nine years old, Justin," his mother said. "You can't vote. Ha!"

"Granddad can make it happen, Mom. He's a judge."

"Dear God," his mother said, "I've given birth to a Republican *and* a budding felon—which are not, by the way, exactly mutually exclusive. Where did I go wrong?"

She loved teasing her father-in-law, and he loved it too. They had been fast friends.

The guys at the firehouse, excepting Isabella and Jorge, backed Justin's view of things, and they loved to rib his mother about it. To get her goat, they hammered in half a dozen Bush/Cheney signs in the front yard of the firehouse. Justin helped. Katherine had to see those signs every time she drove up to work.

She and Jonesie countered with just as many Gore/Lieberman placards in front of the clinic. Granny helped, and so did Isabella and Jorge.

On Saturdays Justin would often bring Gracie. The guys adopted the black Lab as their official mascot. She enjoyed sniffing around the fire trucks and getting her ears rubbed, but her specialty was helping in the kitchen.

Jorge, also known as Beano, did most of the cooking, and he wasn't all that good. He saved his failures — dried out meatloaf, concrete mashed potatoes — for Gracie's weekend visits. He set aside the cardboard donut boxes and let her lick out the flakes of sugar glaze and eat the cardboard. Gracie loved Jorge.

When the weather was good, Justin, Toady and the men would toss around a football or play catch with baseball gloves in the front yard of the firehouse. Gracie liked to play, too, especially Frisbee. She wasn't fast and she was too fat to leap. But she was good at snatching the disc out of Todd's hands just before a throw.

"Gracie!" Off she went with it, and off the rest of them would go in pursuit.

Gracie was strictly forbidden from entering the clinic. County hospital authorities might let Katherine get away with the good-natured political duel with her neighbors at the firehouse, but having a dog in the waiting room would have raised a stink. Katherine didn't agree with the policy — a dog like Gracie, gentle and kind and longsuffering, would have been a blessing to Katherine's fearful and despondent patients. But those were the rules, and Dr. Warren obeyed them.

Until the day Gracie staged a break-in of sorts.

It was a cool, red-leaf fall day. The boys were next door, playing touch football with the firemen, when Gracie spied a squirrel. The chase was on.

At that moment, a family was leaving the clinic. The squirrel saw the open door, which looked like an escape route. Gracie's snout was inches away from that fluttering fluff of the squirrel's tail, and she was barking frantically.

In they went, followed by Justin, Todd, Ben Ray, Jorge, Chris and several others.

The kids in the waiting room squealed. Jonesie screamed. The squirrel and the Labrador raced down the hall and into the supply room.

More barking. The sound of falling boxes of syringes and cotton balls and Band-Aids came out into the hall, and Katherine ran out of Exam One, asking, "What the hell?"

Jonesie armed himself with his folded up Perry Ellis umbrella and headed for the supply closet. Justin and Todd were right behind.

Before they reached the mayhem, an explosion of fur erupted from the room. With Gracie just behind it, slobbering and barking, the squirrel made another pass through the waiting room and came back into the hall. Katherine instinctively went to the end of the hall and opened the door to the outside.

Justin yelled, "Sic 'em, Gracie!"

"Get him, Gracie!" Toady added.

The squirrel saw daylight and made a dash for it. Out went Gracie, and right behind were Justin, Todd, Jonesie, Katherine, five patients, six first responders and three parents.

Gracie was hopping madly around the base of a big red oak, in a slather of barking. The squirrel was in a high branch, flicking its tail in triumph. Katherine leaned toward Jonesie and whispered in his ear, "Holy shit!"

Katherine was in Justin's room at the hospital when she heard a great deal of foot-shuffling in the hallway outside. She stood, moving toward the door to investigate, when Chris McDermott stuck his head in.

"Hey, Doc," he said quietly. "Can we come in?"

"Of course you can." He opened the door wide and the guys and Isabella began to file in.

Everyone from Fire Station Twenty-Six was there, all in dark blue pants and light blue shirts, with badges and nametags and blue caps.

"We were in the neighborhood," Chris said.

"Yeah, right," Katherine replied with a smile that acknowledged the lie. "I'm really, really glad you all came. It means a lot."

"Jonesie's been keeping us updated," Chris said.

"Then you know," she said.

"We know."

They circled around the end of the bed, whispering, looking uncertainly at the ventilator and fearfully and sadly at the still boy in the bed. The sun had gone out of Justin's face. The vigor had gone out of his curls.

Each person bent and touched Justin — on his arm, his foot. Izzy kissed him on the cheek.

"Get better, Justin," one of them said.

"We're pullin' for you, partner," another said.

There were a few sniffles and some shifting from one foot to another.

"Is there anything we can do, Doc? Anything?" Jorge asked.

Katherine shook her head no.

In less than five minutes they began filing out of the room, each with solid hugs for Katherine as they left.

Chris was the last. He held the back of his hand to his eyes, bent to Katherine's ear and whispered, "This is one big fat load of crap."

She put her head against his shoulder. "Yeah, Chris, it is," she said.

After a quiet moment, a long embrace, they separated. He closed the door behind them.

TWENTY-FIVE

Friday morning, Day Seven. After driving home for a shower and clean clothes, Sam felt a need to see his mother. The claustrophobia of the hospital was tightening in him. The waiting stretched out, and nothing seemed to have changed with Justin's condition. Was it ever going to change? It felt good to move, even for a little bit.

His mother's house was ten minutes away, a stately drive through a leafy neighborhood. He punched in the code at the entrance of her estate, and the iron gate swung slowly open. He drove his SUV down the driveway and parked.

He stood for a minute on the front porch. The white fluted columns were as muscular as anything attached to the White House. He'd been there with his parents once, a reception for federal judges and their families. He was Justin's age. President Nixon shook his hand. This was the power of his upbringing, and now it was gone.

With Justin, now, he felt far from the center of knowing, helpless, powerless, out of the loop. Katherine knew everything and he knew nothing, or at least that's what he thought. He didn't realize that she knew nothing, too, or that science was helpless, or that all the facts in the world were worthless.

The personhood of Justin Samuel Moore was disintegrating. The towers that were Sam and Katherine were coming down to dust and pieces. His father could have hammered and hammered his gavel, declaring unfairness, but nobody was listening.

Sam unlocked the massive front door with his key and came in.

"Imogene?" he asked in a big voice. It took a lot to reach through the vast house.

"Up here, honey!"

As big as it was, the house was solid and simple inside. Pretension was lacking; the furniture was traditional, the lighting was practical. Pictures on the walls were of Sam and Justin as young boys, portraits of the two families, ancestors, hunting dogs, landscape paintings. No framed photos of Leo with U.S. presidents or at presentations of honors or diplomas.

The house was his father. The gardens were his mother. Together, it was Sam's growing up.

Sam walked across the foyer and up the stairs. At the top, to the right across the landing, were three bedrooms, including the one that had been his. He went left.

"Sam boy!" cried his mother's companion and retainer as Sam came into the sitting room. "Come give your old Imogene some sugar!"

His mother spent her days in this light-filled room, which was connected to the master bedroom beyond. On the other side of the bedroom was his father's smaller office where he kept his shotguns and golf clubs. Sam paid the family bills at the desk there. On the ground floor, in the library, was where his father had performed his judicial homework.

Imogene set down her knitting in her lap and put her black arms out, and Sam walked up and leaned into them. The sagging arms came around him and brought him close. He held his cheek against hers, then pulled back to see her fully. Her eyes were two brown pools of serenity amid a dark cocoa face and cloudy white hair. The dark was warmth. The wrinkles radiated it.

Imogene had been with the family since Sam's early teens. She'd come every day, help in the kitchen, clean here and there, and at lunch she and Sam's mother would sit at the kitchen table or on the back porch and catch up on their families' news. When guests came for dinner, Imogene stayed later, worked with Sam's mother getting the meal together and then served and cleaned up. She'd get a paid day off after that much work.

She was too old to clean anymore, and the big dinners were a thing of the past. Now she looked after Claire and fixed their small meals. She'd moved into the home full time, and one of the spare bedrooms was hers. She kept an eye on Claire's night sitters.

"Any news, Sam? My little Justin doin' any bettah?"

"Nothing, Imogene. No changes. We're just waiting."

"Oh, honey." She patted the side of his face with a worn-leather hand. "Honey. I don't know what to tell ya."

She sighed as Sam pulled himself up straight and started moving to his mother.

"Miz Cla-ah? Sam's here."

The old woman was sitting in her armchair and facing the big bay window that looked down on the cascading garden that she had created, the creek bed below and, farther down, the slow-moving Trinity River and its accompanying jogging trail. A clutch of white daisies from the garden was in a vase beside her, and a half-full cup of tea.

"Mama?"

She didn't turn.

"Mama, it's me, Sam."

She didn't turn.

He leaned down and touched her cheek with his lips, then pulled up a small chair and sat. Her hazel eyes were far away and locked on the distance. She was nothing but distance.

On the outside, his mother seemed unchanged. She was the essence of Southern gentleness, a friend of the Earth, and the Earth had left its touch within her, on her freckled hands and sun-wrinkled eyes. Her gray-blond hair was in its traditional loose sweep. Her hands were folded in her lap.

Leo had died from the hammer-blow of a coronary as he walked along the sidewalk in front of the federal courthouse. That was not even a year ago. Claire's dementia worsened at a faster pace after that.

It was as if she were fading into her own background. The edges of her self were wearing away. The focus of her attention blurred into a kind of nearsightedness. A particle at a time, her brain was dying.

"Mama, do you remember who I am?"

She looked at him and smiled, but she didn't say anything.

"Mama?"

He sat there for five minutes, then ten. He looked where she was looking, into the heart of beauty. The gardener was keeping the grounds as beautiful as ever. There were heaps and drifts of roses and periwinkles and zinnias, red upon red and white upon yellow.

He wondered what his mother was thinking. Did she see the memory he saw, of the little boy and the grandmother and the white and red and bright orange fish? Or did she have any memories at all?

Finally he got up, pecked his mother on the cheek, and started to leave the room. He looked over at Imogene, and she shook her gray head with resigned negativity, answering his unasked question about his mother's condition.

As he reached the door to the sitting room, his mother finally spoke.

"Javier, it's looking good down there. You've got things looking good."

Sam felt like he needed to go to the office, so he headed downtown after visiting his mother. He'd checked in with

Jenny a couple of times by phone in the last week, but most of each call had been about Justin's condition.

May was a slow month, generally. The tax rush was over, and handling the few clients who had filed for extensions wasn't much of a problem. While he was in the hospital he kept his cell phone turned off. Justin needed to be everything. He was determined to make Justin everything. He had been so wrong about so much. It was time to step up. He didn't know when, or how, but he had to step up. Justin needed him.

After the easy drive into the small canyon of buildings that was downtown Fort Worth, he parked his Lexus in his reserved spot in the bank's garage and walked across its echoing, shadowed stillness to the elevator. Down to floor two. Across the skywalk, through the bank lobby to the group of elevators in the back, and up to the 14th floor and the offices of Moore & Assoc., Accounting & Investments. He went in.

"Hey, Jen."

"Hey, boss!" She gave him an eye-crinkling smile. "It's so good to see ya, Sam."

She was a single mom, late 50s, her children grown, cats for company. She was a wide, warm woman who had always been a help to Sam in putting his clients at ease. Sam was a social bumbler and Jen smoothed things out for him, providing y'all-size smiles of welcome and small, personal comforts. She knew the clients' children and grandchildren by name, whose grandma was sick and where the fish were biting, who liked milk in their coffee or their Dr Pepper from the can. That's what people appreciated — the West Texas, small-town treatment — and Jenny was the real deal.

"Anything going on around here?" He noticed that she'd been reading a novel at her desk, probably waiting for the phone to ring. That was fine. It didn't matter.

"Very slow. I've put all your appointments on hold, told 'em the general situation, and everybody's been nice about it. Mostly. Anything new on Justin?"

"Nothing. Tests. That's all that's happening." He went across the room and sat in a chair facing her.

"Durn it, Sam, I thought maybe since you'd come to the office, that might be a sign that things were better. That maybe you were going to start getting back to your old routine."

"No, Jen. I wish it were true, but no, it's not."

"I'm sorry, Sam. I really am. Is Katherine doing OK?"

"She is. Granny's there, and Jonesie from the clinic. We're taking turns staying with Justin around the clock. Everybody is helping so much."

"That's good, at least. Listen, you give that sweet Granny a hug for me."

"I will."

He stood. "I'm going to go to my desk and look through the messages. I need to check the messages on my cell, too. I won't be here long."

"Sam? One thing."

He remained standing at the entrance to his office. "What's that, Jen?"

"Dr. Boren. He keeps calling."

"And you explained the situation to him?"

"Yes. More than once. But he keeps demanding to talk to you. He's becoming a real pain in the butt."

"Like what."

"Bad, Sam. Rude. Relentless."

"OK." He turned away.

Sure enough, there were close to a dozen pink phone messages from Boren that Jenny had taken down. Some were marked "urgent" or "please call" or "What about the Range Rover lease?" *What an asshole*, Sam thought.

Boren was an oncologist, one of the best in Fort Worth. Katherine knew him well — she knew most of the doctors in the city, or knew of them, because of her committee work in the Tarrant County Medical Society. The networking helped send tax and investment clients to her husband, although Sam wasn't always grateful to be working with so many doctors.

This guy was no exception. Boren had an ego, and a well-deserved medical reputation to back it up. He was good at finding tumors, figuring them out, facing them down; he took each one personally. Whether he saved his patients or not, he always got them more time, quality time, and that to him was a victory. Humility lessons came seldom.

Then came a discouraging word out of left field for Boren, a field he was not so good in - finances.

Oh, he thought he was, which was what was wrong with so many doctors, according to Katherine, and Sam certainly agreed. Ego overflow, she called it. Doctors might be good in one thing — stalking tumors, for instance — but that didn't make them God's gift to humanity in other endeavors, like playing the stock market, understanding the deeper needs of patients, being a parent, knowing the self. Few docs were well rounded. Most were lopsided.

Boren had scored big in the '90s in biotech and telecom shares. He'd gotten bolder as time went on, taken big risks on small dot-com startups. He'd built a five-million-dollar portfolio.

Not anymore. When the stock market took a stomach-bending drop beginning in March 2000, he shifted into pharmaceuticals and bonds. There were still a lot of capital gains that generated taxes, and that's what Sam had been trying to explain to Boren. He was being punished for past successes, even though much of it had been swallowed up in the Nasdaq's plunge.

Another CPA had already gone over this with Boren, but the doctor hadn't liked the results, filed for an extension with the IRS and come to Sam for a second opinion. The dreadful news was the same. The explanation was the same. In the five stages of grief, Boren was nowhere near acceptance of the tumor that had chewed a two-million-dollar hole in his net worth.

During their last meeting — a little more than a week ago — Sam had presented him with some preliminary tax figures for what he owed in 2000 and had suggested Boren take the paperwork home and look it over. The earlier extension, Sam explained, gave them plenty of time to hash things out and maybe bring down the amount owed.

"Look over this Schedule C, Dr. Boren. I listed every expense you gave me, pushed the envelope here and there, right down to office pot plants. See if you can find anything I left out. Then make an appointment for a few weeks from now, and we'll see if we can make things a little more palatable."

Boren agreed, but his anger was bubbling just below the surface. He left Sam's office disgruntled. He wanted this thing resolved *now.*

As Sam sat at his desk listening to his voice messages, his cell phone rang in his ear. He clicked over. "This is Sam."

"Sam. Boren here. Why haven't you returned my calls? Why does that woman who works for you keep giving me the runaround?"

"Look, Dr. Boren, we've had a family emergency. Didn't Jenny explain that to you?"

"Yeah, yeah, I remember something about that. But this is an emergency, too." He punched into each sentence. His voice was fevered and bullying. "I've found some deductions here. Some pretty obvious ones, I might add. For instance, that Range Rover lease. Let me fax that over to you. I think we can link it to the ranch — you know, hauling equipment and all that, but actually it's just Elise taking it on her antiquing jaunts, hauling the kids and all their junk to college, that sort of thing. So, what do you think?"

"Let me ask you something, sir." Sam's voice was penetratingly stern.

"What's that."

"Just what part of family emergency do you not understand?"

"Listen, Sam, I . . ."

"You have been rude to my assistant. You have tried to push your way into my private life during a time of crisis. You have been asked politely to show a little respect, and you have not done that. Are you listening to me?"

His anger. Building, building, so much, so fast.

"Sam, I'm listening. OK. OK. What."

"Are you sure you're listening, Boren?"

So much anger was down there. Everything was wrong. Everything was coming undone.

"Yes, Sam. Yes. What. I don't have all day."

Sam's scream was loud enough to be heard in every office on the 14th floor. "FUCK! YOU!"

And with that Sam took his phone and threw it full force against the wall. It dented the sheetrock and broke into several pieces.

"SON. OF. A. BITCH!"

He lunged out of his office and stood in front of Jenny's desk. "Take that box of paperwork shit from Boren and ship it back to him. Fed-Ex. And charge him for it."

"Yes, sir."

His hands were shaking. His face was red. His voice was quivering.

"Put a message on the phone that says that the office will be closed until further notice, and for them to leave a message. Then lock the door, leave, and I want you to take a paid vacation until I can get back here full time."

"I will, Sam."

"And how dare he treat you that way. Fucking bully. This won't stand."

The tears were pushing from his eyes.

TWENTY-SIX

Once the shower was on and the temperature was right, Katherine closed her eyes and moved into the hardest-hitting water. Almost instantly she could feel the hospital grime coming off — the clammy sweat of coffee, the cold sweat of fear, a thick film of exhaustion. She let the warmth stream through her hair and across her tired, closed eyes. She turned, and the water pounded her back and neck. Her muscles loosened a little. She let it go on and on.

Sam had come back to the hospital at about three p.m. Now, late this Friday afternoon, it was her turn to come home and clean up. He'd told her what had happened with Boren. She didn't blame him a bit.

A high wall of glass blocks separated the shower from the rest of the bathroom. The ceiling was higher — twelve feet — and the shower she took was so long and so warm that she managed to fill the big room with vapor.

She turned off the water, stepped onto the bathmat and put on what Justin called her "fat" robe — pink, extra-plush terry — and plugged in the hair dryer. With the hot air from the dryer she cleared a circle on the vast mirror that covered the wall above the two sinks. She didn't want the circle to be too big. She didn't want to know too much.

It was too much. The face that looked back at her, framed in brown strings of wet hair, sagged and bulged. It was beaten and defeated. Her eyes were full of homemade shadows. The brown of them was gone into a new dark. Justin was one day shy of being in the hospital for a week.

When Katherine came into the bedroom, Gracie was waiting in her usual place, sprawled on the bed with her head hanging off the edge. It put her in easy reach for petting, and that was no accident.

Katherine sat on the bed, bent, and put her cheek into the black fur at the top of Gracie's head. She closed her eyes and inhaled. A dog was there, and a remembered boy, and the boy who made the boy.

Sam and Katherine's first apartment was not much bigger than her bedroom now. The bed was much smaller, and they both had to sleep tight and sideways. That was a good thing.

Katherine smiled to herself. Sam never had any trouble stretching a Trojan to its limits. When she rolled it down on him, it fit like one long, tight leg of pantyhose. It took a big boy to make a big girl happy. He fit the bill. *Oh, baby.*

Those were the days — Hopkins, last months of internship, books and more books. They lived on sex and cereal in that tiny apartment. Those were the only things they had time or money for.

OK, so the box of rubbers was empty that night, time was short and the iron was hot, as usual. What the hell. What could it hurt, just this once?

Oh, baby. He knew how to fill her, and unshielded it was better than ever—Sam's wonderful push and rush and shudder, and her whole body's embrace of him, squeezing the pump, and all of her insides coated and warmed in his liquid light.

She had a dream that night, and the next morning she told him.

"Her name was Miss Buttercup."

"Who?"

They were sitting at the Formica table in the kitchen. There was just enough room among the lecture notes and spreadsheets to fit one cereal bowl each. He had his head in his advanced auditing textbook, and she was pinning her nametag to her scrubs.

"My egg, Sam. I dreamed about her."

"Are we having eggs?"

"Listen to me, Bozo. No, we're not having eggs." She poured the cereal into his bowl and hers. "Raisin bran, like always." Her rotation at the hospital began at seven and would last for a couple of days. She poured the milk.

"OK."

"Sam, dammit, listen to me. I'm worried."

He looked up. "OK. What."

"My egg. Little Miss Buttercup. In my dream she was on this beautiful island beach, stretched out in a beach chair, getting a tan, sunglasses, smashing bathing suit and a floppy pink hat, the whole bit, and here come the Marines."

"The Marines?"

"Yeah. You know, maneuvers. Operation Buttercup. This is where you come in."

"OK. I get it. I'm coming in. I like this part. So what happened?"

"All she had time to do was set down her beach book, tip her sunglasses down her pert little nose and say, 'Oh dear!' before the Marines stormed ashore and pretty much stormed all over Miss Buttercup. They overwhelmed her. She was utterly, utterly ravished."

"So you think I might have hit pay dirt last night?"

"According to my dream, yeah."

"Which means we're screwed."

"Actually, Sam, just me."

"You and Miss Buttercup."

"Yeah."

Sam silently ticked off the months; his fingers tapped against the table. "I suppose it wouldn't be the end of the world."

"Maybe. I'd be through with my internship and we'd be back in Fort Worth."

"I'd be through with school, too. Could you go ahead with your residency?"

"It'd be tough, but yeah."

Sunny Sam brought forth that big smile of his. It dazzled even in the early winter gloom of Baltimore. "*The Sands of Iwo Jima*. Remember that movie? Call me Duke."

"OK, Duke. Don't forget to stop by the store on your way home from class. We need more cereal."

"Yes, Miss Buttercup."

"And milk. And rubbers."

"Aren't we a little late for the rubbers?"

"Yeah. Probably. Whatever, then."

Sure enough, the Marines had hit the mother lode. Nine months later, *oh, baby.* Justin Samuel Moore.

"Gracie, you wanna go outside with me?" Katherine asked. The dog thwapped the bed with her rope of a tail. That was a yes.

Katherine was still sitting on the edge of the bed. She pulled on her underwear and scrubs and socks, then laced up her workday running shoes. Gracie followed her down the hall and across the big room, where long, late-afternoon shadows dulled the yellow walls. The squeak of shoes and click of paws disappeared into the great space above them. They went through the front door and onto the wide front porch.

The sun was low enough behind them to be blocked by the house. Spring clouds, fluffed with the possibility of showers, helped soften the remaining sunlight, making the heat bearable. Katherine sat on the top step and Gracie sat next to her, snuggly. Katherine reached around and rubbed the dog's wide chest. It was a place Gracie couldn't reach on her own, and she loved it.

Nobody was in the triangle park across the street. No cars were passing, no people walking on the bordering sidewalks. Gracie's bent ears lifted slightly with the barking of a distant dog, but she felt no need to answer back.

After a time Katherine felt a wag of a breeze at her feet. Gracie was recognizing someone coming around the side of the house, and in a few seconds Todd appeared with Gracie's leash in his hands.

"Hey, Dr. Moore." (He always called her by her married name, the one that matched Justin's. She didn't care.)

"Toady. How's it goin'."

"Fine." He'd come to take Gracie on a walk, which he'd been doing every day since Justin went in the hospital.

He was Marcie's son without a doubt, blond and wiry just like her, big smile, little nose, tightly wound. Gracie came up to him and lunged her tongue across the boy's chin. The dog didn't have Justin for the time being, but Todd would do in a pinch. Gracie wagged and sat patiently while the boy attached the leash.

"Is Justin OK?"

"Not too good, Todd. But he's putting up a good fight."

"A fight?"

"I just mean he's working hard to get better."

"He'll get better."

"I hope so."

"Mom said the bad place on his face was going away."

"Yeah. From the baseball."

"I did that. The foul."

"I know, honey. But that's not why he's in the hospital."

"Mom said it was because of the dentist. He didn't get enough oxygen."

"That's right."

"Now his brain's kinda messed up."

"Yes. He's in a coma."

"Like he's asleep, but you can't wake him up."

"Something like that, Toady."

"Weird."

Gracie was pulling at the leash, ready to get started, and Todd was about to relent.

"Todd, honey. Come here. There's something I want to talk to you about."

He walked up to Katherine, jerking on the collar to get the dog to turn. "Sit, Gracie!" and the dog sat on the sidewalk at the bottom of the three steps. Katherine smiled. She was amazed. She had never gotten that lazy beast to do anything.

"Pretty good. You've been training her, Todd?"

"A little. Watch this." He took a small dog biscuit out of the pocket of his shorts and held it above the dog's nose. Gracie tossed back her head and grabbed it. "That's not the trick. Gracie is supposed to get still and I put one of these on her nose and then when I say 'Now!' that's when she flips it off her nose and grabs it in the air. But a lot of times she just snarfs it, like then."

"You keep working on it, Todd. She'll get the hang of it."

"What did you want to tell me, Dr. Moore?"

She patted the step beside her. "Come sit here by me."

He moved over a bit and sat. "OK."

She put an arm around his bony shoulder and pulled him toward her a little, close enough to smell the same boy sweat through his T-shirt that she was used to.

"Honey, Justin is pretty sick. In fact he's very sick."

His head went down. He looked at his sneakers. "Is he gonna die?"

She held him a little closer. She looked at his tapered neck and the stubby curls of sweat-dampened hair across it. "I don't know."

Todd reached out and petted the dog, but he still didn't look up or say anything. Gracie bent in and sniffed toward the boy's pocket.

"It's not your fault. Do you hear me, Todd? You didn't do anything wrong. You need to know that."

He bent and nudged the side of his face against the top of Gracie's head. He put his arms around the dog. Katherine kept her hand on the boy's shoulder.

"Loud and clear, Todd. Hear me loud and clear. It wasn't your fault."

His sobs began, blurted out in coughs. Katherine locked her hands around his opposite arm and pulled him into her harder. She bent to him and put the side of her face against his damp hair.

Her voice fell to a whisper. "It wasn't your fault."

TWENTY-SEVEN

When Katherine arrived at the clinic, the parking lot was empty. Evening was approaching. She had spent a couple of hours at home, and now she was missing her other home. She was only going to stay for a few minutes.

After punching in the code of the alarm, she went back to her office. Her feet echoed in the empty hallway.

She turned on the light. *Damn.* Her desk was covered with three tall stacks of charts, just as she had left it. Where was the chart fairy when she needed him? But it was just as well. She was the only one who could fill in the blanks, and even if it were a long time before she got back to the task, she would probably remember enough.

The routine. The difficult, fulfilling routine of her long days. God was she missing it. This was her life, and it was gone, and maybe it was gone for a long, long time. Maybe the rest of her career would be spent tending to one utterly helpless patient. Persistent vegetative state.

She could deal with that, couldn't she? Especially if there was no other choice. Yes, she would deal with it. That's what doctors did. Buck up. Steel yourself. Deal with it.

Katherine reached into the pockets of her lab coat, and her heart sank. Nothing there. She had changed into a clean coat at home, and now in her laundry hamper was a lab coat containing a half-full pack of Winstons and Jonesie's butane lighter. She'd have to stop by the house on the way back to the hospital.

But what about the Physicians' Desk Reference? Was it possible there could be an old, neglected pack there? Sure, smoking them would be a stale and dry experience, but this was desperation.

Oh my God! She pulled back the book from the shelf behind her desk and there was a pot of gold – a brand new pack of Winstons, a new lighter and a sticky note: "You're a bad, bad girl, but what else is new? Sending my love, Jonesie."

She smiled. She rejoiced. She lit up. She rejoiced again.

The smoke warmed her breath and prickled her brain. She closed her eyes and let the gentleness of it settle into her.

When she went to the window and cranked it open, the spring breeze of new grass and fresh earth circled in, thanks to the fire guys' work on the community garden nearby. The wind began playing with the curtains. She blew her smoke into the opening, and the breeze took it and scattered it back across her face. That was good, too.

She went to her chair, eased back, closed her eyes and blew out a long breath toward the window. A light blanket of calm and contentment settled over her.

If only it could last. If only this were a true oasis of genuine safety, the great peace she longed for, but it wasn't. It was a chemical mirage.

It was better than nothing, of course, and she took it. Whatever worked.

"Look at her, *doctora*!" Mrs. Ramirez screeched as Katherine walked into the examining room. It happened only a few weeks ago, and the memory was clear. It shredded her blanket of peace. "Just look!"

The mother had taken Yolanda's blouse off, her pants, her shoes and socks, and the girl — nine years old, Katherine read in the chart with the first glance — was standing next to the scale in her pale-flowered blue panties, shivering with shame. Her arms hugged her nakedness. Tears fell across her bunched brown face.

"Diet? What diet? She won't do no diet!"

Katherine remembered them from an earlier visit. Same scene, same problem, and she had tried to talk to the woman about getting her daughter — the whole family — on a sensible diet. Nutrition. Meals on time every day. Fruit for snacks. Positive reinforcement. Encouragement. But Mrs. Ramirez didn't speak enough English to get even half of it. Plus she was a stupid, arrogant woman.

"The little pig, *cochinita,* that's what I call her," she continued in her off-key opera of a voice, gesturing extravagantly with her cheap bracelets jangling and her Wal-Mart rings glittering shabbily on her chubby fingers with their neon-red nails. She was packed like a bratwurst in black polyester. "She just eats too much, that's all that's wrong — tell her to stop, *doctora*. She go from a little pig to a big pig, *cochinota*, I tell her.

"The diet you give us. Chicken breast? Tuna? Who's got that kind of money? Oranges? Grapes? Or the time? I got a job, you know, and my man's gone off to I don't know where. I work hard, fixing hair all day. Shampoos. Nails. These women. *Dios mio*! They come late, keep me late, I come home and Yolanda's eating doughnuts from the store. *Ay*!"

Katherine looked up from the chart, her dark eyes narrowing. Her uncombed brows arched over her tortoise half-rims. She absently took the stethoscope from its draped perch around her neck, warming it in her hands as she prepared to listen to the girl.

"Tell her no more doughnuts. Don't eat *nothing*. It's that simple. Be a little hungry. That's a diet, right?"

This was too much. Katherine could feel her buttons being pushed. "I need to examine Yolanda in private," she said with a reinforced professionalism in her voice. "Mrs. Ramirez, I need you to go to the waiting room. *La sala, por favor*."

"But what about the diet? You gonna tell her to quit eating so much? *That's* a diet."

As she was talking, Katherine — with just the presence of her formidable body and a hand out, gesturing — escorted her into the hallway. "Yes, Mrs. Ramirez, I'll tell her."

She closed the door. "My God," she whispered at the laminated wood, and turned.

Katherine went to her swivel stool across the room. It wasn't easy getting her six-foot frame to curl that low (she had the stool twisted down to its lowest level, to put her even with her small patients), nor to get her ample bottom perfectly centered so the spillover was balanced on either side.

She pulled herself across the room with the heels of her running shoes, rolling over to Yolanda, who stood by the scales. The doctor skimmed across the last page in the girl's chart as she moved.

At her last visit Yolanda was four feet ten inches, one hundred thirty-six pounds. Katherine set the chart down on the paper-covered examining table, then reached over and took the girl's thick shoulders in her hands. She came down the arms with her hands, stroking gently, and separated the girl's hands from their covering position. Katherine began every exam with a full, deep once-over.

Yolanda's belly pooched over the rim of her underwear, and the lower cheeks of her buttocks pushed out at the back. There was a roll across her middle, and another above that — breasts enough for a training bra, but they were only fat. Katherine looked across her face, the roll of a second chin, the buried dimples, the eyes squeezed to a half-squint — dewy brown, shy, ashamed. Her chocolate-rich hair was a bonnet of ringlets around her forehead, and in the back was a swirled ponytail, fastened with a pink plastic clip.

"Please don't make me weigh," Yolanda said in a small voice that broke in the middle with a leftover hiccup.

Katherine instinctively pulled the little girl into the folds of her lab coat, and Yolanda's battered spirit burst open all over the doctor's shoulder and against her ear. Katherine pulled the girl in closer, put the back of her hand into her curls, and they rocked together just a little.

"You don't have to, honey," she said quietly. "I'm not gonna make you weigh."

Memories of Katherine's mother came pouring into her. Her early days had been marked by the same kind of towering, berating, controlling mother. Weight had been an issue, and shame had been her mother's weapon of choice. Her mother, on the other side of the dining room table, would drill her with a stare if she reached for a second helping of potatoes. She got tent dresses for her birthday. Her school lunches from home contained dry wads of stinky tuna fish on brown bread. Faye Jean's derisive anger was particularly fierce in the evenings after a couple of bourbons.

But Granny came along and pulled her to safety, and Katherine's lifetime struggle with her weight became bearable. Granny fried less and served more vegetables, and never said a word about the weight. Katherine's teen-age spurt in height took care of a majority of the little-girl fat. Now it had come back, of course, but that was another story and a struggle for another day.

Katherine reached over to get a tissue from the box on the stainless steel cabinet. Yolanda took it, dabbing it around her eyes. Katherine got the clothes from the examining table. She held open the pants and helped Yolanda into them. She held out the blouse for the girl to reach her arms through. Katherine was talking as they put on the clothes.

"Yolanda, did your mom make you get on the scales before I came in here?"

"Yes."

"She told you what you weighed?"

"Yes."

"I want you to tell me what it was. You can whisper it in my ear if you want."

Katherine pointed to her ear as she leaned forward, and Yolanda said, through a cupped hand, "One forty-two."

She wrote it in the chart, then glanced at Jonesie's notes: "Refuses to weigh. Can you try? Mom says school nurse recommended dr. visit. Y. shows excessive thirst — headaches — night sweats — feeling faint. Mom = M.L.B."

Katherine smiled to herself. M.L.B. was part of a code she and Jonesie had developed to keep the medical records under the radar screens of government inspectors. Jonesie was never one to hold back on his opinions about Major League Bitches, and boy was he right on this one. In the office now, she finished the cigarette and snubbed it out on the side of the empty trashcan.

Before Yolanda finished buttoning her blouse, Katherine listened to the girl's chest and back with her stethoscope. She looked in Yolanda's nose and ears with the otoscope. All clear. She took her blood pressure. Too high, but not dangerous.

Katherine walked back across the room and opened a drawer. As she worked, she asked Yolanda to sit on the edge of the exam table. She spoke toward the wall. "Bad news, honey. I'm going to need to draw some blood."

Yolanda shrank back and Katherine turned toward her. "Does that mean a needle?"

"Afraid so. Bee bite. For just a minute."

"It'll hurt a lot."

Katherine didn't deny it. She came back to Yolanda and put the supplies on the exam table next to the girl — a syringe, tubes, cotton wipes and a Band-Aid. "You're going to be a brave girl. *Entiendes?*"

"OK."

"I don't want you looking at what I'm doing over here," Katherine said as she tied the rubber strip around Yolanda's upper arm. "Promise? No peeking?"

"Promise." The girl looked at the poster of the digestive system on the wall.

"Now make a fist, honey, grip real hard."

Katherine began patting the forearm with two fingers, trying to work up a vein. She found one, wiped it clean with the alcohol pad, pulled the cap off the syringe with her teeth and came down with the needle.

"Here comes the bad part, honey," she said around the cap in her mouth.

"Ow! That hurts! It hurts!"

Katherine pushed the tube into the back of the syringe and Yolanda sucked in through her teeth. Her mouth grimaced.

"Relax your hand, sweetheart."

The burgundy blood pumped in — second tube, third tube — "one more, almost done, almost done" — and then the doctor released the armband, withdrew the needle, recapped it and pressed a cotton ball on the wound. Last was the Band-Aid.

"Good girl!" Katherine said. "You were very brave!"

"That's it?"

"All over." She reached down and put one arm around Yolanda. "You did real good."

"Am I all better now?"

"Yolanda, honey, I don't know. I'm worried about you. We've just got to get you eating better."

As they talked, Katherine dropped the used syringe in the plastic compartment attached to the wall.

"I know. Mama says I'm fat."

"I don't mean that. I'm talking about inside you, some of the chemistry deep inside you. That's even more important. I don't want you to get diabetes. It's bad stuff."

"I shouldn't eat doughnuts."

Katherine wrote Yolanda's information on the blood sample tubes. "Right. And exercise. You've got to get lots of exercise. Jump rope, run on the playground, whatever you can do. *Entiendes?*"

"OK."

"Listen, Yolanda, I know it's not easy. Lord knows I'm fighting it all the time myself. Everything I'm telling you I need to do, too. Honey, we big girls have got to stick together. We've got to help each other." She smiled big, and Yolanda smiled back. Solidarity.

In a minute they came back into the waiting room together. Katherine had her arm over the girl's shoulder. Mrs. Ramirez stood, anxious to leave.

Yolanda had a sucker in her mouth. Her tears were gone. Her smile was triumphant.

"You have a very brave girl here, Mrs. Ramirez," Katherine said. "We had to take some blood, and she . . ."

"Is that candy in your mouth?" the mother asked. "Yolanda, what did I tell you about candy?"

"It's sugarless," Katherine said. "I gave it to her."

"Let me have it," the woman demanded, holding out her hand, and Yolanda reluctantly pulled it from her mouth and gave it to her. Mrs. Ramirez dropped it into the wastebasket beside the clinic's front door.

"No candy! I told you that, Yolanda!" As the mother pushed through the door, pulling the girl by the hand, she turned back toward Katherine. "You should have seen what she did at Halloween. A pig!"

Seldom was Katherine caught off guard, but now she was left speechless. The door closed in her face.

She had planned to sit with the mother in the waiting room and explain her treatment plan: Yolanda's initial blood test would get a glucose level, and if Katherine's suspicions of impaired glucose tolerance were confirmed by the results of that test and others, then it would mean a fasting plasma glucose test as a follow-up. Type Two diabetes was likely, and they needed to get on it.

Now what?

Defeat, probably. Ignorance and brutality win another one. This was medicine on the front lines. Stress and more stress. The bullets were flying, and when one of these psychic fragments hit a child, the wound lasted a lifetime.

Jonesie was sitting at the reception desk, taking in the drama. When Katherine turned toward him, her face was streaked with tears.

The second cigarette was half gone, but Katherine's memories had pushed away the serenity she had achieved in the first few puffs.

Dealing with bullies, she was thinking. *It might be a parent. It might be another kid. Hell, LIFE is a bully. It comes in and roughs you up and steals things from you and ridicules you when you make mistakes. You have to do the best you can with it. Sometimes you fight back, sometimes you compromise, sometimes you get even. Fight here, retreat there, help soften the blows to the little ones if you can.*

You just keep going. If at all possible, don't let the bastards win.

The day after the incident with Yolanda, Katherine called Child Protective Services. Francine was her go-to gal at the agency when Katherine needed to put a scare into someone. Yolanda's mother didn't legally fit the category of a child abuser, but Francine could let Mrs. Ramirez know that the state had been notified of a possible problem. It might help.

Katherine thought back to her growing up in Granny's neighborhood. It could be a rough place. People were poor, working hard, stressed to the max. Bullies were hard to avoid.

Once, in seventh grade, on the school bus, Jesse Romero told Katherine that if she got any taller he was going to be able to see under her dress without bending over. He leaned over on the seat next to her to see what he could see.

She didn't appreciate that. Her knee did the trick. Jesse's nose didn't stop bleeding until fourth-period algebra.

And now, with Justin, they were coming to the last mile, the worst challenge, the greatest burden, the biggest bully of them all. How could you fight someone you couldn't even see?

Her boy had been knocked to the ground, and he wasn't moving. He was fighting for his life, and she couldn't help him fight back. She couldn't do a thing.

TWENTY-EIGHT

Katherine left the clinic and arrived at Children's Medical about seven in the evening. She should have been refreshed after her time away from the hospital and her long shower in her own bathroom, but there was no escape from the burdens of Justin's condition. An empty present fed into an emptier future. It infected everything.

She got on the elevator in the lobby and punched the button for three. She was wearing her scrubs and her lab coat.

Two male interns were in the back corner talking in low voices, but not low enough that Katherine couldn't hear.

"Goldfinger's got this one kid. Total broccoli is what I'm hearing."

"What happened."

"Something about a dentist. I don't know. Anaphylactic . . ."

Katherine pulled the emergency stop button, and the elevator shuddered to a halt between floors. When she turned toward the young men, her anger had added six inches to her height and was pounding blood through her reddening face.

The interns shrank back against the corner of the elevator. The shock of the stop and the obvious level of her anger left them cowering. She towered over them, and so did her voice.

It was the brown one who had been doing the talking. Singh was his name. Katherine's bulging eyes went right up to his and stared him into blinking.

"You fucking little *piss* ant! What do you mean talking about a patient in this hospital with such arrogance and insensitivity. What if that kid's parents had overheard you?"

"Ma'am, I . . ."

"I was the chief resident here, I am on the board of this hospital and I am a good friend of Abe Goldstein's, who I believe you were referring to and who has quite a bit of sway with the intern program."

"I didn't mean . . ."

"Your behavior is reprehensible!"

The other one said, "Dr. Warren, there were no civilians on the elevator. Peter would have never talked that way if there had been."

"Fuck off, buddy! This is between me and Singh here."

They were silent, waiting for Katherine's next move. They didn't have to wait long.

"Take off that white coat, Singh. *Now!*"

He freed the three buttons with fumbling fingers. "Yes, ma'am." He pulled his arms out of the sleeves.

When he handed it to her, she wadded it up and threw it on the floor of the elevator. First, she stomped on it, rattling the whole elevator, and then she wiped her feet on it and kicked it into a corner.

"You're not fit to serve here, Singh. Do you hear me?" She pushed in the stop button and punched floor two, where Goldstein's office was.

When the doors separated, she stepped out into the hall and turned toward the young man: "Now get out of my hospital, Singh, and don't come back until someone from the program calls you." As the elevator began to close in front of her, she thundered, *"Do. You. Under. Stand?"*

The doors were closed, but Katherine heard a faint, quivering, "Yes, ma'am."

She headed down the hallway of offices. Her voice had lost none of its strength; she punched into every word. "Son of a *bitch*!"

Dr. Goldstein was probably gone but she decided to try him anyway. She went to his office and knocked. No one answered. She tried the door and it opened.

"Abe?"

No one there. She called him with her cell phone.

"Goldstein," he answered.

"Abe? Katherine. You around? I'm here at your office."

"I'm on my way down. Be there momentarily. Go on in."

Katherine entered.

Abraham Napoleon Goldstein. His name was his story.

Half Jew, half Cajun, he was the most popular nerd at Lafayette High and, later, a shoo-in for membership in the wildest fraternity at Tulane. He had the brains, which got him in good with the jocks who needed help in chemistry lab. His dad was a wholesale liquor distributor with all of southern Louisiana as his territory, so Abe was the boy to go to when it was party time. His mother was a nurse, which meant he had ready access to rubbers. But his chief claim to fame was his expertise as a duck caller. He was born with a natural ability, like a good horn player, and his swamp-bred uncles put a final polish on his talent. He was Louisiana state champion three years in a row in his age category.

Duck season was a very big deal in Lafayette, and getting Abe to sit in a blind with you among the cypresses in December was the pinnacle. Boy, could he call in them ducks.

His specialty was the lonesome hen call. It was deceptively simple — a series of single quacks mimicking the plaintive, wistful, yearning song of a female mallard advertising her availability. It took restraint. It required the perfect pitch of desire, and he had mastered it. He could break a duck's heart.

They fell for it every time. Abe could call a mile-high mallard out of a flock. Even today his oldest friends still called him "Lonesome" Goldstein.

Abe's office was his story, too. On the walls were stuffed birds — a pintail, a wood duck and a greenhead mallard. His bookshelves contained a display of two-dozen duck calls, some of finest polished cherry wood and some crudely hand-carved. It was a delight for his young patients to come in and try them out. Often the second-floor halls of Fort Worth Children's Medical Center were filled with choruses of quacks. (It was also a subtle message to some of his colleagues whose skills he had no use for.)

Justin, through the years, always insisted they stop by Dr. Abe's office as part of his mother's hospital chores. The boy did considerable quacking, and Abe, like a gentle grandfather, would step in to give him some pointers. Abe would quack. Justin would respond. Gradually the child's quacks got closer to the mark.

When Justin was seven Abe gave him a duck call, and that was unfortunate. When Sam and Katherine were craving sleep, storms of loud but imaginary ducks circled among the high ceilings of the Moores' home. Gracie barked back in some ancient response buried in the subconscious of her retriever breed. It was the call of the wild, and it was relentless.

Katherine was sitting in the visitor's chair, facing toward the desk, when Dr. Goldstein came in from behind her. He gave her a peck on the cheek and went to his desk.

"What's up, Katherine?"

"I had a run-in with one of your interns in the elevator a few minutes ago."

"Yeah?"

"A kid named Singh. Another one whose name I didn't get."

"Peter Singh. Yeah. Seems to be pretty much on the ball."

Katherine reached into the bowl of mini Tootsie Rolls on Goldstein's desk. He got one, too.

"Anyway, he and this other guy were talking, and I overheard them. They were talking about Justin. Singh called him broccoli."

"Shit. That's not good."

"Well, I went ape shit, called him a fucking little piss ant. I made him take off his coat and I stomped on it, then sent him home."

"You stomped on his lab coat? I like that. Nice symbolism."

"Anyway, I never told him I was Justin's mother. Maybe you should call him, tell him that, then scare the shit out of him about what's going to happen to him."

"Yeah, OK, that sounds about right. What do you think is a fair punishment? He's a smart kid, good diagnostic sense, knows his stuff. I think he's mostly just a wise-ass intern."

"And weren't we all, Abe."

"I was the worst of the lot at Tulane."

"I'll tell you what I want. I want him to write you a short essay on compassion, and tell him that I'll be reading it. And I want him to come up and visit Justin. All I think we need to do is to try to get his heart going in a better direction. I wouldn't want you to kick him out of the program. That's much too harsh."

"Tell you what, I'll have him up to the boy's room by tomorrow afternoon, and I'll have a little chat with him first. It'll be the worst day of his life."

"Yes. That's what I want. That's what he needs."

They had another Tootsie Roll apiece. Abe had started eating them when he quit smoking several years back. Lots of them. "And I've got the roll to prove it," he liked to say, grabbing his gut just above his belt.

"Let me tell you what's happening with that dentist, Katherine."

"Shields. Yeah. What's the latest."

"You know us Jews tend to run in packs, and so I know a lot of good, mean Jew lawyers."

"Are there any other kind?"

"Not that I'm aware of. The ones I've put on the case are real pros. Circumcised bulldogs, you might say. They'll sink their teeth into your ass and won't let go.

"And this is the kind of case they love, Katherine. Blatant injustice, appalling professional incompetence.

"Most good lawyers know how to get their pound of flesh. These guys, they won't settle for anything less than a pound and a half. In fact that's their starting offer."

She laughed.

"Anyway, they've scared the shit out of him with the state board, already gotten him to close his practice, and they're working with his lawyer to get him to surrender his license permanently and to get his malpractice insurance to pay all of Justin's bills."

"Good God, Abe. All that in less than a week?"

"Hey, that's no problem for these guys. They're doing this as a personal favor to me.

"By the way, you want anything else from this fucking moron of a dentist? They can probably get you at least one of his balls. Maybe both."

"No. This'll do, I think." She smiled again. "Mostly I just want that fucker out of business." She looked into her friend's round and deceptively gentle face. "Abe, thank you for having my back. God, I appreciate you so much."

They sat silently for several long moments. The air in the room somehow seemed to grow much heavier.

"Katherine, I've been working on Justin's latest test results this evening."

She made sure both feet were firmly on the floor. She stiffened. "Yeah?"

"I need more time."

She breathed. "OK."

"But not much more. I'm going to stay late tonight, and I think I can have something for you by tomorrow sometime."

"All right." She looked in his face, and all she could see was data. No emotion. No hint of where this thing might be headed. Goldstein was a pro.

"Tomorrow, Katherine. I'll call you."

"I'll be here, Abe," she said with a long, resigned exhalation. She stood. She turned toward the door. "Thank you," she said.

TWENTY-NINE

"Kath! Kath!"

Sam was shaking her. Saturday, Day Eight, five a.m. His loud, desperate whispering jostled her sleep. Immediately she was sitting up on the couch in the waiting room but her head was struggling to catch up, swimming toward a surface of light that seemed miles above her.

Once the light arrived he was still a jumble of urgency. She was nothing inside but questions.

"What? Honey, what?"

Sam's hands were seizing her still. His breathing was all over the place. His voice lunged.

"Justin," he said, and he began to cry. "Justin."

"What, Sam. Please tell me. Please."

"Kath, he smiled at me."

"Oh my *God!*"

She was up and she was running. The door to the waiting room was open and she ran toward the hallway light. The door to Justin's room was slightly ajar and she burst in.

"Justin!" she cried.

Sam flipped on all the lights in the room. By the time Granny startled awake and pushed herself upright in the recliner in the corner of the room, Katherine was next to the bed, leaning over the boy, cradling the side of his face in one hand and looking at his closed eyes. "Justin? Justin, can you hear me, honey?"

She was looking and looking into the boy's empty face for some sign of warmth. "Justin, can you smile for me like you did for Dad? Please? Just a little?" Tears were in her eyes, threatening to fall. Her voice was cluttered with tears.

"Justin?" Sam asked.

Granny was standing on the other side of the bed. "Did he . . . ?"

"He smiled at me, Granny," Sam said. "I saw him smile."

It blew up so fast, this white-capped wave of hope. It knocked Katherine off her feet and caught her up, and she was bobbing, reaching, struggling for the ground. She put her hand on Justin's shoulder, shook him, and looked and looked. "Justin?" she kept asking. "Justin honey?"

Slowly she realized there would be no response. As she quieted inside, steady reason began to take back control. Katherine straightened and stepped back. She looked at the monitors.

It was insane, she knew it was insane, but she had gone there nonetheless, praying that her lifetime of science and her religion of rationality had been wrong, all wrong. She was willing to throw it all away for just one smile.

The nurse, Brenda, who had been in the room all this time, had stepped back from the stampede and was standing in the corner next to Granny, somewhat bewildered. They'd interrupted her work charting vitals.

Katherine turned to her. "Did you see anything, Brenda?"

She was a night-shift stalwart who'd been around the peeds ward for years, before Children's Medical had been built, and she and Katherine had known each other from the beginning. Brenda was no-nonsense, sturdy, square-built, quiet, fully attentive, but now she seemed to have been taken by surprise. Her dark stubby hair shook "no," and her eyes blinked with some astonishment behind her glasses.

"I'm sorry, Dr. Warren, but I didn't see anything. I was checking the oxygen levels on the respirator, not paying attention to Justin's face, when all of a sudden your husband rushed up and started shaking the boy and crying."

"You didn't see it, Brenda?" Sam asked. "You didn't see the smile?"

"No sir." Brenda came closer and stood by Katherine. "I'm sorry, no, I didn't see anything."

"Nothing on the monitors?" Katherine asked. "Absolutely nothing out of the ordinary?"

"No ma'am. Absolutely nothing. Heart, respiration, all the same."

Justin was perfectly still, completely blank, mannequin-empty. The heart monitor blipped along. The respirator pumped and hissed. Sam straightened and stepped back. He saw what Katherine saw, and sighed. The hope was beginning to drain back out of him, and the old, pale despair was taking its place. He fought back.

"Then I was the only one who saw it," Sam said. "I guess I was the only one. But I know what I saw."

"I believe you, honey," Granny said to him.

Katherine turned toward the door. "I'm calling Abe."

Dr. Goldstein had spent the night on the couch in his office, reading his notes and going over the latest test results on Justin's condition. He'd slept only a couple of hours when his cell phone rang. He was on his way upstairs in a flash.

His wiry gray hair was squashed, his eyes were gray bulges, his tie loose and disjointed, and his lab coat was a wrinkled mess.

Katherine followed him into Justin's room. "Nothing on the monitors?" he asked her.

"No. In fact, Brenda was in the room when it happened."

"She didn't notice anything out of the ordinary?"

"Nothing."

Dr. Goldstein listened to Justin's heart. He waved his penlight across Justin's eyes, and the light bounced off a crust of black ice. The eyes said everything.

"Where's Sam?"

"Across the hall."

They went to the waiting room. Granny greeted Abe with her usual manhandling hug, then went back to her guard post in Justin's room. Goldstein sat in one of the armchairs and Sam brought them all coffee. He sat next to Katherine on the couch facing Abe.

Sam still appeared stunned and confused, and his voice was thready and parched. "It was a very little smile, Dr.

Goldstein," he said. "I couldn't sleep, and I was standing by the bed. That background light was on behind the bed. I looked at Justin and there it was. Just for a second, very small, a smile. Up, then down. It was just a little something."

"Yes," Goldstein said.

"I saw it, Doc. I know I saw it."

"I have no doubt that you did, Sam."

Abe and Katherine walked down the hall together toward the nurses' station. At a sufficient distance for privacy, they stopped. Katherine leaned back against the wall.

"You really think Sam saw something, Abe?"

"Honestly, no. I've seen this sort of thing happen before. People are exhausted, stressed to the max, and hope is the only fuel keeping them going. The border between sleep and wakefulness is as thin as a sheer curtain. The light in the room is dim. You see what you want to see, what you *need* to see."

"Understandable."

"Let him down gently, Katherine, if at all."

"Of course."

He paused. He took a drink, and the coffee glistened the lower edge of his moustache.

"Katherine, it's time for our talk."

A wave of fear slithered up in her. She looked at him but said nothing. He was avoiding eye contact.

"This morning, alone, just you and me."

"OK, Abe."

He looked beyond her. "Give me twenty minutes or so to freshen up, and then meet me downstairs in my office."

She had to find enough breath to answer. It took a second. "All right."

THIRTY

Once again Katherine sat in the ratty office chair across the desk from Dr. Goldstein. She had her Styrofoam coffee cup in her hand, her lab coat armor on, her scientific shell up. She had washed her face and done some defensive hair brushing.

Of course this was going to be bad. She was face to face with one of the finest pediatric neurologists anywhere. He had devoted a week of study to her son, brought in all kinds of specialists, spent most of last night going over a book-length compilation of studies and scans and consultations.

The verdict was going to be pronounced, and she was convinced she knew the ruling: persistent vegetative state. Irreversible. Undeniable. Incontrovertible. No mistake. No way around it.

But she was wrong.

Abe's dark eyes were weary-sad, wet with strain, puffed and heavy-lidded. "I'm sorry," he began, but then he had to clear his throat and start over.

"Katherine, I'm sorry. Justin is dead."

He rolled his chair up as close as he and his gut could get, reached across his desk and took her hand.

"Yes," she said, but it wasn't much of a word. Mostly it was an exhalation and a professional acknowledgement that she'd heard him speak. That she'd heard something – something like a blunt force of wind, sheared of meaning. It whirled through her head, bounding. Her body shuddered.

"His condition has done nothing but deteriorate, Katherine. From the moment he came into the ER until now. It's undeniable. Complete absence of intracranial blood flow. His brain is dead."

Goldstein's words kept coming, the wind kept rising, but nothing much was getting through to her. He waited. He gave her breath time to fully return, her awareness a chance to re-collect into a self again, the jet of noise to fade. But she was still tangled in his beginning words.

Dead? He's dead? My son is dead?

It was the way doctors delivered news to each other, a one-two punch of unvarnished reality, and the worst was over. Except she hadn't been ready. She thought she was, she thought she'd steeled herself with girders and concrete, but inside her iron-ribbed structure was the heart of a mother, not a physician. You can't do much with a floppy heart like that.

She should have known, and Abe, too, what would follow. Her choke of tears, her wail of loss — they should have expected that — all in a gush — but neither was ready. She should have arrived with Kleenex in her pocket, not the worthless instruments of medicine — a stethoscope, prescription pad, pens. All Abe could find was a coffee-stained paper napkin, and he pushed that across his desk to her and patted her hand and looked bewildered.

What dumb-asses they were. What emotional klutzes. She looked up from her napkin and Abe's old eyes were full of tears, too.

"You have . . . no doubt?" she finally asked. "What Sam saw this morning? For sure it was nothing?"

He wiped his pudgy nose with the back of his hand like a little boy. "No doubt," he said, tears running down his face. His foot was bouncing under his desk.

"And persistent vegetative state? What happened . . . ?"

"We've gone far beyond that, Katherine."

Dr. Goldstein's hand wasn't big enough to handle all his tears. They wouldn't stop. The old man of science couldn't make them stop.

THIRTY-ONE

After her meeting with Abe Goldstein, Katherine found herself in front of the hospital on the same shaded concrete bench where she and Jonesie had shared laments and cigarettes a day or so before. She didn't remember getting there. She found a burning cigarette in her hand. She didn't remember lighting it. The meeting with Goldstein obviously ended somehow. She couldn't remember their parting words.

She looked at her watch. It was almost noon. The meeting must have been at least an hour long, closer to two. Her attention had whipsawed, holding steady for moments on something he said, then falling between his words, dispersing, collecting, dispersing into a dark and free-falling future.

Even before her talk with Goldstein she was chambered in the same kind of physical, mental and emotional exhaustion she remembered from her intern days, when the demands and instructions and demonstrations of her seniors lost all weight and floated about her in thought bubbles, just out of reach. In this last week her nights had been half-awake in rolling fear and her days had been half-asleep in rolling exhaustion. Her focus was as shallow as glass.

Sam shattered it this morning. The smile, the hope, the upside down of everything.

Then Goldstein. The enormous crush of more facts, an unexpected blow, a fist of news that knocked her back and sent her flying.

Now Katherine had to struggle back into focus, into rationality. Justin needed her, now more than ever. She had to do the right thing for him, and she already knew, in her heart and below her consciousness, what that was. Both she and Sam had been dumped into the deepest sea. Both of them were struggling for anything — anything — to hold on to.

That was the first thing, just to hold on. Not to get anywhere necessarily, at least not right away. Not to really solve anything, figure out anything. Just to hold on. Going over this with Sam would help her, too, in a process of thinking aloud. If she could get him to something like solid ground, maybe she could get herself there, too. As she thought about how she was going to do that, the truth was already beginning to form inside, bubbling up from the deep.

She had to get back to Abe's words. They were still in her mind somewhere, behind the clouds, and she had to rediscover them and look at them, firm them up with meaning and keep them within reach. Some of his words were crystal beads of clarity. Some, she realized, were probably lost forever.

"Electroencephalogram grossly abnormal," she remembered him reading from one of the reports on his desk, looking down through his smudgy glasses and holding his forehead against a prop of fingers. "CAT scan shows extensive cavities of dead tissue in both cerebral hemispheres, and spotty islands of loss in the band of cerebral cortex remaining around the cavities."

Med school. Gross anatomy. She bounced out of the present and into the past.

She remembered opening the skull of her cadaver to see its contents, the bumpy gray jellyfish and its lacy tentacles of blood vessels. She remembered placing a sliver of brain tissue under the microscope: It was a cellular honeycomb, each cell a circle within circles, smaller and smaller — neuron, synapse, dendrite, axon — spiraling into smaller components than her lens could reach.

It had been an overwhelming, Grand Canyon moment for her when she first looked over the rim of her microscope that day and imagined the life that had been in those cells. There before her eyes had been the landscape of being: a circulating dance of infinitesimal lightning storms in the chemical sky, all of it adding up to a smile, a self, and – because the whole is always more than the sum of its parts, and for lack of a better word – a soul.

She was a scientist who was not afraid to say that word. *Soul.* The spiritual essence, a force of light, radiant quarks of energy adhering to the walls of the most central cells of the brain. A kind of Higgs boson of the deepest dimension, the particle that gathers the energy that enlightens the world from within. The eye behind the eyes, illuminating the way of consciousness amid a universal crush of darkness. A little something that is everything.

Since her med school days she had seen too many little souls not to believe in them; they were most evident in their absence. She had seen them depart from dying children, leaving behind a very real place of emptiness, a hole in the universe that didn't go away for the longest time.

Katherine went back to her dream of the other night, down into the gray enfoldments of Justin's brain. She had been looking for that central light in him, the birthplace of the aurora of the self.

Hidden, maybe. Buried under a heap of bruised darkness, but something that could be uncovered and reignited.

It was down there, wasn't it? The muted light? The injured sunrise? The essence of a boy named Justin?

She could not find it. The light was not there. That dream had told her the truth, just as Goldstein was telling her now. The cells that contained the boy's home of light had dried up and disintegrated. Every red branch of every vascular road led down to an empty tomb.

He was gone. He was gone. He was gone.

The science was overwhelming. The path was becoming clear. The facts were shouting to her, and the facts were everything.

She was going to have to take Sam by the hand and lead him there. Together, into the fire and out the other side.

THIRTY-TWO

Katherine left her haven in the park and went upstairs to Justin's room. She asked Sam to meet her in the waiting room. She told Granny they were going to need some private time.

In the hallway Katherine called Jonesie and asked him to hold off coming to the hospital until two that afternoon, and she also asked him to call Father Red to see if he could join them then. Luckily Jonesie had this Saturday off work. She told him that Dr. Goldstein was going to update the family on Justin's condition. And that it was bad, very bad, and that she was going to need him more than ever.

Jonesie didn't ask for details. He knew. He had maybe always known. He said that nothing — nothing in the world — could stop him from being there.

Sam knew, too. Not a lot, not why, but that what Katherine and Goldstein had discussed was not good. The look in his wife's face was grave and gray. Her voice was defeated. Her hands, her confident hands, were quivering.

She had no plan, she had no words, she had too many feelings. She knew that Sam, on the couch across from her, was looking at her. He was waiting for her to speak. She was waiting, too, but the words weren't there.

"Kath?"

How long had she been staring into inner space? Five minutes? Ten?

"Kath?" Sam asked again.

She was hunched over in the armchair, looking down at her hands. The first clear feeling finally came up in her, and it was weight.

"Are you all right, Kath?"

Just weight. Her hands, her arms, her shoulders, her head, all through her and over her, weight. Dumb, blind weight. The burden of the world.

"It must have been bad," Sam said. "What Goldstein talked to you about."

She turned. She looked at him, but she didn't see much. There was too much water in her eyes. He was a run of colors.

"Yeah," she said.

She leaned back and crossed her arms and closed her eyes. Maybe that would help with the water. But when she opened them again, nothing had changed. She had to put her hand up to her eyes to dam up the tears and keep them at bay.

"I didn't think it could get any worse," he said.

She moved, finally. She went to the couch and sat next to him. She took his big hand into one of hers and continued working at her eyes with the other. "Remember on Tuesday when Abe said it was like Justin had gone down and down the stairs, to deeper and deeper levels of unconsciousness?"

"Yeah. Two steps up from the bottom was what he said."

"Not anymore. Justin's at the bottom of the stairs, Sam. In the last few days he's gone lower. And for sure he's not coming back. He can't."

She looked at him. All it took was a glance to see that his barriers went up almost instantly. The look in his drooped eyes was flat and inward. Before he said another word, she knew he was going to put up a fight.

"But, Kath . . ." He stood. He turned away from her, walked toward the window and looked out. "He's the same. Justin looks exactly the same. He's not coming back? What the hell does that mean?"

"Inside, no, Sam, he's not the same. All the tests are showing that he's been losing ground. I saw the scans, these big areas of dead brain cells. Abe read me the reports. Down, down, down."

"What about what I saw this morning, Kath? I saw Justin smile, clear as day."

"We've been over this, honey." Katherine stood, too, and went to him. She took back his hand. "The tests indicated nothing happened physically in Justin when you thought you saw something, and nothing has happened since. Have you seen anything since then, Sam? Has anybody else?"

"I don't guess so."

"It's like there's been an avalanche inside him, Sam, this collapse of dead brain cells, and it's continued and continued, an infection of darkness that keeps spreading. He's trapped down there. We can't get to him. He can't get to us. The barrier is impassable."

"I can hear a heartbeat, Kath. It's right there on the monitor. Right there, a heartbeat, blip, blip, and the lines move.

"He's down there, Kath. Justin's alive. Maybe we can dig down to him somehow."

"Nobody is down there, Sam." She put her hand on his shoulder and leaned toward him. "I said it wrong. He's not trapped down there. Nobody is down there. Everything that was Justin has been destroyed."

He pulled away from her. "I don't care what you say. If there's a heartbeat, there's somebody there."

She could see the muscles in Sam's neck straining and tightening. He was locked in a stare, looking beyond the window and the hospital and to his memory of this morning.

She knew where Sam's mind had gone – to that smile he thought he saw, the smile that never was, the smile that wouldn't die.

She was a long, long way from reaching him.

THIRTY-THREE

"Science and all its hard data — I'm not so sure, " Sam said after a long period of thoughtful silence — at least an hour. They remained in the private waiting room, struggling inside themselves for words that might reach the unreachable. "The hardness, I mean.   What Dr. Goldstein keeps coming up with, all those tests. Are you sure? Can you be absolutely certain?"

"I don't think I'm following you, Sam." Katherine was on the couch next to him, although there had been periods of quiet pacing, times at the window, more coffee.

"Like in accounting. You hear kind of the same thing — you know, hard numbers, numbers don't lie, that sort of thing — but really they're as soft as clay, and that's the scary thing. You can make almost anything out of numbers. You can prove anything almost. There can be art in accounting, some magic, some sleight of hands. You've got to be wary."

"And even supposing the data is hard, Sam, it's really the interpretation that's too damn flexible."

"Yeah. OK. I see your point."

"In medicine, with Justin, we've got plenty of hard data. His EEG doesn't lie. His brain either emits consistent waves or it doesn't. His body either says yes or no — moves or doesn't — when his reflexes are pushed.

"Justin's body doesn't answer when we knock, Sam. Like Abe said, lights are on but nobody's home. Except in

Justin's case, even the lights are hardly on. Barely a nightlight - breath and a heartbeat that are forced on him by machinery."

"But it's something, Kath. His heartbeat. It's right there. It's real. It's hard data. Doesn't that count for anything?"

"It's a muscle, Sam. That's all the heart is. It contracts and expands. A mechanical, electronic bundle of pipes and muscle, nothing more. The air being forced into Justin keeps it going. That's not life, it's robotics."

"But isn't that better than nothing?"

"It's the same thing as nothing."

Sam took a long breath inward. He closed his eyes, opened them, looked at the floor, looked over at her. "Kath, I don't get it. You keep pushing this thing toward the negative. Every time I try to come up with something positive, you shoot it down."

Pushing? Shooting him down? He had no idea how weakly she was defending Goldstein's position and how much she was avoiding the hard truth that she had heard this morning. She let go of a deep, long sigh. She was so grateful that Abe had set up this afternoon's meeting with the family, which was to begin momentarily. He would do better. He was stronger, more objective. He had a better handle on the facts.

She reached out and touched Sam's knee. "I'm sorry to sound so negative, Sam. I'm just trying to keep you — all of us — in reality. But maybe I'm making things worse, and I'm sorry.   I   don't   mean   to   hurt   you."

THIRTY-FOUR

Dr. Goldstein was sitting in an armchair. On the couch facing him were Granny and Father Red. Sam and Katherine were in folding chairs on either side of the couch. Jonesie was sitting off to the side, next to the coffee pot. He had brought a cake, cookies and sandwiches, which were sitting on the counter in the little kitchen. Nobody had touched a thing.

"Is this everybody?" Dr. Goldstein asked.

"This is it, Abe," Katherine said. "We're not much of a family, I suppose. Sort of a loose assortment of orphans, more than anything. You know, seeds and stems."

"I lean more to the stem side of the family," Father Red said with a laugh.

Jonesie raised his hand. "Hayseed here." Jonesie was from the scrawny little West Texas town of Cisco.

Dr. Goldstein gave the smiles time to flourish and to fade, and to take some of the tension from he room. "I think we can begin," he said.

Katherine felt a small, simple wave of gratitude. Abe did not expect her to carry this burden alone. "You've got too much skin in the game here," he'd said at their private meeting that morning. "You're a family member, too, after all, and have a god's plenty on your plate already. I'm going to take charge. I'll walk your family through this the best I can."

Look how well her attempt to brush back Sam's fog of hope had gone. She had wanted to give him just a glimpse of the inevitable, and she had failed. She was going to need all the help she could get.

Granny was not happy about being there. She wanted to be with Justin. That was her job, keeping an eye on him, but Katherine had insisted, and so she relented.

Abe removed his glasses, leaned his head back against the back of the armchair, and closed his eyes. He folded his hands across his unruly gut and took in a long, reverse sigh. Then he opened his eyes and spoke to the ceiling. "This is a God damned tragedy."

After readjusting himself in his chair, he looked one at a time into the faces of his audience. "The news is not good," he said. "The news is terrible."

Eyes went down, went off to the side. Beyond the closed door, the shuffling of foot traffic in the hallway came forward.

Father Red gently pushed his voice into the empty space. "I didn't think this situation could get much worse," he said.

"I'm sorry, sir. I'm very sorry to say it, but yes, it has," Dr. Goldstein said. "We've come to the end of the line."

"I can't believe that," Sam said. His desperation was starting again. "I just can't believe it. I can't accept it. Are you saying there's nothing more we can do? Already, you're giving up?"

"Nothing," Abe said. "I'm sorry, Sam. Nothing we can do."

Voices began to crowd in on one another.

"What I don't understand is how things could get any worse than they already were," Sam said. "That's what I was trying to get Katherine to explain to me. It seems like nothing's really happened to Justin. You can't tell anything from looking at him."

"His color's about the same," Granny said. "Not great, not terrible."

"I know you've been running a lot of tests," Jonesie said. "And the results . . ."

"Worse," Goldstein said. "Progressively worse. I'm sorry."

"Maybe you should tell them about the tests, Abe," Katherine said. "Maybe that will help."

"Sure. There are a dozen or so tests altogether," Dr. Goldstein said. "I'll tell you about some of them, all of which, by the way, we did twice, some of them three and four times. I wanted to be absolutely certain. I've had other doctors come in behind me and recheck my work. I've consulted with some world-renowned experts at other hospitals. I've looked at every possible alternative."

"And of course Katherine's been part of all this, too," Sam said.

"Every step of the way," Katherine said. "The best I can, Justin's biggest advocate. But you've got to understand that a lot of this is beyond my level of expertise."

"Before this ordeal, Justin's health was robust," Goldstein continued. "If anybody could recover from an injury this severe — if anyone deserves the benefit of the doubt — it's this boy. This healthy, healthy boy. That's why we've been so thorough with the tests."

"And there's been nothing to dissuade you from your conclusion, Dr. Goldstein?" Sam asked. "Nothing to give you pause, to raise any doubts?"

"Nothing. I'm sorry. Nothing."

"The tests," Katherine said. "Tell us . . ."

"Like I said, quite a number of them." Goldstein leaned forward. "Some simple, some more complicated. Several of them involve the eyes.

"Maybe some of you've seen me or another of the doctors open Justin's eyelid and shine a bright light into his eye. We use a penlight like this one." He unclipped the light from the front pocket of his lab coat and held it up. "The light activates the optic nerve and sends a message to the brain. In the normal brain, the brain sends an impulse back to the eye to constrict the pupil. In Justin's brain, there's no impulse. The pupil remains fixed. It's true in both eyes."

Katherine added: "At first, when Justin came into the hospital a week ago, we could get a little reaction."

Goldstein clipped the penlight back into his pocket. "In a similar test we drag a cotton swab over the cornea while we hold the eye open. Normally, the eye will blink. In both of Justin's eyes, there's no reaction."

"And the more complicated tests?" Sam asked.

"There's what we call the CBF study, Sam. Cerebral blood flow. We inject a mild radioactive isotope into the bloodstream. Then we use a radioactive counter over the head to measure the amount of blood flow into the brain."

"And Justin?" Sam asked.

"Nothing," the doctor said. "Negative. The study is indisputable, Sam."

"That what."

"That Justin is brain dead."

This froze them in place. For what seemed like half a minute not a muscle twitched, not a chest moved in or out. Not even Katherine's. The words stunned her all over again. The gavel came down with a piercing crack.

Hope was as enmeshed in her breath and blood as in anyone else. But to extract it from the others, especially Sam, where so much more hope had built up, was going to take persistence and time.

Sam broke the silence. "I can't . . . I just can't make sense . . . how it could get so much worse? And so fast? How does it happen?"

"OK, Sam, let's look at that," the neurologist said. "It gets complicated, so bear with me. It involves the chemistry of the brain on the cellular level.

"This process. The ischemic cascade. That's the term for it."

"The ischemic cascade," Sam repeated.

"So then, ischemia," Dr. Goldstein continued. "It has to do with inadequate blood supply - and we are talking about the brain here — which is what happened when Justin stopped breathing in the dentist's chair. A cascade is a series of events in which one event triggers the next. A causes B, causing C, affecting A again, triggering D and E, sometimes in a circle, sometimes linear. The ischemia caused neurons to die in his brain, which caused a chemical reaction that affects other neurons, causing more to die, which causes more to die in various chemical reactions caused by increased calcium in the cells, lactic acid, glutamate, calpain — a process called excitotoxicity — and so on, down the line. This can go on for days after the initial triggering event. Like I said, it's very, very complicated."

"You can't turn it around?" Sam asked.

"No," Abe said. "There is a tipping point, Sam. Once the cascade reaches that point, science cannot turn it back. Justin has passed the tipping point."

"And the brain," Jonesie said. "It dies."

"The dying process," Goldstein said. "Around. Down. Cell to cell. Destroys everything that was Justin, personality, memories — a massive die-off across the frontal lobe. Muscle control. All the way down into the brain stem, the control room of our involuntary muscles, those that keep the lungs breathing and the heart pumping. Machines are keeping those systems going in him now."

"Legally," Katherine said, "brain death is death."

"Brain death is death," Goldstein said. "Yes."

Katherine gently guided them to the inevitable. "And that's where we are, and that's why we're here. The facts are telling us that it's time to turn off the machines and let him go."

She and Goldstein stopped. They let the words soak in. They let the room breathe.

Sam was stricken. His voice was injured. His eyes were in retreat. "This is not right," he said finally. "This just can't be right."

Father Red reached over and put his hands on Sam's forearm. He patted it. Sam didn't notice.

"Katie, I was wonderin'," Granny asked, "what harm it would be if we did nothin'. You know, just waited some more."

"Yeah," Sam said. "Do we have to make a decision now? What about what I saw this morning? Shouldn't we give that smile a chance to show itself again?"

A confusion of hope, a grasping and shoving of hope and denial, took over.

"Sam, we've been over this and over this," Katherine said. "What you saw. There was nothing . . ."

"And if we did wait," Sam asked Dr. Goldstein, "how long could Justin survive in this condition? Besides, there's been talk about a rehab hospital." He turned to Katherine. "Remember? You said . . ."

"I like the idea of not rushin' into anything," Granny said. "What Sammy said."

"As physicians, we always try to come down on the side of life," Dr. Goldstein said. "But then there are certain extreme cases where quality of life is so compromised, so far from acceptable. That's when we consider the removal of life support."

"Wait a minute," Sam said. "The removal of life support? *Now?*"

Katherine reached over and took his hand. "Sam, yes, that's what we're here to talk about. I thought you understood that. I've already mentioned..."

"Kath, no . . . I guess I didn't . . ." He was looking at her hand in his. "That it was this bad. Already this bad."

The extraction of hope from Sam and the others. So slow, so painful, step by bloody step. Every psychic muscle held on to hope for dear life, and Katherine knew that and experienced it herself. She hated this process. God how she hated it. But she had to push forward.

Abe stepped in. "Sam, I'm sorry to say that yes, it's time to put this out on the table. We have to look at the options, all bad."

"Let me tell all of you of my deep concerns," Katherine said. "The way I'm trying to think this thing through. It's Justin — the kind of life he would have in a coma, on life support. I try to imagine what it would be like, and to me it looks like a cold and confining future. I try to imagine being paralyzed, catheterized, turned, bathed, bottom wiped, and all of it takes place in an eternal darkness. Imagine it. Imagine being sentenced to a lifetime of that. To me it sounds like a living hell."

"But maybe it's nothing, Kath," Sam said. "If he's truly in a coma, as deep as Dr. Goldstein says, it's absolutely nothing. Totally dark, totally empty. And we could wait it out."

"I need to insert myself here, and correct a misconception," Dr. Goldstein said. "I don't know how long Justin could survive in brain death, on life support. If he were in what we call the persistent vegetative state, which is where we were a few days ago, then yes, I would be all for sending him to a rehabilitation facility and hoping for the best. He might survive for quite a while. And yes, occasionally, very rarely, extremely rarely, people recover consciousness in such situations.

"But this . . . no. Survival? Probably not for long. The chances of him ever being the same boy again are zero. If you decide to donate his organs to prolong the lives of others, then I don't recommend waiting for more than a day or two. His organs won't be viable if we wait too long."

"A decision in a couple of days?" Sam asked. His broken face was breaking further. The lines were deepening.

"Sam," Katherine said, "that's where we've been trying to lead this discussion. The biggest decision of all. Trying to make meaning out of this senseless mess."

"Well I'm not ready. I'm not near ready." Sam's stricken eyes and cluttered voice were pleading. "I need more time. There is a life in that bed across the hall. A boy. My son."

"But what about Justin?" Katherine continued. "That's what I keep asking. That's what I want you all to ask yourselves. What would *he* want? Will you all please, please, think about *him*? He was a boy on the run, and now he's been slammed to the ground and practically tied to a bed. His life is one hundred percent the opposite of what it was."

Science, she was thinking. *My precious science, my life's calling, is what got Justin into this fucking mess — the miracle of a pain reliever gone wrong — and then science stepped in again and saved his life. Now, thanks to science, he's been turned into the living dead.*

Father Red stepped in: "I think Katherine is right. We need to consider what's best for Justin, not for anybody else. That's the big question, the hardest question."

"Red, sometimes I wonder if keeping Justin alive is selfish, and maybe the easy way out," Katherine said. "It keeps us from making the tough decision, and living with the consequences. It keeps *our* hope alive, as long as he's still breathing, even with the help of a machine. But what about Justin? That's what I keep thinking about. That's what I keep going back to. What would Justin want? What about *his* hope?

"We have a chance to set him free, and I'm thinking we ought to take it. I'm thinking that's what he'd want."

THIRTY-FIVE

The questions for Dr. Goldstein ceased, and he began gathering his papers. When he went to the door, Katherine followed him, and in the hallway they talked for a moment in low tones.

"I'll call you tomorrow, Katherine."

"Tomorrow's Sunday, Abe."

"I realize that. I'll call you tomorrow."

"OK."

"I'll have my cell phone on. You call me if there's anything, anything at all. Questions, concerns. If you and Sam want to talk some more, I'll be right over."

She put her arms around him and whispered in his hair-strewn, chimp-size ear, "I love you, Abe."

Dr. Goldstein wasn't good at hugs, but he did his best.

People were thrown into their separate inner turmoils, and periods of long quiet developed. A few got up and went to the window, others got a soft drink or more coffee, all absently.

Granny didn't stay long. "My boy needs me, Katie. I'm going back over there."

"OK," Katherine said.

She and Granny touched hands as Granny headed for the door. "Y'all talk all you want. I've got a job that needs doin'."

Katherine flashed back in her memory to her teenage years at Granny's house, her long periods of isolation in her little bedroom with Bob Dylan and her diary. Granny would come home from the day shift at the hospital and have to knock on Katherine's bedroom door.

"You're broodin' too much, Katie. We don't have time. Help me get supper on the table."

That's how you did things with Granny. You just kept moving. It made life so much simpler. It solved most things.

Growing up with her, Katherine didn't have any trouble absorbing that work ethic. In fact, she had trouble keeping out of the way of it. If she slowed down, there was a good chance Granny might run her over. Keeping busy was a form of self-defense. You better go with Granny's flow or the flow would take you down.

Sam, Katherine, Father Red, and Jonesie congregated into an intimate group on the couch and the armchairs.

The priest began: "Katherine, I'm honored to be here. It shows great trust to allow me into such an intimate and difficult moment in your lives."

"I wanted your special perspective, Father Red," Katherine said. "Justin loves you so much, and with your long experience in dealing with lives in crisis, I believe your insights are invaluable. Something more than science. We've already gotten the scientific perspective here. We need more."

Father Red lived a second life that few people knew about. On the surface he was the headmaster of Justin's Episcopal school. He loved the children and they loved him back. He gave a kind of twinkling strength to them with his jokes and laughter, and they returned it.

But when the school day was done, a life of fear and doubt was his, and he did the best he could with it. Most evenings were without his priestly uniform and included an Alcoholics Anonymous meeting. That's when he referred to himself as just another loser among his fellow losers, getting by, helping out a little if he could, and being helped, and being grateful.

"I'm sorry to say I don't have any answers, really, at least not the kind you're probably hoping for. Nothing easy. Nothing simple.

"But I can tell you this for sure. This situation with Justin is not something you can simply think your way through. This is not the time for philosophical arguments, legal arguments, scientific arguments, even theological arguments.

"Deciding what to do here is a question for the heart. You've got to let the heart speak its truth, and its words are not easy to discern. There's lots of background noise, guilt and fear and all kinds of things."

"My heart is so confused," Sam said. "It's broken."

"Just be as quiet inside as you can be, Sam. That's what I do. I listen to the silence, and I listen hard, and I try to be patient. That's what I call prayer — not asking for anything, just listening.

"The silence is not empty. The silence will eventually speak to me.

"I don't know if it's God speaking, or just a higher version of myself, or maybe both. It doesn't matter. All I know is that this silence is the center of things. It's where the rubber meets the road.

"It's the heart that must accept the facts, not the mind, in a situation like this. And the heart will take its time, and you will know when it has decided. Out of the silence will come a knowing."

Father Red called himself a Battlefield Christian. He knew that about all you could do was to try to stop the bleeding and then to crawl over to the next grunt and do it again, and let him holler, and don't promise anything you couldn't deliver such as a new leg or an end to the pain or a different future. He'd learned that in Vietnam as a redheaded kid of a medic, and he brought home a shitload of baggage. Then seminary, then a wife. He drank up that marriage and almost his career.

Hope didn't do any good when some guy was bleeding all over you. He needed pressure on the wound. He needed morphine.

Hope? Hope was a waste of time. Prayer, too, probably — at least the kind that asked for things — although he kept that secret deep inside. He wasn't sure anymore why he put on the collar. But then again, what could it hurt? He tried not to promise too much. The fog of war? What about the fog of *everything.*

In the heart of his heart he knew that God's miracles were few and subtle, that the laws of nature prevailed. God didn't thunder. The heave of gravity, the spiral of particles, the birth and death of cells and stars — God was a mere whisper between the comings and goings of his creation. A bare, small whisper of light. A little something among the grandeur and the silence.

Red prayed that Sam and Katherine might hear it and be comforted just a little, but he couldn't lead them there. You had to stumble into it all by yourself.

Sam wandered away from the conversation and was standing at the window. He remembered. When Justin was six, his favorite bedtime book was *Hank the Astronaut.* In fact, Justin had decided he was going to be an astronaut just like Hank, and that was the dream he and his dad nourished together for several of those early years. They'd been to the Johnson Space Center in Houston, and Sam had been working on a plan to get them to Florida for a launch of the shuttle. Justin had decided his dad was going to be an astronaut, too, and they'd go into space together.

In the book, when Hank the rookie goes out on a space walk to check for possible damage to the Atlantis, he gets in trouble. His lifeline gets tangled and threatens to come loose. How can the veteran commander — Col. Hodges — get Hank back in?

The book talked about the deadly cold and vast silence of space. If an astronaut lost his connection to his tether, he'd slowly, helplessly slip into the dark. The air in his suit would run out. He'd be swallowed in the deep.

Justin always paused when they got to that page. Sam could feel him shudder and tense, then breathe when the commander managed — at considerable risk to himself — to untangle the rookie and reel him back into the safety of the shuttle.

"You'd pull me in, wouldn't you, Dad? Just like Colonel Hodges?"

"Of course."

"You'd do whatever it took to get me back home."

"Whatever it took, Justin. I love you that much."

"Promise?"

"Scout's honor."

Staring out the window, Sam looked and looked into the darkness that Justin had become. Where was he? Where was the hope? Where was the way back?

"I was thinking about something that Abe mentioned to me this morning," Katherine said to the little group.

"What's that," Jonesie said.

"Abe said, 'The world is the brain. The brain is the world.'"

"You can't have one without the other," the priest said.

"Exactly," Katherine said. "Based on everything we know, Justin has no awareness of his existence. If you don't have that, what do you have?"

"I guess that's death," Sam said. "I guess that's what it is."

But then he added, "If the injury's permanent. If there's no way back."

Granny, sitting alone in the room with Justin, went way back. She was maybe ten years old, something like Justin's age.

They lived on a farm near Pampa at the top of the panhandle of Texas. It was the 1930s, and the dust storms were terrible. Her father was barely hanging on to his livelihood, but he kept trying. He kept working. He put everything he had into that old farm.

"Ellen," her mother said to her one evening, "go call your daddy in for supper. He's out in the barn."

Granny went and stood at the back door. It was the blackest black duster she had ever seen. She couldn't even see the barn. The wind was terrible. There was no use hollering.

Her daddy had tied a rope from the back of the house to the barn. It was the only way you could get there when the dust was this bad.

Little Buddy wanted to go too. Her brother was six. He wasn't right in the head.

"Hold onto my sash, Buddy," she told him. "Keep the other hand on the rope. You just follow me."

He smiled. That's all he ever did. He couldn't talk much.

They inched along the rope together. You had to almost close your eyes against the wind and sand. The tumbleweeds went bouncing by. He was behind her, holding on.

But when they got to the barn he wasn't there.

"Buddy!"

She turned back, inched back down the rope toward the house, looking and looking. Was that Little Buddy with her sash in his hand, stumbling in the drifts of sand? Was that him disappearing into the gritty wind?

"Buddy!"

It was her little brother and soon he was gone. Her father went looking. Her mother too. They wouldn't let her leave the house, and for a long time she was alone. Their voices went away and the wind was everything.

They couldn't find him. It was all her fault. He got swallowed up.

Jonesie collected the foam coffee cups that were scattered around the little kitchen and threw them out. He wiped down the counter and shook the cookie crumbs out of the sponge and into the sink. He inspected the coffee pot and decided to make more. He went inside himself, to his own darkest corner.

Billy was like the boy next door. He was shy and blond and quiet, and he loved ballet and good music and the best art. He loved Jonesie.

You put perfect friendship and perfect sex together, and you've got something. They had the very best for ten young years.

Then Kirby tore his meniscus. His dance career was over, and that's when he started nursing school. That's when Billy came down with the stuff. The junk. The black death.

Kaposi's sarcoma. The red-brown lesions came and grew and multiplied until the boy who had been Billy was gone. He was a stricken little old man, all bones, depleted.

Jonesie would bathe him and hold him and carry him to the bed. He would sit up with him and study his nursing texts. Billy said that when he looked in the mirror it seemed like he'd already been cremated, and laughed.

Jonesie never left his side. Billy's dying was a slow, slow retreat from the world, deeper and deeper into the self, and beyond. They were lying in bed and holding each other when Billy left.

Jonesie kept the urn of ashes in a cabinet beside his bed. He liked to keep them close.

When Katherine and Dr. Goldstein had talked this morning, he had recommended, for Sam's sake, that they follow the procedure known as non-heart-beating cadaver donation.

Justin would be taken to an antechamber next to the operating room in the main hospital, and Sam and Katherine would be with him to the end. He would be removed from the ventilator and his heart would be allowed to stop. After no more than two minutes Sam and Katherine would leave, and the team of surgeons standing by would take the body into the OR to procure the organs.

"I think Sam will be reassured," Abe said, "when he hears the heart stop and I make a formal pronouncement of death."

"If we get to that point. If he even agrees to ending life support."

"Yes."

"I think he's got a long way to go, Abe. A lot more struggling, and he's going to have to get there himself. I'm not going to push him. And if Sam says no, then my answer is no, too. We can't have a split decision here, and I will yield."

Father Red walked over to Jonesie, who was working at the sink. "I've been thinking about what I'm going to tell the kids in chapel. They all want to know about Justin. He's a popular kid."

"Have you figured out anything?" Jonesie asked.

"I guess I'll tell them the truth, that I don't know why something like this happens.

"They won't like that answer. They think adults know everything, especially the ones who dress in black.

"But it's the truth. I don't know, and I don't think I ever will."

Push, they said. It was time to push.

Katherine bore down. The lights were bright in her face, and her sweat was turning the light into jewels.

The pain had a purpose, the best purpose in the world. It had a goal. It had a shape, and the shape emerged with a gush of blood and splendor, and he was Justin Samuel Moore.

Now he was leaving. He would go quietly. This pain was the ugliest thing in the world. It didn't have a purpose.

Father Red divided people into three categories: the broken, the not-yet broken and the unreachable.

Here I am among the broken and the breaking, and I am grateful to you, Lord. It is a privilege that you have led me here.

The wound was the light. The priest knew that. The wound was the way in, and the way forward. It shattered a person's inner being the same way stained glass breaks the spectrum of light into a dazzlement of colors. After a time, after the bulk of the pain subsided, a person could begin again, and the world was new, draped in a softened light.

For Father Red, his life had taken him through brokenness to complete surrender and a new kind of openness to the world. The wound was a gift that led to a humble simplicity, a hollowing out, and room to grow in another direction. Even the great, grave silence at the heart of things had become a comfort.

This profound pain, he believed, was humanity's only real hope in the world, this process, the way of the cross. Sam and Katherine were on this path, and he prayed for them. He prayed that they could keep going. He prayed that they would arrive — broken, remade — into the peace and the truth that passes all understanding.

It was late afternoon when Peter Singh arrived at Justin's room. He was in scrubs, and he had his ID badge dangling around his neck. Granny was the only one in the room. Granny and Justin.

"My name's Peter," he said.

"Granny," she said. "I'm that boy's Granny."

Peter smiled shyly and went up to the bed. Justin was on his side, facing the wall, and Peter looked into the empty face. He looked at the picture next to the bed, the boy and the dog running together. He saw the baseball glove on the shelf next to the bed, and he picked it up. A ball was inside. Peter forced his hand in and absently began tossing the ball into the glove.

"What position did Justin play?"

"Right field," Granny said. "He was real good."

"I played right field, too. In high school. I wasn't big enough to play in college."

The conversation paused and Peter continued tossing the ball into the glove.

"What's going to happen?" he asked.

"I'm not sure," Granny said. "I think we're gonna have to let him go."

Peter put the ball back in the glove and put the glove back on the shelf. He reached down and touched Justin's arm. He put his hand on Justin's hand.

When he looked up his hazel eyes were washed and wet. "Granny, would you tell Dr. Warren that Peter Singh stopped by?"

"I will, honey. I sure will."

Sam was looking out the window in the family room. Katherine was somewhere behind him.

"How many neurons are in the brain, Kath?"

"I think it's somewhere around a hundred billion."

Sam liked it when things added up. There was a small satisfaction every time he went to the calculator and added and multiplied and subtracted and got the figure that matched his expectation. The bottom line.

But this time? One hundred billion neurons minus one hundred billion neurons equaled what.

Equaled zero. Equaled nothing. Forever and forever, nothing.

The tests. The facts.

Slowly, slowly, the great weight of the truth was working through Sam, pushing him toward surrender to and acceptance of the utter mystery that lies at the end of everything.

It was going to be worse than merely being unable to pull Justin back to safety by his tether of oxygen. They were asking him to cut the cord. He would stand by and watch the boy sink away into the dark like a burial at sea, the deep black sea.

"Promise, Dad? Promise to get me back?"

"Scout's honor, Justin."

Sam looked down into the night from the waiting room window. He could go too. He could dive down after

Justin. He wouldn't find him but it wouldn't matter. They would be free, at least, sharing the same emptiness.

Granny was alone in the room with Justin. She pulled her chair up next to the bed.

Granny never did have a lot of use for the God part of church. The sermons and the Bible readings and the hymns were something she got through on the way to the social hour afterward, greeting her neighbors and checking on their needs and tidying up the place after everyone left.

Now it was different. Now something way more important had come along. She put her head down on Justin's chest and closed her eyes and prayed for the first time in years and years.

Can't you take me instead, Lord? Can't you leave the boy alone? He ain't botherin' nobody.

She wasn't sure anybody was hearing her. She tried again.

Listen here, you longhaired sorry son of a bitch. You already took one of my boys, and that one was more than enough. This time you take me instead.

She bowed to the weight of it all. *You hear me?* She was screaming inside. *I said take ME. Take ME!*

She hadn't cried in a long time, either, but she did now. Her head was down and her old white curls were shaking with her sobs.

After standing at the window for the longest time, Sam turned. Nobody else was in the room. They must have said goodbye, but he didn't remember.

The night had descended fully. He didn't know what time it was. It didn't matter.

He sat in the armchair and put his socked feet up on one of the folding chairs. He sat up all night. He didn't sleep.

Without another word from anyone, in the silence of himself, the darkness slowly, slowly added up in him and did its work. The last of his hope — weighed down by the authority of science and the evidence before him — Justin's empty eyes — was displaced by inevitability.

Katherine came into the waiting room at five a.m. It was Sunday, Day Nine. Sam was still in the armchair, his feet up, his eyes open.

"Are you OK, Sam?"

"Yeah."

She got him some more coffee, and she brought her own. She sat on the couch across from him. She waited.

"I figured out the smile, Kath," he said. "Justin's smile."

"Yeah?"

He looked at her, and his tears greeted hers. "He wanted me to know that he was all right. That it was OK."

"Yes." She put her hand on his knee.

"Kath, he was saying that he loved me, and that he knew that I loved him."

"Yes."

"And that it was time to say goodbye."

THIRTY-SIX

Sam noticed a woman coming somewhat shyly down the hall, looking at room numbers and pausing in front of Justin's. No, not a woman, a teenager. Her blond hair was piled haphazardly on her head, and her eyes were dark with sleeplessness and fear. She had a silver stud in one nostril. A butterfly tattoo was visible on her upper chest just above the line of her halter-top. He noticed the stars tattooed on her hands, and the bright blue fingernails.

"Hi, is Dr. Warren . . . ?" She looked at the closed door and back to Sam. "This nurse told me she might be here."

It was about eight on Sunday morning. Katherine had gone downstairs to take a shower in the doctor's lounge. Sam was standing in the hall by Justin's door, waiting for her to return so that he could go downstairs and walk for a little while.

"Well, right now she's gone," Sam said, "but I expect her back any time now. Is there something I can help you with?"

"That's all right. I just wanted . . ."

Sam turned to his left, distracted by the sound of the elevator opening. Katherine came out, in new scrubs and lab coat, worn down in her walk, not nearly as fresh as her clothes.

"Brandi?" Katherine asked.

"Hi, Dr. Warren."

Katherine came up and took the girl around the shoulders. At the same time she reached out and squeezed Sam's hand.

"Are you all right, honey? Is Monique . . . ?"

"She's not any better," Brandi said. "She's worse."

"What did Dr. Humphries say? You finally got to see her, I suppose?"

"I didn't understand much of it. Can you, like, come look at Mo again?"

"Sure," Katherine said.

"Is that another one of your patients in there?" Brandi asked, looking at the closed door of Justin's room. "Justin Moore" was the name next to the door, and "NPO" was next to his name. Through the windows she could see the boy with the assemblage of machines around him.

Katherine said yes, it was her patient.

She introduced Sam, and asked if he could come see the baby, too. Brandi said sure. "You're not gonna believe how cute she is, Sam," Katherine said.

Sam went along, not quite certain why. The anger that had been in him several days before was gone, and he didn't know why, and he wasn't sure where it had gone. So much was being washed away.

After a long walk down the hall and to the opposite wing, they went around the corner to the nurses' station, and Katherine asked for Monique's chart. They went to her room.

The child was listless, more jaundiced than three days before, and her little belly was swollen. Katherine sat in a chair beside the crib bed and looked over her chart. Brandi moved her *National Enquirer* out of the way before she sat in the other chair. Sam stood by the door.

Katherine reviewed the lab results again. Monique was suffering from antitrypsin deficiency, a genetically caused liver disease. They had begun treating her with cholestyramine, and it would be months before they'd know if the treatment could turn things around. Katherine explained this as she went along, reading parts of the chart to Brandi.

"What did Dr. Humphries say, honey?" Katherine asked

"She said if Monique doesn't get better, she might need like, you know, a liver transplant."

Katherine looked displeased. "Yes, it's possible. But it's a long time before we'd know that." She folded the chart and gave her full attention to Brandi. "Monique could get better with the treatment. In fact she probably will."

"She said Mo could die if she couldn't get a transplant."

Katherine's look of displeasure increased. She was not at all happy with Humphries' communication skills. This sort of possibility, remote as it was, didn't need to be introduced at this juncture. She and Humphries would be having a talk.

"I suppose that's possible, Brandi, but it's highly unlikely, and even if she needed a transplant it would be a long time from now before we'd know. Monique has so much going for her. I wouldn't worry about it." Katherine stood, walked to the crib and reached over the railing to touch the child's forehead. "You've got a baby tiger here. She's a fighter."

"I know. She gives me hell all day, or at least she did until she got sick. Now I'm starting to, like, miss her little fits."

Sam came over to the bed and stood beside his wife. He too reached in, playing with the baby's springy hair. Monique smiled and wrapped her little hand around Sam's index finger. Sam couldn't stop himself from smiling back.

"We're gonna turn this around," Katherine said. She draped her arm over Brandi's shoulder and gave a squeeze. "Don't give up hope, Brandi."

The girl responded with a tentative "OK."

As Katherine and Sam were walking back to Justin's room, he asked, "You really think Monique's going to be all right?"

"Sam, yes, I do. I always tell the truth to my patients and their parents. Always."

"So Justin . . . he wouldn't be . . ."

"A donor? No. Not in this case."

"But . . ."

"But yes, kids like Monique, Sam. Desperate kids. Justin could give a second chance to some of them."

He didn't say anything. He looked away. He went down and down inside himself as they continued walking.

They stopped in front of Justin's room. Sam looked deep into Katherine's worn down face.

"I'm ready," he said. "I'm OK with it."

    She took him in her arms. They held and held and held.

THIRTY-SEVEN

Two hours later Katherine was pulled into another drama. She couldn't say no. She couldn't help it. She suffered from empathy overload, and it wouldn't quit pulling her along.

She had been down on the second floor, talking with Abe, and was getting on the elevator heading back up to Justin's room.

"Jesse?"

"Katherine?"

It was Jesse Romero. She hadn't seen him since junior high school, although his kids were her patients. He was a big man with a wrestler's build, a trucker. His gimme cap said Mel's Van Lines. He was on the road a lot.

"So what brings you to our fine hospital?" she asked him.

"Jesse Junior got shot."

"Oh my God, Jesse. Is he gonna be OK?"

"I think so."

"Can I come see him?"

"Sure. I want you to."

Katherine ignored her stop on three and went up with Jesse to the fourth floor.

There was a convention going on in Junior's room. Brothers, cousins, mother, grandmother. One baby. A couple of tough-looking characters. Jesse Sr. motioned for them to leave, and it took a while for the crowd to disperse. Junior (pronounced *hune-yor*) was dozing in the bed, still working off his anesthesia, and the shuffle of shoes didn't wake him. Katherine came up to the bed.

She'd been treating Junior and his three younger siblings since the clinic opened, but she hadn't seen him in several years. This was typical. Once boys reached a certain age, they'd usually quit coming. Macho pride and all that, what with the possibility of an Anglo lady seeing their private inadequacies.

Junior was fourteen. She could see that the boy in him was retreating, and in its place was the heavy shadow of a downy moustache, pimples, a jaw line. But his eyelashes were boyishly long, and in a flash she saw the old shy smile as his dark brown eyes opened and he recognized her.

"Hey, you, tough guy."

"Dr. Warren?"

"So what the hell have you done to yourself *now?*" She'd treated him for a broken arm, a sprained ankle, the usual boy stuff.

"I got shot."

"Where."

"The belly."

"Well, let's take a look." She pulled down his blanket and pushed his hospital gown to the side, keeping things discreet. "You trying to turn yourself into Swiss cheese?"

"It was an accident. There were these older guys. They . . ."

The wound was dressed and appeared to be dry. She palpated the area, and all seemed well. "What are you doing hanging with bangers? That's not how your mama raised you."

"No ma'am. It was just..."

"Listen, let me go get your chart. I'll be back in a minute."

"Well look who's here," Katherine said as she walked up to the med-surge nurses' station. "My favorite Nee-gro surgeon."

Laurence Wellborn spoke down toward the chart he was working on. He didn't have to turn around to recognize her. "If it ain't my favorite honky-ass pediatrician."

She came up and put an arm around his waist. He was dressed for work, in scrubs, shoes in plastic booties, scrub cap.

"So what's new, my friend," he said. He put down his pen and turned to her.

"I ran into a patient's dad a few minutes ago. Surgery on the boy last night, GSW to the gut. Romero."

"He's one of mine. Yeah, last night."

"What can you tell me about him, Laurence? I was just in his room looking him over. It appears you didn't kill him."

"Not this time." He smiled. "I gave it my best shot, but he pulled through."

Dr. Wellborn pushed the chart toward her. "He's all yours."

She picked it up and began skimming it.

"Complications?" she asked.

"Naw. The bullet nicked his spleen, somehow made it through the rest of him without much damage. First we thought it had lodged in his spine, but we found it in the large intestine. One lucky kid."

She looked up from the chart and smiled. "The happy butcher saves another one."

The surgeon grinned back. "Well, apparently." He leaned over and gave her a smooch on her ear. "Listen, darlin', I got another appointment with destiny in ten minutes, and I better go scrub in. Let's us get together sometime, maybe a barbeque at my place. It'll be fun to get the kids together."

"Sure, Laurence." He didn't notice her wince. "Gimme a call."

Katherine came back in the room and walked over to the bed.

"I was just talking to your surgeon, Jesse. He said you were damn lucky. That bullet could have easily put you in a wheelchair for the rest of your life."

"I told him that already, Dr. Warren," Jesse Senior said. "God spared him this time."

"And if that bullet had gone a few inches lower, Junior, you'd be singing in St. Rita's boys' choir for the rest of your life."

His father burst into laughter, and the boy gave a nervous chuckle. "Listen, Junior, did your dad ever tell you what I did to him on that school bus in eighth grade?"

"Oh Lord. I'd forgotten all about that," Jesse Senior said.

"I'll let you tell the story to Junior later." She turned to the boy. "Let's just say that your dad got an early look at what women's lib is all about."

Jesse Senior put his hand up to his nose. "Yeah, a real education."

Katherine looked at her watch. "Gentlemen, I must be going. But let me tell you one more thing, Junior. There's a saying — what doesn't kill you makes you stronger. You've heard that?"

"Yes, ma'am."

"Well here's the second part of that: What kills you makes you dead.

"Think about it, Junior. Dead. I'm talking casket, flowers. Your mom is crying and crying. Your girlfriend is a mess. You're dead."

The boy's voice was a little shaky. "I promise I'll think about it."

She bent down to him. "OK, bro, give the old lady doc a hug," she said. Junior reached his arms around her and their cheeks touched. She gave him an extra squeeze.

Jesse's father and Katherine stepped out of the room and closed the door. They leaned against the wall in the hallway. He got tears in his eyes when he told her about the shooting, the midnight call from the police, the long night they'd had in the surgical waiting room.

"Can you be his doctor through this?" Jesse Senior asked.

"I can't, Jess. That's for the doctors at the hospital. But maybe I can see him later at the clinic for a follow-up."

"Sophia will want to see you. She loves you so much."

"I love her, too. And give those little ones a swat for me, tell 'em I said to eat their vegetables."

"I will."

He put his hand out to shake hers, to smile, to thank her, but it was all too much. His head went down, his hand went to his face, and he began to quake with a relief of sobs. He couldn't speak.

"It's gonna be all right," she whispered to him. She put a hand on his arm. "Jesse, Jesse, the worst part is behind you."

Dr. Goldstein spent most of Sunday in his office scheduling meetings. Sam and Katherine met later that evening with the hospital's attorney, the hospital administrator and with the surgeon in charge of the transplant team, Jerry Weintraub.

Sam and Katherine, so weary, with hardly a question or comment, signed what seemed like a hundred documents.

The procedure would take place the next morning.

THIRTY-EIGHT

Dr. Goldstein arrived in Justin's room at four-thirty Monday morning. He was the first.

Abe appeared more rumpled than usual, as if he had slept in his clothes again. Actually, he had — on his office couch downstairs — although little sleep had taken place. There was more tossing and thinking than rest, and now the rumples covered his face as much as his dented lab coat. The knot of his tie was wavy. He'd done a poor job of shaving. His eyes were dark lumps.

"A long night, I suppose," he said to Katherine.

"Long and uneventful, Abe," she replied. "You, too?"

"Yeah. I went over the results of every test. Just once more. I had to."

"Nothing, I suppose."

"Nothing."

He checked the monitors. He opened Justin's chart and looked over the top page. He closed it. He sighed.

Jonesie came in with a tray holding four Styrofoam cups of coffee, a milk carton, packets of sugar and plastic spoons.

"My savior," Katherine said, reaching for a cup.

"Excellent, sir," Goldstein said as he reached for the second cup. Jonesie smiled.

Granny got one and patted Jonesie on the cheek.

"Jonesie, thanks," Sam said, and took the last one.

Katherine doctored hers with a hefty splash of milk and two packages of sugar. Dr. Goldstein added three packs to his.

Jonesie had combed his blond swath of hair and washed some color into his boyish face. He was the freshest-looking among them. He had spent the night in the waiting room across the hall.

Sam's drawn, bristled face seemed to carry the heaviest burden. His hair slumped on his head and his head slumped on his neck and his neck was hardly holding the weight. The burden was everywhere on him and seemed to have taken inches from his height.

He and Katherine had stayed with Granny in the room with Justin all night. It was the second night in a row that neither of them had slept even an hour.

Katherine looked better. Professional stamina had taken hold. She'd pulled enough all-nighters in her career that she had learned to manage them. Yes, her eyes were shadowed and puffed, and her hair had gone wayward, but that wasn't much different from her usual look.

Justin needed her. For a few more hours he needed her more than ever, and she wasn't about to submit to circumstances. She was going to be clear and steady, solid, present. She didn't bend an inch. Not an inch.

Within the half-hour the team came in from the OR. Two techs, in green scrubs, heads covered in clear plastic caps and their feet in protective gear as well, began to unhook the monitoring equipment from the wall and wrapping the cords around the machines.

Jerry Weintraub, head of the transplant team, darted around the room giving orders to his techs. He was garbed like the OR techs, Katherine's age, fresh and intense. "Any last-minute questions, Katherine?" he asked.

"No, Jerry," she said. "Sam?"

He didn't answer. He was looking at the med techs preparing Justin's attached equipment for the long journey down the basement hallway under the street and to the main hospital next door.

"Sam, honey?" Katherine began. "Dr. Weintraub asked..."

"I'm going to carry him," Sam said. His voice was clear and firm. "This is my son. I'm going to carry him."

Everyone stopped.

"OK, Sam," Dr. Weintraub said after considering this for a moment. "We will make that happen."

He turned to the techs. "Unhook the IV, please, and the catheter and the monitors. Nancy, you'll be following with the vent. We need to keep that going, but that's it." He went out into the hallway and told the young man who was standing beside the rolling bed to take it back to the OR.

Katherine helped Sam get his hands in the proper place when he lifted Justin. She straightened the boy's gown and got his hands to his chest so they wouldn't dangle. With the proper positioning achieved, Sam brought the boy close to his chest and nestled his chin and cheek against Justin's curly head. He turned, and the procession began.

Father Red, in black with a white surplice and green satin stole, joined them at the elevator. He was carrying his Book of Common Prayer. The group, which included Katherine, Granny, Jonesie, the techs, Dr. Weintraub and Dr. Goldstein, went down the large elevator to the basement.

It felt strange to Katherine to see the pipe-ribbed basement hallway again. She remembered ten days ago, the journey from the ER to Children's, the gray, long way toward uncertainty, all of it undergirded by the anticipation of a future of hopeful waiting. Things *could* turn around. They *could*.

The procession moved along at the pace of a dirge. Sam led the way, holding Justin in his arms, holding him close. Nancy followed with the vent, which was attached to the boy's trach tube by a long plastic hose. The second surgical assistant walked with her.

Katherine was next, walking with Granny. Then Father Red limped along next to Jonesie, and last came Goldstein and Weintraub.

The defeated. All of them.

THIRTY-NINE

At last they arrived at the end of the hallway. Sam led the way into the elevator, and the others found room behind him.

When the doors opened onto the surgical floor of the main hospital, a clear, deep voice filled the hallway. It was Chris.

"Ten . . . SHUN!"

Twelve firefighters — six on each side, forming a corridor — came to attention, staring ahead. They were in dress blues.

"Sa . . . LUTE!"

Slowly, slowly the honor guard of men and one woman brought their white-gloved hands to their foreheads.

Sam stepped out of the elevator and walked forward between the lines of firefighters. Tears were running down his face. His arms were too full to reach up and stop them and hold them back. Justin's bare legs swayed as his father moved. The others followed.

FORTY

In the OR anteroom Sam laid Justin carefully on the waiting gurney, and Katherine helped get the boy situated under the covers. The techs hooked him up to a heart monitor, and the ventilator was rolled up next to the bed.

The assistants locked the wheels on the gurney and departed. Dr. Weintraub, with a touch to the hands of Sam and Katherine, departed as well. It was time for him to gown up and scrub in. The rest of the surgical team was waiting for him in the operating room next door. Granny and Jonesie went to a waiting room across the hall. Jonesie held on tight to her, and she held tight to him.

A nurse remained. Father Red was standing off to the side. Dr. Goldstein and Katherine stood on one side of the bed, and Sam was on the other. She brought Justin's hand up and let her closed lips slide across the ridges of his fingers, remembering as deeply as she could his smell of weeds and dust, his shy touch, his morning smile. She kept his hand in hers, and Sam took up Justin's other hand. They closed their eyes. It was the silent prayer of hands across the great divide.

After a minute Dr. Goldstein stepped forward. "Shall we proceed?" he asked.

Katherine hesitated. Her voice was gone. She nodded.

Sam did the same.

The doctor paused, reached, and disconnected the ventilator from the trach tube at the boy's neck with half a twist of his wrist. He stepped back. If Justin should start breathing on his own, the doctor would reattach the vent and give the boy an instant boost to his breathing, and they would call off the whole procedure.

Katherine's breath stopped, and so did Sam's, unconsciously holding it in sympathy with Justin's. It seemed as if the only breath in the room, in fact, came from the ventilator, heaving and sighing uselessly.

They watched Justin's covered chest, waiting, holding the boy's hands, listening for life. Not a twitch, no gasps, not an indentation in the sheets.

Then Justin's chest heaved, fell, heaved, reached for a breath and strangled on the attempt. Sam had been warned that this sort of physical reaction was likely, the spontaneous struggle of a body at the end of its time. Sam did not move. He held back with all he had.

Katherine watched the heart monitor. Eighty beats per minute. Ninety. The desperate heart.

One hundred beats per minute. One ten. After one minute off the vent Justin's heart was racing, straining, struggling, frenzied. But it was all going according to science. Cold, cold science. The numbers rise, the numbers fall, the numbers disappear.

"V-tach," Goldstein said as the heart monitor went into spasms of beeps and seismic jumbles on the screen.

Justin's chest stayed perfectly still. The line on the monitor went flat, and the beeps became a long whine. The boy did not attempt another breath.

Goldstein reached over and turned off the monitor to silence its awful, empty tone. When he switched off the ventilator, a second, heavier blanket of silence settled over them.

Father Red began to read from the Book of Common Prayer: "Into your hands, O merciful savior, we commend your servant Justin. Acknowledge, we humbly beseech you, a sheep of your own fold, a lamb of your own flock, a sinner of your own redeeming. Receive him into the arms of your mercy, into the blessed rest of everlasting peace, and into the glorious company of the saints in light."

Katherine stood aside as Dr. Goldstein came forward, pushed down the blanket, bent over Justin with his stethoscope, listened to the still heart, withdrew. He looked up at the clock on the wall. He put one arm around Katherine. "Time of death, five-forty-two a.m., May Twenty-First, Two-Thousand-One."

Sam watched as the boy was released into the deep. Justin was adrift, receding into a speck, falling away and falling. Then he was gone, and then he was forever gone.

The priest concluded: "May angels surround him, and saints welcome him in peace."

Katherine took her stethoscope from the pocket of her lab coat. She had to know for herself. All six feet of her bent down to her son — bending double almost — as she put the silver medallion to Justin's chest, closed her tear-filled eyes and listened. Sam put his hand on hers.

Then, beyond the reach of science, within him, within her, something stirred.

Deep, deep in his chest, in the vast silence of that empty tomb, in the still cavern at the bottom of the stairs, in the darkened prison at the end of the world, there it was.

From branch to branch in the shadowed, swaying willow, a hop and a hop, and the little brown bird was gone.

A flutter of air, a flicker of light, the freedom of wings, and the boy was gone.

Into the soft and always dark, a little something, gone.

FORTY-ONE

An hour later, from the roof of the hospital, the helicopter revved and rose. Katherine heard it, and so did Sam.

Justin's heart was aloft.

We go on.

Epilogue
Thanksgiving Day
Nov. 22, 2001

FORTY-TWO

"Hold still, dammit."

"I'm trying, Jonesie, I'm trying. How much is it gonna hurt?"

"You'll hardly feel a thing."

Katherine was sitting on a chair in her bathroom at home, wrapped in her pink terry bathrobe, her hair wet from the shower and steam still hovering in the high-ceilinged room. She watched in her lighted vanity mirror as Jonesie descended with the tweezers, aiming for one of the major hairs that grew between her eyebrows.

"You're sure? You promise? It won't hurt?"

"A simple little pluck."

Suddenly — trying to catch Katherine a bit off-guard as she dodged about with her small fears — he squeezed and yanked.

Her scream curdled through the house. She covered the place of pain with both hands and bent double in her chair.

"For God's sake, Kath." He put one hand up to his hip. "What a drama queen."

As she pushed her fist into her forehead and moaned, Sam came in from the living room, wearing his robe and house shoes and carrying a section of the morning paper. "What's going on in here? It sounds like something out of the Bates Motel."

"Your wife is a fashion wimp," Jonesie said, holding the tweezers up and clicking them menacingly. "A simple little hair extraction, and she folded."

"I never thought of fashion as a blood sport," Sam said.

"It's true," Jonesie said. "I've always told Katherine, beauty takes sacrifice. If your shoes don't twist your toes and your bra doesn't pinch your lungs, then you're not living up to standards."

"Whose standards?" Katherine asked, leaning toward the magnifying mirror to get a better look at the red spot between her eyebrows. She gingerly touched the place with her index finger. "Gay standards?"

"What other standards are there?" Jonesie asked.

Sam had gone back to his newspaper in the living room, and Jonesie was looking through Katherine's closet as she sat on the bed and combed her wet hair. He was scraping the hangers down the rod as he sorted through the clothes, looking for something appropriate for their Thanksgiving celebration.

"Katherine, where are your things?" *Scrape.* "Your real clothes?" *Scrape.* "The nice stuff?" *Scrape.* "All I'm seeing in here is lab coats and scrubs and sweats. The person whose closet this is obviously has no life. Just work. Work, work, work. There is not one bit of *fun* in this closet!" He continued tisking and scraping, shaking his shapely blond hair and narrowing his manicured eyebrows. "Are you hearing me, missy?"

"I gave a bunch of stuff to St. Rita's a month or so ago for their rummage sale."

"In heaven's name, why? You and I had picked out some nice things, Kath."

"But nothing fit anymore."

"And you think they won't ever fit again? Honey, I'm putting you on a regimen after the first of the year. I'm gonna make you *sweat,* sweetheart!"

"I know, I know, Jonesie. It's just . . . I just had a moment of real discouragement." She paused. "Ever since the funeral and all that food, I've lost all control. God knows we've talked about it enough."

He left the closet and sat on the bed beside her. "Honey, I know." He put a long, tender arm around her shoulder. "It hasn't been easy."

"I had one of those come-to-Jesus moments. I took off my clothes and stood in front of the mirror."

"Oh God. Not good. I take it you and Jesus weren't happy with what you saw."

"It was horrible, Jonesie. Horrible! There were two huge funeral hams attached to my backside, one on each cheek. *Huge*!"

"Honey, I'm so sorry." He held her shoulders, leaned back and looked at her. "We'll work on those hams. We'll get rid of those hams."

"Promise?"

"Promise. New clothes, slimming and well-fitting. A makeover. I've got someone I want you to see. Jonathan — that's the name of his salon, too. You need to know people in order to get in with him, and I can get you in. He's known as the Hair God."

"The Hair God? Are you saying I need divine intervention?"

Jonesie reached over and fluffed at her sad, sodden mop. "Yes, sweetie, I'm afraid I am." He looked at her and shook his head discouragingly. "I'm thinking, too, that maybe Jonathan can come up with a solution for that hideous pelt of fur between your eyes. A waxing of some sort, maybe, or a shot of Botox to deaden the area before the chicken-plucking begins. I don't know, something major. But the hair, honey. We've got to do something with this hair."

"And my hands? These awful paws?" She held both hands up, their backs facing him, and Jonesie shook his head in dismayed agreement.

"I'm seeing more cuticles than nails, and that must change. We can do it, sweetie. Definitely."

"I feel like a failure, Jonesie. A fashion failure."

"I'm not disagreeing with you, honey. But we're going to turn things around. Kath, I promise."

She let her head fall against his chest. "I'm ready. Bring on the sweat."

Sam folded the markets section of *The Wall Street Journal* and set it beside him on the couch. He crossed his arms, leaned back and closed his eyes.

The wider world came flowing in on him. It had been two months since September Eleventh, and none of the dust of the towers had settled. All that bloody dust and loss and waste.

Was this ever going to end? Will the memories never stop?

A bluebird September morning erupts. The airliner is absorbed into the side of the building as cumulus flames bubble out.

It seemed so similar to that Saturday morning in May. You are doing everything right, and then suddenly everything goes wrong. Before you know what hit you, the second plane comes arching over the skyline, low, banking toward the other tower. A baseball, a loose tooth, a dentist, the ceaseless dark. Before you understand what happened, they are using the word *irreversible*.

Sam knew. A person's world can wobble and fall, and keep falling, and not stop falling. He knew — and for those hours and days in September, the wider world knew also: There is no such thing as solid ground.

Not really. You can't count on much of anything.

Jonesie found Katherine a pair of slacks (elastic waistband) and a decent top (a drab, dirty ivory, without a smidgeon of snap, but it was passable). He couldn't talk her out of those atrociously comfortable running shoes of hers. But so what. At least it was better than the scrubs. It would have to do. The guys wouldn't care . . . although he might try at least once more to talk her into something with just a little bit of heel.

He and Katherine were in the kitchen, starting on the prep work for their part of the Thanksgiving meal — washing the lettuce, peeling the potatoes. They worked well together in the kitchen, just as they did at the clinic, helping without getting in each other's way — so well coordinated, in fact, that they didn't have to say much about the task at hand.

"Kirb, I was thinking about our Saturday morning cooking classes," Katherine said.

"Yeah."

"Not just helping parents fix the right things for their families. I want to think about including more kids. You know, these latchkey kids who wind up doing a lot of their own cooking. Do some very simple, nutritious recipes that they could follow. And maybe do a field trip or two to the convenience stores nearby. Show them what to buy, what to avoid."

"We'd have to teach them to avoid ninety percent of the stuff in those stores, Kath."

"I know. But there's bound to be a few things that would work."

"Oatmeal, maybe. What's wrong with that for a dinner? Instant is fine Add a few raisins, some cinnamon, low-fat milk, sweetener. Beats the hell out of another damn burrito."

"Excellent idea, Jonesie. This is excellent."

"And you want to attract a crowd to the cooking classes?"

"You bet."

"Free donuts!"

Katherine laughed big and deep. It had been so long since Jonesie had heard it. "I'm there!" she said. "Donuts!"

It was nearing noon, the food was prepared, and Jonesie was helping Katherine with the finishing touches of her makeup and reintroduced his pleas for more fashion-forward shoes. Sam stepped out on the front porch for a look around.

The day was mild and clear, and Sam was comfortable in his sweater and slacks. It would all be changing soon. A major cold front would be coming in this evening.

The weather guys were talking about high north winds and a chance of sleet.

That was the way of Texas weather. Tonight might be harsh and tomorrow formidable, but it never lasted long. Winter never wore out its welcome. By Friday afternoon or Saturday the ice would be gone and the weather like this again. A sweater would be enough.

He looked out over the yard. The new cold would shrivel the last of the roses, and it would be time to prune the bushes close to the ground. Maybe this weekend he could get out and work in the yard. The weeds, too, had been accumulating, and the daisies and phlox needed cutting back as well. There was a whole weekend of work to do. He was going to ask Katherine to help. They hadn't worked alongside each other in a long time.

Things were changing. Katherine still worked too hard, but she had pulled back. She had resigned from the hospital board and all the committees she had been on. She'd done enough. Let somebody else have a shot at changing the world. Jonesie had always joked to her that they would have to pry her cold, dead hands from her stethoscope at the end of her career, but maybe not. Maybe she would just let go someday.

She and Lydia were working better together, sharing the load, and Katherine was getting home on time for supper every day, most days. She wasn't going to the hospital as often. She was letting a hospitalist take over most of that work.

Gracie stood close to Sam's legs, leaning forward in a Labrador pose, poised for action. Kids, other dogs, anything.

Todd usually came by late in the afternoon for a walk. Why couldn't he be early just this once?

Sam remembered how, during the grand Thanksgiving meals they used to have with his parents, Justin would occasionally leave the table, run into the den, check the television for whatever football game was dominating their interest at the moment — usually it was the University of Texas Longhorns vs. Texas A&M Aggies — and then return to the table with the score and a rundown of the last play, complete with dramatic flourishes and a bit of editorializing. "Those rotten Aggies just scored a touchdown!" Or, "We gored 'em, Granddad! The 'Horns just gored 'em, right in the guts!"

Justin was master of ceremonies, too. He had learned a repertoire of jokes from Father Red, who began each morning service at the school with a prayer and a corny joke. Justin brought every one of those jokes home with him, trying them out on his parents. The best ones he trotted out at family gatherings, and his audience loved them.

"Knock, knock," Justin had said at the Thanksgiving dinner two years ago.

"Who's there?" Jonesie asked on cue.

"Dwain."

"Dwain who?"

"Dwain the tub! I'm dwowning!"

That one got the laughs, and Justin took a bow.

"Hey, Dwain," Jonesie said to Justin a little later, "can you pass the gwavy?"

More laughs. Those guys were a team.

Today it was going to be different. For the first time since their days at Johns Hopkins, Sam and Katherine would be packing up their meal and celebrating Thanksgiving away from home.

Sam went around the side of the house, through the gate and to the garage. Gracie hopped in the back of the Volvo, but it was a little early for her. Nevertheless, she rode with him out of the garage, down the driveway and under the porte-cochere, wagging all the way. Based on what he had overheard from the bedroom, it was going to be at least thirty minutes before Jonesie finished supervising the last of Katherine's makeup and talked her into different shoes. He could be relentless when it came to shoes.

Granny had already parked her pickup at the clinic when Sam drove up. Jonesie got the salad and potatoes from the back of the station wagon, Katherine got the flowers and the other salad, and Sam went to help Granny. She had two chocolate pies for him to carry, but first he got one of her breath-crippling hugs, which he had always thought were more like wrestling moves than greetings.

After more kisses and embraces, the four of them headed across the winter-browning lawn to the fire station, Gracie wagging at their heels. They had to pick their way through the foot-tall American flags that lined the driveway and sidewalk. Neighbors had put them up after Nine-Eleven.

"Oh dear," Jonesie said. "I think I see what looks like a culinary disaster."

Sure enough, next to the side of the firefighters' building was a tipped over turkey fryer. Water and peanut oil were mixed in puddles beside it. On the brick wall behind it was a large black scorch mark. Gracie went over to check it out.

They surveyed the mess for a moment and then went to the side entrance, which led directly into the kitchen and dining area. Gracie followed. She loved seeing the guys. They had great crumbs.

"Happy Thanksgiving!" Katherine called out.

"God dammit, Jorge," his boss Chris was saying, "what am I gonna say if the chief finds out we damn near burned down the firehouse?"

Jorge seemed pleased at the chance to change the subject. He turned away from the upbraiding. "Happy Thanksgiving, you guys!" Sam handed him one of the pies. Jorge was the cook and in charge of the kitchen.

"So what happened, Beano?" Katherine asked.

"I was frying the turkey and we got a turkey call," Jorge said. "It didn't sound like it was gonna take that long, so I left the turkey cooking."

"It was bad," Waylon said. "Some poor guy's turkey fryer got out of hand like ours did. Damn near burned his whole house down."

"So did we," Chris said, with a half-serious angry look toward Jorge. "Caught it just in time."

"And what about the turkey?" Katherine asked.

"It sorta survived," Beano said.

"Sorta?" Jonesie asked.

"Well, we fried the hell out of it. Now it's about the size of a quail. I had to throw it out."

Gracie walked over to the trashcan. She seemed pleased with the possibilities, based on a sniff.

"Can Gracie have this tiny turkey?" Jorge asked, walking over to the corner and pulling the petrified bird out of the trash.

"Sure," Katherine said. "I don't see what it would hurt."

Gracie took it from Jorge gingerly and stole away under the table with it. She spent the rest of the afternoon doing some serious gnawing.

The guys were setting out the plates, the utensils and napkins. Jorge opened the oven to check on the marshmallow-covered sweet potatoes. Green beans were cooking on top of the stove.

"So have we got a Plan B here?" Sam asked.

"Fried chicken," Isabella said. "I was on my way to the Colonel's place to get maybe three buckets." She was the rookie, and rookies were saddled with these sorts of tasks. "You think that'll be enough, guys?"

"Better make it four," Sam said. He got two twenties out of his wallet and handed them to Isabella. She smiled.

"This'll really help, Sam," she said. "Thanks." She put on her jacket and headed out the door.

Ben Ray noted, "We thought about thawing out some more burritos, but we're getting pretty tired of 'em."

"Y'all are still working on those burritos?" Katherine asked. "God, how many did you get, do you suppose."

"Couple a hundred maybe," Jake said.

"It's got to have been more than that," Chris said. "I think we've already eaten at least that many."

Not only did the firefighters receive flags and honks and waves and flowers from people in the community after Nine-Eleven, but plenty of cakes and flan, cookies and *pan dulce*. And enough homemade burritos to feed — and kill — an army. Bean, chicken, beef, you name it.

Something similar happened when Justin died. The clinic was filled with flowers from people's gardens. The sympathy cards came in by the bundles. People brought statues — a dozen Virgin Marys and one Jesus, some of them hand-carved, others from Wal-Mart — and Jonesie did the best he could with them in an arrangement near the front door.

"Chicken ain't bad," Granny said in the middle of chewing after the meal got underway. "Not as good as mine, but not bad."

"Beats the heck out of Jorge's leather quail, I'm sure," Chris said.

Katherine looked around the two tables, into each kind face. These people, she was thinking. This steadfast family. They went all the way to the end of the journey with her, to the funeral, to the grave. Mourners overflowed the chapel at St. Alban's Episcopal Day School. They almost overflowed the campus, and it took three police motorcycle escorts to get the half-mile trail of cars to the cemetery. The firemen were pallbearers. They led the procession of cars in Ladder Sixty-One.

As the meal began to wind down, Katherine stood with an announcement. "All right, guys. As you know, we're planning a very big Christmas party at the clinic, and it's only two weeks away. Sam will be Santa Claus, I'll be Doctora Clause, and I'm gonna need a bunch of elves. Volunteers?"

There was a lot of moaning. Jonesie's was the only hand that went up.

"Listen up," Chris said with a rumble of authority. "I don't want to hear any complaining. Every damn one of you is gonna be a goddamn elf. You got it?"

"You, too?" Jorge asked.

"Yeah, me too," Chris said with resignation. "Randy and Jack'll be there. They love seeing their dad looking like a fool."

Quite a bit of money had come in to Justin's memorial fund. Katherine had decided it would all go toward Christmas toys. No school supplies, no socks or underwear.

Toys. That's what Justin would have wanted. The elves would be busy.

Katherine looked around the room, pointing at each of them. "Humpty, Dumpty, Grumpy, Lumpy, Bumpy, Frumpy . . ." She looked at Jonesie. "What about Fluffy."

"Fluffy it is!" Jonesie said, and they all joined him in big-hearted laughter.

About two-thirds of the way through the meal the buzzer sounded and the dispatcher announced a house fire over the PA system.

The guys stood with a ruckus of chairs scraping the floor. They headed toward their equipment and the trucks, still chewing.

"Probably another turkey call," Jorge said as he headed toward the door. "Save me some of Granny's pie."

"Will do," Katherine said.

"Maybe not," Sam said.

After cleaning up the dishes, putting away the leftovers and locking the door, Sam, Katherine, Jonesie and Granny headed back to their cars.

Granny slipped once in the grass but Jonesie was there to keep her on her feet. Katherine had been noticing that Granny was getting a little wobblier lately. She was working at the nursing home only once a week now. Katherine had asked her if she'd like to come live with them.

"Pardon my French, but hell no," Granny had said. "I got my own life. If I drop in my tracks, so what."

As they began their drive home, only a block from the clinic, Katherine said, "Slow down, Sam. I think that's Yolanda."

He slowed. The girl was walking down the sidewalk. "Yeah, it's her," Katherine said, and Sam stopped at the curb opposite the girl. Katherine rolled down the window with a button.

"Need a ride, honey?" Katherine asked.

"Hi, Dr. Warren. I don't guess so. I need to walk. You know, like you said, exercise."

"Good for you!" Katherine replied.

"And I only ate one piece of pie."

"Good girl. Excellent. Me, too!"

It looked like Yolanda had lost at least ten pounds. Katherine had gotten her on medication, and her pre-diabetes was under control.

"Everything going well at home, honey?"

"I'm living with my Aunt Theresa now. She's real nice."

"Oh, good, Yolanda. I'm so glad. Listen, you tell your aunt to bring you to our Christmas party at the clinic in a couple of weeks. I want to meet her."

"OK."

"You be sure and have a happy Thanksgiving," Katherine said.

"You, too, *Doctora*."

Katherine raised the automatic window as Sam eased away from the curb.

Jonesie leaned forward from the back seat. "You had o*ne* piece of pie? I counted..."

"Shut up, Jonesie. It's Thanksgiving."

Halfway home Katherine's cell phone rang. It was her mother. Oh God.

"Honey, I've got the most exciting news. Harold and I announced our engagement during the Thanksgiving meal with his family this afternoon. Can you believe it? We're planning a beach wedding in the Bahamas at Christmas." Then she did her usual stage whisper, "Honey, he's loaded!"

"I'm so happy for you, Mom."

Her mother went on and on. Harold was in arms and ammunition, lived in a huge house in the River Oaks section of Houston, not far from the president's father. Her sales commissions this year were heading for a record. The ring Harold got her was to die for.

Katherine remembered her mother's behavior at Justin's funeral. She wailed. Her grief spilled out all over the place; she practically rolled on the floor. She had begged

Katherine to open the casket for the mourners, and Katherine had refused. They nearly came to blows over it, and Jonesie had to intervene.

After Katherine got off the phone, Jonesie asked, "So how many husbands is this for Faye Jean?"

"I don't ask," Katherine said. "When I've asked before, Mom has been coy. 'Honey, some of them just weren't worth countin'. I call 'em no-counts.'"

"Did she invite me to the wedding?" Jonesie asked.

"Sorry, no," Katherine said. "She didn't invite me, either."

Jonesie's health hadn't been good lately. His energy and weight were low. It was one of his periodic flare-ups of HIV. He needed rest, good food and probably another round of chemo, and Katherine was worried about him. She asked him if he'd like to stay at their house for a while, but he said no.

What a godsend he had been to her this past year. Jonesie was the most generous person she had ever known.

Katherine had stayed home for two months after Justin's death, and Dr. Lydia was called on to step in. Jonesie came to the rescue then, too.

It wasn't as bad as he expected. After Lydia had become a mother, she'd gotten a little less rigid, let the records slide, cuddled her patients. Jonesie told Katherine, "I think she's set down her chainsaw for good."

At Jonesie's suggestion, Lydia had brought in a crib and set it up behind his receptionist desk, and the poor guy took on baby-sitting duty besides phones and records and nursing. And as hard as he tried not to, he fell in love with little Simone. He even admitted to Katherine, "Who knew lesbians could have such cute kids?"

Jonesie did his best to keep most of his generosity secret. He had kept the fire guys informed all the way through Justin's ordeal. They came up with the idea for the honor guard, and Jonesie — leading from behind — choreographed things, making sure the firefighters were ready when Sam came off the elevator.

"Justin was one of us, and he deserved that honor," Chris told Katherine later. "We are a band of brothers, and Justin was our little brother. He was family."

None of them would have admitted it out loud, but Jonesie was a brother to them, too.

FORTY-THREE

In the great room at home, in his armchair beside the fire, Sam leaned back and closed his eyes and listened. Winter had swooped in right on schedule, early on Thanksgiving night. Sleet pelted the roof and the windows like blowing sand. It came in ripples and waves. Limbs brushed the walls outside. Some of the wind had found its way inside, settling into the bones of the old house, and that made the fire all the more comforting.

The TV weather forecaster had urged Thanksgiving travelers to get home before it hit. Texans weren't any good with icy roads. The freeways weren't safe, what with all those pirouetting pickups.

Sam and Katherine could stay home tomorrow; they wouldn't have to get out in this mess, and he was grateful for that. In the morning he'd make another fire, and they could drink their coffee and take their time with the newspapers.

It was nine p.m. He and Katherine were sitting beside each other in front of the fire, he in the armchair and she at the end of the couch, eating a piece of Granny's pecan pie (she had made one just for them) and drinking cups of decaf. Katherine had her CD cassette of arias playing through the big Klipsch speakers on either side of the fireplace. The voices trilled and soared in a matchup with the wind.

For a time, Sam and Katherine drifted into separate worlds of quiet. The fire called them into themselves. The dance of flames was hypnotizing. In such a big fireplace Sam could build a healthy, beautiful fire, the logs of old oak piled into a pyramid. Even now, with the fire mostly gone, it lit up half the giant room and made a lamp superfluous. The fire added a circle of warmth around them. The light and heat and music created a room within a room, a second and intimate home inside the cathedral of darkness that surrounded them.

Nothing about the last five months had been easy. People talk about closure, but neither Sam nor Katherine had experienced it. They'd have a good day or two, and then the past would reclaim them and pull them under.

This shit. This rage. This boiling mess of guilt and regret and heaving waves of sadness. Closure? You couldn't close the door on something like that. Nothing could contain it.

After weeks and weeks in her darkened bedroom, Katherine emerged and did what she'd always done, which was to follow Granny's advice. Sam got on board with it, too.

Get to work. Keep moving. Don't brood so damn much. Think about somebody else.

It would work for a while. Then it wouldn't. The closed door would swing open and all the old memories would take them down again, claw them back into grief.

The cycle would probably never end. The dust would never settle. But they would keep going.

That's what people do. That's what Granny did. Keep going.

Sam took the empty plates and coffee cups into the kitchen. Katherine asked for wine, and he brought back glasses of red for each of them. He settled in again.

The wine was warming. For a while the music came forward, and the fire danced. The cassette played randomly from five CD's. Now it was Rossini's turn.

Katherine went back to Justin's last days. She remembered telling Sam that their son had been destroyed in the collapse of brain cells, that no one remained beneath the rubble, that he was an empty tomb.

But it wasn't true, was it. That last minute of his life, when she had stooped to hear his final heartbeat: Something remained, and a little something — a last flutter of life — was set free. Deep in the leaves, the little brown bird flew away.

What was it? The light behind the light, the mystery that illuminates the mystery, the particle that propels the particle. There was no answer. Science must go quiet in the end.

It didn't take long for Katherine to fall away. The careworn caregiver, halfway through her wine, nine-thirty p.m., lost her hold on the day. She opened the curtain of leaves, she came inside, and the safe dark was hers.

After a time Sam got up and went through his routine, checking each door and turning out the last of the lights. In their bedroom he turned on the security system. In the den he switched off the music. He used a key beside the mantel to turn off the gas to the fire.

Yes, he knew, bolting the doors and arming the house was a useless thing to do. The thief had already broken in and taken the thing most valuable to them. But Sam did it anyway. It was his job to protect them. You do the best you can. It doesn't mean you quit trying.

So much had changed in him since May. What used to anger him about Katherine's life of missionary zeal — all the time it took away from their life together — didn't bother him any more. The big things had become small and the small things nonexistent. Ambition waned in him. Circumstances had dismantled much of his ego.

He looked, instead, for the quiet glory in each day, and he usually found it. He cherished his time with his wife, instead of resenting the time he didn't get. He let the markets rise and fall. He planted more roses, and he wandered the neighborhood with Gracie. He remembered all the good days with Justin, and he didn't cry as often.

Moments of the deepest harmony, of purity, of perfect simplicity would come up in him. You had to set aside the self to let in the light of those moments. You couldn't just make them happen. You had to slow down, and that's when they'd surprise you, coming in the back door when you were looking in another direction. This was the rich life and it wasn't easy, but it was possible.

Now here came Christmas, and he had reluctantly agreed to be Santa Claus at the clinic's party. Saturday afternoon he and Katherine were meeting Jonesie at the costume shop for the fitting of his red suit. He was going to just have to stand there and take it as Kath and Jonesie preened him and pruned him. Jonesie would insist on more "snap" to his beard. Kath would want just the right stuffing for his gut. They would both insist on some vibrant ho-ho-hoing, and that would mean some practicing.

Well, so what. He was going to be drooled on, peed on, barfed on, and Katherine had told him to get ready for that, and Jonesie had said, "Now you'll know what our days are like." He smiled as he thought about it.

The day after the clinic Christmas party, he and Katherine were leaving for a two-week stay in Hawaii. It was going to be a surprise for her. Jonesie had helped him arrange everything.

Katherine's feet were up on the leather ottoman. Her head was resting against the back of the couch, nodded to the side. Sam brought Granny's quilt in from their bedroom and carefully covered her from her socked feet to the top of her shoulders.

He sat beside her on the couch, put his feet up next to hers on the ottoman and slipped under the other half of the quilt, which had become more worn and ratty than ever. Gracie was sleeping at the other end of the couch, spread out.

Sam was in easy reach of her velvet ears. The dog didn't stir, and neither did Katherine.

Beneath the blanket he found her hand and held it. He leaned over and very lightly kissed her closed eyes.

Without the gas, the fire had faded to almost nothing. The wood had burned down to a small scattering of charred rubble. Only a bit of flame remained, a rosebud of fire. Small wrinkles of light came from the back of the fireplace and fluttered out into the tall, tall darkness of the room.

It wasn't much — a little heat, a little light, one hand in another.

That which remains, he was thinking. This day, this life. A little something to be thankful for.

He closed his eyes. Sleep was calling. The fish of many colors were waiting for him there, and a boy, and a smile that would never die.

The End

Acknowledgements

I am especially grateful to William Gulledge, M.D., for shining a light on the dark truths of the injured brain; to the fine people of Harvard Square Editions, who aren't afraid to roll the dice; to Kathryn Lang, late of SMU Press, my editor then and good friend now, for hanging in there with me, scolding gently and encouraging greatly; to Kelli Johnson, R.N., for nursing guidance through the E.R. and elsewhere; to my son, James, for the Spanish and baseball tutorials; and of course to Kay, my longsuffering spouse, who kept me propped up and staggering along through years of rejections and all thirty-seven versions of this sucker.

More books from Harvard Square Editions:

Dark Lady of Hollywood, Diane Haithman
Gates of Eden, Charles Degelman
Growing Up White, James P. Stobaugh
Sazzae, JL Morin
Calling the Dead, R.K. Marfurt
Close, Erika Raskin
Living Treasures, Yang Huang